'Jon McGregor is one of the finest and most versatile novelists writing today. *Reservoir 13* is a unique feat of communitarian storytelling, full of humanity, humility, drama and mystery. Turning within a natural almanac, the lives of its characters ebb and flow as the years pass, as they encounter tragedy, conflict, the best and worst aspects of each other. It's rare to find a writer with symmetry and understanding of both the natural world and its residents – especially the edgelands – rarer still to find an author of such compassionate reach and existential balance, but McGregor writes with such grace and precision, with love even, about who we are and where we are, that he leaves behind all other writers of his generation'   SARAH HALL

'If you don't yet know you should read novels by Jon McGregor, then I can't help you'   EVIE WYLD

'Devastatingly good'   LINDA GRANT

'Brilliant'   CYNAN JONES

'*Reservoir 13* is a masterfully paced and grippingly controlled read that finds the shadows, the wildness, in the ordinary heart of a community'   COLIN BARRETT

'Haunting and heartbreaking – his best yet'   *Observer*

'Brilliant brilliant brilliant'   NINA STIBBE

'This is a book quite unlike anything I have read before. There's a hypnotic pull to the narrative, which has an irresistibly cumulative effect: in time I felt intimately immersed in a community traumatised by tragedy. Moreover McGregor writes with rare grace and integrity, and with such exquisite care the reader would be hard-pressed to find an infelicitous syllable, still less a word or phrase. If people were not already aware that here is one of our most accomplished living writers, they certainly will be now'

SARAH PERRY

'A truly magnificent piece of work. By the end I felt bereft. In fiction, a lot is made of word choices and individual sentences – praise heaped on their capacity to surprise and delight; *Reservoir 13* moves beyond that: it's the sequencing of word choices, sentences and narrative decisions – who to follow and when – and how these come together that gives the book its beauty, humanity and elegance'

STUART EVERS

ALSO BY JON McGREGOR

If Nobody Speaks of Remarkable Things
So Many Ways to Begin
Even the Dogs
This Isn't the Sort of Thing That Happens to Someone Like You

Reservoir 13

Jon McGregor

4th ESTATE • London

HarperCollins
PUBLISHERS
Since 1817

4th Estate
An imprint of HarperCollins*Publishers*
1 London Bridge Street
London SE1 9GF

www.4thEstate.co.uk

First published in Great Britain in 2017 by 4th Estate

2

Printed and bound in Great Britain by
CPI Group (UK) Ltd, Croydon, CR0 4YY

MIX
Paper from
responsible sources
FSC **FSC® C007454**
www.fsc.org

FSC is a non-profit international organisation established to promote
the responsible management of the world's forests. Products carrying the
FSC label are independently certified to assure consumers that they come
from forests that are managed to meet the social, economic and
ecological needs of present and future generations,
and other controlled sources.

Find out more about HarperCollins and the environment at
www.harpercollins.co.uk/green

The river is moving.
The blackbird must be flying.
     – Wallace Stevens

i.m.

Alistair McGregor

1945–2015

1.

They gathered at the car park in the hour before dawn and waited to be told what to do. It was cold and there was little conversation. There were questions that weren't being asked. The missing girl's name was Rebecca Shaw. When last seen she'd been wearing a white hooded top. A mist hung low across the moor and the ground was frozen hard. They were given instructions and then they moved off, their boots crunching on the stiffened ground and their tracks fading behind them as the heather sprang back into shape. She was five feet tall, with dark-blonde hair. She had been missing for hours. They kept their eyes down and they didn't speak and they wondered what they might find. The only sounds were footsteps and dogs barking along the road and faintly a helicopter from the reservoirs. The helicopter had been out all night and found nothing, its searchlight skimming across the heather and surging brown streams. Jackson's sheep had taken the fear and

scattered through a broken gate, and he'd been up all hours bringing them back. The mountain-rescue teams and the cave teams
and the police had found nothing, and at midnight a search had
been called. It hadn't taken much to raise the volunteers. Half the
village was out already, talking about what could have happened.
This was no time of year to have gone up on the hill, it was said.
Some of the people who come this way don't know how sharply
the weather can turn. How quickly darkness falls. Some of them
don't seem to know there are places a mobile phone won't work.
The girl's family had come up for the New Year, and were staying
in one of the barn conversions at the Hunter place. They'd come
running into the village at dusk, shouting. It was a cold night to
have been out on the hill. She's likely just hiding, people said.
She'll be down in a clough. Turned her ankle. She'll be aiming to
give her parents a fright. There was a lot of this. People just wanted
to open their mouths and talk, and they didn't much mind what
came out. By first light the mist had cleared. From the top of the
moor when people turned they could see the village: the beech
wood and the allotments, the church tower and the cricket
ground, the river and the quarry and the cement works by the
main road into town. There was plenty of ground to cover, and so
many places she could be. They moved on. There was an occasional flash of light from the traffic on the motorway, just visible
along the horizon. The reservoirs were a flat metallic grey. A thick
band of rain was coming in. The ground was softer now, the oily

brown water seeping up around their boots. A news helicopter flew low along the line of volunteers. It was a job not to look up and wave. Later the police held a press conference in the Gladstone, but they had nothing to announce beyond what was already known. The missing girl's name was Rebecca Shaw. She was thirteen years old. When last seen she'd been wearing a white hooded top with a navy-blue body-warmer, black jeans, and canvas shoes. She was five feet tall, with straight, dark-blonde, shoulder-length hair. Members of the public were urged to contact the police if they saw anyone fitting the description. The search would resume when the weather allowed. In the evening over the square there was a glow of television lights and smoke rising from generators and raised voices coming from the yard behind the pub. Doubts were beginning to emerge.

At midnight when the year turned there were fireworks going up from the towns beyond the valley but they were too far off for the sound to carry and no one came out to watch. The dance at the village hall was cancelled, and although the Gladstone was full there was no mood for celebration. Tony closed the bar at half past the hour and everyone made their way home. Only the police stayed out in the streets, gathered around their vans or heading back into the hills. In the morning the rain started up once again. Water coursed from the swollen peat beds quickly through the cloughs and down the stepped paths which fell from the edge of the moor. The river thickened with silt from the hills and plumed across the weirs. On the moor there were flags marking where the parents said they'd walked. The flags furled and snapped in the wind. At the visitor centre television trucks filled the car park and journalists started to gather. In the village hall the trestle tables were laid with green cups and saucers, the urns rising to the boil and the smell of bacon cobs drifting out into the rain. At the Hunter place there were voices coming from the barn conversion where the parents were staying, loud enough that the policeman outside could hear. Jess Hunter came over from the main house with a mug of tea. A helicopter flew in from the reservoirs, banking slowly along the river and passing over the weir and the quarry and the woods. The divers were going through the river again. A group of journalists waited for the shot, standing behind a cordon by the packhorse bridge, cameras aimed at the empty stretch of water, the breath clouding over their heads. In the lower field two of Jackson's boys were kneeling beside a fallen ewe. There was a racket of camera shutters as the first diver appeared, the wetsuited head sleek and slow through the water. A second diver came round the bend, and a third. They took turns ducking through the arch in the bridge and then they were out of sight. The camera crews jerked their cameras from the tripods and began folding everything away. One of the Jackson boys bucked a quad bike across the field and told the journalists to move. The river ran empty and quick. The cement works was shut down to allow for a search. In a week the first snowdrops emerged along the verges past the cricket ground, while it seemed winter yet had a way to go. At the school in the staffroom the teachers kept their coats on and waited. Everything that might be said seemed like the wrong thing to say. The heating pipes made a rattling noise that most of them were used to and the mood in the room unstiffened. Miss Dale asked Ms French if her mother was any better, and Ms French outlined the ways in which she was not. There was a silence again in the room and the tapping of the radiator. Mrs Simpson came in and thanked them for the early start. They all said of course it wasn't a problem. Under the circumstances. Mrs Simpson said the plan was to follow their lessons as normal but be ready to talk about the situation if the children asked. Which it seemed likely they would. There was a knock at the door and Jones the caretaker stepped in to say the heating would be working soon. Mrs Simpson asked him to make sure the yard was gritted. He gave her a look which suggested there'd been no need to ask. When the children were brought to school Mrs Simpson stood at the gate to welcome them. The parents lingered once the children had gone inside, watching the doors being locked. Some of them looked as though they could stand there all day. At the bus stop the older children waited for the bus to the secondary school in town. They were teenagers now. It was the first day back but they weren't saying much. It was cold and they had hoods pulled tightly over their heads. All day they would be asked about the missing girl, as if they knew anything more than they'd heard on the news. Lynsey Smith said it was a safe bet Ms Bowman would ask if they needed to chat. She did finger-quotes around the word *chat*. Deepak said at least it would be a way of getting out of French. Sophie looked away, and saw Andrew waiting at the other bus stop with Irene, his mother. He was the same age as they were but he went to a special school. Their bus pulled up and James warned Liam not to make up any bullshit about Becky Shaw. It snowed and the snow settled thickly. There was a service at the church. The vicar asked the police to keep the media away. Anyone was welcome to attend, she said, but she wanted no photography or recording, no waving of notebooks. She wanted no spectacle made of a community caught in the agony of prayer. The wardens put out extra chairs, but people were still left standing along the aisles. The men who weren't used to being in church stood with their hats bent into their hands, leaning against the ends of the pews. Some folded their arms, expectantly. The regulars offered them service books opened to the correct page. The vicar, Jane Hughes, said she hoped no one had come looking for answers. She said she hoped no one was asking for comfort. There is no comfort in the situation we find ourselves in today, she said. There is no comfort for the girl's parents, or for the family members who have travelled to the village to support them. No comfort for the police officers who have been involved in the search. We can only trust that we might meet God among us in these times of trouble. Only ask that we not allow ourselves to be overcome by a grief which is not ours to indulge but instead be uplifted by faith and enabled to help that suffering family in whatever way we are called to do. She paused, and closed her eyes. She held out her hands in a gesture she hoped might resemble prayer. The men who had their arms folded kept them folded. The warden rang the bell three times and the sound carried out through the brightening morning and along the valley as far as the old quarry. At the end of the month the sun came out and the fields softened. The still air shook to the thump of melting roof-top snow. There were rumours and only rumours of where the parents might be now. They were beside themselves, it was said.

In February the police arranged a reconstruction, bringing actors over from Manchester. There had been no leads and they wanted to make a fresh appeal. The press were allowed up to the Hunter place and given instructions on what to film. The day was clear and edged with frost. The press officer asked for quiet. The door of the barn conversion opened and a couple in their early forties appeared, followed by a thirteen-year-old girl. The woman was slim, with blonde hair cropped neatly around her ears. She was wearing a dark-blue raincoat, and tight black jeans tucked into calf-length boots. The man was tall and angular, with wiry dark hair and a pair of black-framed glasses. He was wearing a charcoal-grey anorak, walking trousers, and black shoes. The girl looked tall for thirteen, with dark-blonde hair to her shoulders and a well-acted look of irritation. She was wearing black jeans, a white hooded top, a navy body-warmer, and canvas shoes. The three of them got into a silver car which was parked outside the barn conversion, and drove slowly down to the road. The photographers ran alongside. At the visitor centre the actors waited for the photographers to get into place before climbing out of the car and setting off towards the moor. The girl lagged behind and three times the actors playing her parents turned and called for her to hurry up and join them, and three times the girl responded by kicking at the ground and slowing a little more. The two adult actors held hands and walked ahead, and the girl quickened her pace. This sequence of events had been drawn from police interviews, it was later confirmed. The two adults kept walking until they'd gone over the first rise and dropped out of sight, and a few moments later the girl dropped out of sight as well. The cameras photographed the empty air. The press officer thanked everyone for coming. The three actors came back down the hill. Work started up at the cement works again and the roads were silvered with dust. The freight trains came shunting through the hill and around the long bend between the trees. A pale light moved slowly across the moor, catching in the flooded cloughs and ditches and sharpening until the clouds closed overhead. On the riverbank towards the weir at dusk a heron stood and watched the water. A slow fog came down from the hills overnight. At four in the morning Les Thompson was up and bringing the cows across the yard for milking. Later in the day the vicar was seen driving to the Hunter place. She was inside for an hour with the missing girl's parents, and she didn't speak to anyone when she left.

The investigation continued. By the end of March the weather had warmed and the parents were still at the Hunter place. There was no news. Jane Hughes went up to see them again one morning, and on her way past the Jackson place she saw Jackson and the boys out front of the lambing shed. They wore the looks of men who've been working hard but see no need to admit it. They had mugs of tea and cigarettes. The smell of breakfast being cooked came from inside the house. It was only when they saw the first children on their way to school that Will Jackson remembered he was due at his son's mother's house, to fetch the boy for school. The van wouldn't start so he took the quad bike, and he knew before he got there that the boy's mother wouldn't be happy about this; that it would be one more thing for her to hold against him. When they got back to the school the gates were locked and Will had to call Jones out of the boilerhouse to let them in. He took the boy down to his class. Miss Carter accepted his apologies, and settled the boy down, and asked Will if he might think about the class coming to visit at lambing time. He told her they'd started lambing already and she looked surprised. She asked if there weren't more to come and he said if she wanted to arrange a school trip she'd have to put something to his father in writing. It was the most she'd heard him say in weeks. When he got back to the yard his brothers were all inside the shed. They'd lost a ewe while he'd been gone. There was a meeting of the parish council. Brian Fletcher had trouble keeping people to the agenda, and eventually had to concede that it was difficult to pay mind to parking issues at a time like this. The meeting was adjourned. The police held a press conference in the function room at the Gladstone, and announced that they wanted to trace the driver of a red LDV Pilot van. The journalists asked if the driver was considered a suspect, and the detective in charge said they were keeping an open mind. The girl's parents sat beside the detective and said nothing. In the afternoon the wind was high and the clouds blew quickly east. A blackbird dipped across Mr Wilson's garden with a beakful of dead grass for a nest. There were spring-tails under the beech trees behind the Close, feeding on fragments of fallen leaves. At night from the hill the lights could be seen along the motorway, the red and the white flowing past one another and the clouds blowing through overhead. The missing girl had been looked for. She had been looked for all over. She had been looked for in the nettles growing up around the dead oak tree in Thompson's yard. Paving slabs and sheets of ply had been lifted before people moved away through the gates. She had been looked for at the Hunter place, around the back of the barn conversions and in the carports and woodsheds and workshops, in the woodland and in the greenhouses and the walled gardens. She had been looked for at the cement works, the huge buildings moved through with unease, people nosing vaguely behind pallets and forklifts and through the staffroom and canteen, their hands and faces slick with white dust when they ghosted on down the road. At night there were dreams about where she might have gone. Dreams about her walking down from the moor, her clothes soaked and her skin almost blue. Dreams about being the first to reach her with a blanket and bring her safely home.

By April when the first swallows were seen the walkers were back on the hills. At the car park as they hoisted their packs they could be heard speculating about the girl. Which way she might have headed, how far she might have gone. North and she'd have been over the motorway by nightfall. East and the reservoirs would have been in her way. West and she'd have come to the edges, where the heather and soil frayed out into air and the gritstone rolled away from the hill. The weather she'd have been walking through. And in those shoes. There were so many places to fall. How was it she hadn't been found, still, as the days got longer and the sun cut further into the valley and under the ash trees the first new ferns unfurled from the cold black soil. In the evenings the same pictures were shown on the news: an aerial shot of the search party strung across the moor; the divers moving through the water; the girl's parents being driven away; the photograph of the girl. In the photograph she matched the description of what she'd been wearing and her face was half-turned away. It made it look as though she wanted to be somewhere else, people said. The girl's mother was again visited by detectives. Sometimes there were new questions. At the school before the children arrived Miss Carter filled aluminium jugs from the dinner hall with water and arranged in them cut branches of willow tight with buds. On the allotments the purple broccoli was sprouting, the heads snapping off cleanly and too sweet on the tongue to get a decent harvest home. Surveyors were seen up on the land around the Stone Sisters. There were rumours they worked for a quarrying firm. The annual Spring Dance was almost cancelled, but when Irene suggested holding it in aid of a missing-children's charity it became difficult for anyone to object. Sally Fletcher offered to help organise it, once Irene had looked pointedly at her for long enough. The divers roped up again, slipping into the reservoir while the herons sloped away overhead. The trees came back into leaf. A soft rain blew in smoky clouds across the fields.

————

At the butcher's for May Day weekend there was a queue but nothing like there once would have been. Nothing like the queue Martin and Ruth needed to keep the shop going. Martin had been keeping this to himself, although it was becoming obvious and nobody asked. Irene was at the front of the queue telling everyone what she knew about the situation at the Hunters'. She did the cleaning there, and knew a thing or two. You can imagine what it's like for the girl's parents, she said. Having to watch us all down here just getting on with things. Ruth saying but surely the village couldn't be expected to put life on hold. Austin Cooper came in with copies of the *Valley Echo* newsletter and laid them on the counter. Ruth wished him congratulations, and he looked confused for a moment before smiling and backing away towards the door. Irene watched him go, and asked if Su Cooper was expecting. Ruth said yes, at last, and from the back of the queue Gordon Jackson asked would there be any chance of getting served before the baby was born. A breakdown truck came slowly down the narrow street, with a red LDV Pilot van hoisted on the back and a police car following. The van was wrapped in clear plastic. Martin wiped his hands on his apron and stepped outside to watch it pass. Gordon came out with him and lit a cigarette. Martin nodded. That changes things, he said. Fucking breakthrough is that, Gordon said. The swallows returned in number, and could be seen flying in and out through the open doors of the lambing shed at the Jacksons' and the cowsheds over at

Thompson's, and the outbuildings up on the Hunters' land. The well-dressing committee had a difference of opinion about whether to dress the boards at all this year. Under the circumstances. There'd never been a year without a well dressing that anyone could remember. But there'd never been a year like this. In the end it was agreed to make the dressing but to keep the event low-key. There were sightings of the girl. She was seen by Irene, first, on the footbridge by the tea rooms, walking across to the other side. Quite alone she was, Irene said. Her young face turned half away and she wouldn't look me in the eye. Gone before I got to her and I couldn't see which way she went. I knew it was her. The police were told, and they went searching but they found nothing. There were lots of young families in the area that day, a police spokesperson said. But I know it was her, Irene said again. There was rain and the river was high and the hawthorn by the lower meadows came out foaming white. The cow parsley was thick along the footpaths and the shade deepened under the trees. Stock was moved higher up the hills and the tea rooms by the millpond opened for the year. In the shed Thompson's men were working on the baler, making sure they'd be ready when the time came for the cut. The grass was high but the weather had been low for days. The rain on the roof was loud and steady. The reservoirs filled.

———

The van had been found behind storage buildings at Reservoir no. 7. The area had been searched in the days after the girl went missing, which meant the van had likely been placed there at a later date. Somebody may have seen that van being moved. Somebody may remember who was driving that van. Police were appealing for any witnesses to come forward, and were trying to trace the owner. The number-plates were false and the chassis number had been filed. The van had been removed from the scene and was subject to a thorough forensic examination. A creeping normality had begun to settle over these press conferences. The chairs were put out, the cameras set up in the usual place. There was a weariness to the proceedings. There was a volume to what was not being said. The room emptied and the chairs were stacked away. The floor was swept and the lights turned off and Tony went back to the bar. The wild fennel came up ferny bright in the shelter of the old quarry, and when Winnie went to pick some she found knotted condoms lying around yet again. It was the knotting that surprised her. A man in a charcoal-grey anorak with the hood up over his head was seen standing on the far side of Reservoir no. 8 for a long time, before turning and walking up into the trees. Martin Fowler went to the incident unit in the square, and told them what he knew about the driver of the red van. This was after a conversation with Tony. Martin had mentioned knowing the man's name was Woods, and Tony asked why he hadn't told the police already. Martin said this wasn't the type of bloke you wanted to be talking to the police about. Tony was persuasive. There were gaps in the story Martin told the police about Woods. The gaps were to do with scrap metal, poaching, and red diesel. Woods was known to be involved in these enterprises, and Martin had been drawn in on occasion. The police didn't want to know. They wanted to know where Woods was, and why the van had been hidden, and why the van had been seen at the time of the girl's disappearance. Martin was reluctant but the information was obtained. Later in the pub he spoke tensely to Tony about repercussions. Woods is one of those as values discretion, he said. Man's connected. Just so you know what you've got me into here. Martin, come on now. She were thirteen. Think on. You don't know Woods though, Martin said. But if I did I'd have gone to the police quicker than you did, Tony told him. They watched each other while Martin drained his glass and walked out. By the evening there was a photo-fit on the news. The police said they were keen to eliminate the man from their enquiries. At the cricket pavilion the teenagers gathered to drink. Sophie Hunter had a bottle of wine she'd sneaked from her parents' cellar that she said would be years before it was missed. They were a long time trying to open it, and in the end Liam used a screwdriver to force the cork down inside the bottle. They were talking about the girl again. James Broad said he wondered if they should say something after all. The others told him there was no point. They'd discussed it before. It wouldn't make any difference, Lynsey said. She's gone.

It would only get the rest of us into all sorts of shit. You weren't the one who was there, James said. It was just a mix-up, Deepak told him. You didn't do anything wrong. They sat on the pavilion steps and drank the wine, and they asked each other if it was working yet. None of them quite knew how they were supposed to feel. When the wine was finished they'd long stopped talking. Sophie hid the bottle underneath the pavilion steps and they all went home. There was an unexpected warmth in the air and they stumbled against each other more than once. Their voices were louder than they realised.

The girl's parents were seen near the visitor centre, walking up the hill with a pair of detectives. From a distance their movements looked stiff and slow. They took a wide detour around the area where she'd last been seen. The flags had been taken down and there was nothing to mark the spot. No one would know it, unless they knew. They followed the old bridleway which led past Black Bull Rocks towards the reservoirs. They were gone for most of the afternoon, and by the time they came back there were photographers waiting in the car park. It had been more than six months and still there was nothing. No footprints, no clothing, no persons of interest, no sightings on any CCTV. It was as though the ground had just opened up and swallowed her whole. Journalists used this phrase by way of metaphor or hyperbole; people in the village knew it as a thing that could happen. Questions were asked about how much longer the parents would stay. The Hunters had cancelled all the bookings in the barn conversions, but it wasn't known how long that could go on. Little was seen of them, and if the Hunters knew anything they weren't passing it on. It was known that Reverend Hughes was visiting. More flowers and candles were left at the visitor centre, and the question of what to do with them was broached. It was understood that the girl's father had been seen out, walking. It wasn't known what he was trying to achieve. Irene said he was taking it badly, and was asked what the hell other way she'd imagined him taking it. Woods was found working security on a building site in Manchester. He was arrested and questioned at length. There was nothing to link him to the missing girl, and he had an alibi for the night in question. It hadn't been his van that was seen, as it turned out. He was released, and immediately rearrested on a number of other charges relating to theft and handling. In the hay meadow south of the church there were groups of wild pheasants moving through the grass, the mothers steering their young with nips and cries, whole groups scattering at the slightest noise. Cathy Harris walked around the edge of the meadow and crossed the river with Mr Wilson's dog. As she entered the woods she let the dog off the lead and squeezed between the gapstone stile. People wanted the girl to come back, so she could tell them where she'd been. There were too many ways she could have disappeared, and they were thought about, often. She could have run down from the hill and a man could have stopped to offer her a lift, and taken her away, and buried her body in a dense thicket of trees beside a motorway junction a hundred miles to the north where she would still be lying now in the cold wet ground. There were dreams about her walking home. Walking beside the motorway, walking across the moor, walking up out of one of the reservoirs, rising from the dark grey water with her hair streaming and her clothes draped with long green weeds.

The last days of August were heavy with heat and anything that had to move moved slow. At the allotments the beds were bursting with beans and courgettes, the plants sprawling over the pathways. The bees stumbled fatly between the flowers and the slugs gorged. The first lambs were ready to sell and Jackson's boys were busy making selections and loading them into the trailer. At the cricket ground the annual game against Cardwell was lost. The girl's mother came to the church from time to time. She arrived just before the service began, escorted by the vicar to a seat in the side aisle which was kept free for her, and left during the closing hymn. There was an arrangement. Jess Hunter sometimes waited for her in the car outside. People understood they were to leave her be. When it came to sharing the peace she shook hands briefly, with a smile that some said seemed defensive and others took as grateful. Late in the summer the teenagers held their own search party. It was James's idea. They could walk up over the moors, go as far as Reservoir no. 13, check all the places they knew about that the police wouldn't have thought of. If they found anything they'd be on the news. Liam said they could take some cans, make it a party. A search party. Lynsey said it was messed up making a joke about it. They headed out early, Liam and James and Deepak, Sophie and Lynsey, each telling their parents something different, meeting at the car park by the allotments and cutting up through the beech wood while the morning air was still cool. They had ideas about what had happened to Becky, based on what they knew about her, and what they thought themselves capable of in the same situation, and on what they knew of the landscape. They'd seen her the previous summer, when the family had stayed at the Hunter place for a fortnight, and they'd spent more time with her than people seemed to know. It made them feel involved. By midday their pace had faltered in the heat and they stopped at a fork in the tracks. At the bottom of the hill there was a ruined barn where Jackson stored feed and equipment. They were thirsty and they shared the only two cans of lager they'd managed to get hold of. There were crickets in the heather and a beetle moving on Lynsey's hand. The sheep pushed in and out of the barn, looking for shade. Did they search that place? Deepak asked. Obviously, Liam said. I searched it myself. I borrowed one of those thermal-imaging cameras; nothing.

Deepak gave him the standard slap for bullshitting. They searched everywhere, said James; so what are we doing? No one answered. Lynsey and Sophie had their eyes closed already, and in the midday sun Sophie's skin was starting to burn. There were butterflies feeding on the heather. An aeroplane went overhead. What time is it? asked Liam. About twelve, James said, his eyes closed, guessing. The heather sprang firmly beneath him. They were all lying closer to each other than they were used to. Someone's stomach gurgled and no one acknowledged. There was a distant sound of traffic, and farm machinery. They slept. At some point James saw a man walking up the path towards them, poking at the heather with a stick, and as he came past he didn't seem to see the five of them lying there. He was wearing a charcoal-grey anorak. James stood up and the two of them nodded, and James meant to say he was sorry about the man's daughter but all that came out was *sorry*. The man nodded again and kept walking. Later James wondered if this had happened at all. It would have been too hot to wear an anorak. In the afternoon the five of them made it to the top of the hill overlooking Reservoir no. 8, and it turned out that Liam had brought vodka. They found a mine entrance they hadn't seen before and went in with torches, scratching a line in the mud behind them and putting the wind up each other. When she was very scared Lynsey grabbed on to Deepak's arm. By the time they came out again it was dark, and in their confusion they went down the wrong side of the hill. When they finally got home they were in more trouble than they thought possible. Their parents were furious and held them close, and there were police officers waiting to have words.

Su Cooper redecorated the small bedroom in their flat above the converted stables, ready for the twins. Austin had offered to help, but she'd told him he had too much on with the *Echo* and she wanted to just get it done. He'd asked if there was something she meant by this. She hung animal-print curtains at the windows, and assembled the second cot more easily than the first, and fixed hooks in the ceiling to hang mobiles from. She folded the tiny white clothes into the drawers, and stacked nappies on top of the wardrobe, and arranged toys along a shelf. It was a small room, but everything the babies would need seemed to fit. It was a small flat. The space had once been sleeping quarters for the stable lads. It had never been meant for a family to live in. But Su and Austin had loved it since they'd first moved in, and they were determined to make it work. She'd bought storage baskets which slid neatly beneath both cots. She knew there was a danger in preparing the room so thoroughly, so soon. There were people who had super-stitions about this kind of thing. She knew her mother wouldn't approve. But she wanted it done. She wanted to be ready. She didn't yet know people well enough to assume they would help. She didn't know how Austin would rise to the challenge. She suspected he might not. She suspected he was the kind of man who would gaze lovingly at his infant without realising it needed a nappy change, or another feed. He would provide for them, she knew. She had waited until she was sure of that. But he would have no idea what to do. This she was prepared for. He was a sentimental man, and, when it came to anything besides the business of writing and editing and printing, completely unpractical. She wound the babies' mobiles, and listened to the whirring tunes, watching the snails and frogs turning circles in the sunlight. She'd closed the door behind her before the music had stopped. The badgers in the beech wood fed quickly, laying down fat for the winter ahead. They moved through the leaf litter in a snuffling, bumping pack, turning up earthworms and fallen berries. Their coats were thickening. The river turned over beneath the packhorse bridge and ran on towards the millpond weir.

The clocks went back and the nights overtook the short days. The teenagers walked home from the bus stop in the dark. A man fitting the missing girl's father's description was seen walking further and further away from the village; at the far side of Ashbrook Forest, past the last of the thirteen reservoirs. There were reports of a man in a charcoal-grey anorak walking on the hard shoulder of the motorway. The bracken was rusting in swathes across the hill. There were dreams about the missing girl being found face-down in pools of water, and dreams about her being driven safely away. Mischief Night passed and it wasn't what it had been in recent years. No one quite had the spirit, besides whoever filled the telephone box with balloons. Jackson's boys brought the flock down to the bye field and spent the day clipping around the tails, getting ready for tupping. At the school the lights were seen on early, and there was black smoke rising from the boilerhouse. In the staffroom Miss Carter was running through the week's lesson plans with Mrs Simpson. When they were done Mrs Simpson asked Miss Carter how she was settling in. Miss Carter nodded quickly and said it was fine, it was only that she was finding it hard to get to know people. Mrs Simpson laughed and said she knew what Miss Carter meant, and had she tried marking up the register with little portraits to jog her memory? Miss Carter said she hadn't meant the children. I thought you meant settling into the area, she said. Mrs Simpson apologised and said that to avoid confusion Miss Carter should know she'd never ask anything about a teacher's private life. We're only worried about what happens within these gates, she said. At the reservoirs the dams were inspected again, and areas of concern were noted. In the dusk the woodpigeons gathered to roost.

————————

In November Austin Cooper and his wife came home with twins, and carried them up the steps to their flat above the converted stables. When he turned to close the door he stood on the threshold for a moment, looking down at the street, as if expecting or perhaps even hearing applause. It would have been deserved, was his feeling. He'd never imagined finding the kind of deep friendship he'd found with Su, and ten years later the twins' arrival was the kind of extra he'd long trained himself not to expect. At some point, in some life, he must have done something right. Irene saw him closing the door, saw the deep glowing light from their windows, and remembered bringing her own Andrew home some fourteen years before. But when she got to the Gladstone and told people there, all anyone could say was sweet buggering hell, those steps; how's she going to get a twin buggy up and down those steps? Austin didn't sleep that first night. He made hot drinks for Su while she phoned her parents and friends and told them the news all over again, and later he walked in and out of the bedroom to look at the rest of his family sleeping, and finally he lay down beside Su and listened to the different sounds of breathing in the room: Su's long and measured; the twins' fast and shallow, as though they'd only just come up for air. In the night there was crying and waking and feeding and changing, but amongst it all there were moments when the breathing was the only sound in the room and Austin felt he had only to stay awake to keep them safe. That this was the only thing required of him now. In the evening when Su had been on the phone to her parents he'd tried to pick out some of what she said. He knew the words for mother and father and children, but beyond that he was lost. He thought he knew the word for happy, but Su spoke so quickly to her parents that he could never be quite sure. He assumed she was happy. Mostly she just seemed tired. It was so long they'd been hoping for this; she'd been trying so hard and now all the strain in her body had nowhere useful to go. It looked a comfortable sort of tiredness, a relief. He could tell already, from the way she held the twins and the way she moved around them, or leant across and made small adjustments while he was holding them, that she knew exactly what she needed to do. And that she knew without even being surprised. It was one of the things that kept delighting him about Su, this equanimity. As though she'd known all along that life would be like this. The very first night they'd spent together, the look on her face in the morning had seemed to say well, now, of course this has happened. What else did you expect? Early in the morning the lights were seen on downstairs, where Austin had converted the stables to an office for the *Valley Echo*. The white office lighting was stark against the dawn and the dome of his head was just visible through the window as he worked on the last few pages of the next issue, adding something to the announcements column while being careful not to exploit his position. And when the issue appeared through letterboxes and on shop counters a week later there was only this for the few who didn't already know: *Su Lin Cooper and Austin Cooper announce the safe arrival of their twin sons, Han Lee Lin and Lu Sam Lin, and thank everyone for their kind wishes.*

At the school the lights were seen on early in the hall. Preparations were being made for the Christmas assembly. Jones had cut holly and fir from the woods, and Mrs Simpson was on her knees arranging it around the nativity scene. Miss Carter asked Jones to hold the bottom of the ladder while she took some tinsel up. Ms French couldn't help noticing, glancing across from her half-finished wall display of shepherds and cotton-wool sheep, that Miss Carter was wearing a skirt. Also that Jones was not keeping his eyes down. She didn't like to interfere but she thought it best to ask Jones to put the chairs out instead. When Miss Carter looked down to see no one holding the ladder she stood very still, and looked at the wall in front of her, and tried not to think about how recently Jones had polished the floor. She found herself thinking about Tom Jackson's father, Will, and about him not seeming the type to wander away from a ladder like that. She held on tight. There were carols in the church with candles and the smell of cut yew and holly. Olivia Hunter sang a solo verse of 'Silent Night'. She was eight years old and blithely confident. Her voice trembled a little on *all is calm, all is bright,* and at the end of the verse she beamed as she waited for the congregation to join in.

At the village hall the production of *Jack and the Beanstalk* was finally staged. The costumes and scenery had all been kept from the year before, and most people had been happy to keep the same parts. The hall was full on the night of the show. Lynsey Smith had shot up over the year, and was looking less boyish than when she'd been cast. But she climbed up the beanstalk with just the right recklessness, and when she disappeared into the curtained rafters Cathy Harris, playing Jack's mother, did a good job of looking bereft. Afterwards the chairs were cleared and the bar opened and trays of mince pies brought out. Richard Clark was seen in the audience for the first time in years. He'd been staying with his mother for a few days. He hadn't got there until his sisters had been and gone, which his mother was used to now, and he was out of the country before the year was through. He was a busy man. Some years she was glad to see him at all. He lived out of a suitcase, it seemed, and this was no way to live for as long as he had done. They didn't really sit down and have a conversation the whole time he was there, and when he left for the airport she didn't even know where he was headed. He was a consultant, was as much as she knew. There seemed to be a new lady friend but he hadn't mentioned a name. When he was gone she changed the sheets on the bed and opened a window to air the room and the sound of church bells came into the house. They were holding another service to mark the year since the girl's disappearance. There were no extra chairs this time, and no one left standing at the back of the church. Jane Hughes said many of the same things she had said the year before. And still we have no answers, and all we can do is wait. She closed her eyes and held out her hands and let the silence settle. The missing girl's name was Rebecca, or Becky, or Bex. She had been thirteen at the time of her disappearance. She'd been wearing a white hooded top with a navy-blue body-warmer, black jeans, and canvas shoes. She would be taller than five feet now, and her hair may have altered in both style and colour. The investigation remained active, a police spokesperson confirmed. The girl's mother was seen on the side of the moor, walking the same paths and tracks she'd always walked. There was more rain on the way, or worse. A cold wind blew shadows across the reservoirs and on the higher ground a flurry of thin snow whirled against the tops of the trees. The goldcrests fed busily deep in the branches of the churchyard yew.

2.

At midnight when the year turned there were fireworks going up from the towns beyond the valley but they were too far off for the sound to carry to the few who'd come out to watch. The dance at the village hall went ahead, and was enjoyed by those who attended. A year was long enough, they thought. The streets were quiet and there were no police now but in the sharp night air it still felt recent. Will Jackson was seen with the teacher from his son's class at school. The snow came down thickly overnight and for a time it seemed the road might be closed. By noon the sun was out and the drains were gulping meltwater from the road. A blackbird inched under the hedge in Mrs Clark's garden, poking around in the wet leaf litter for something to eat. In the eaves of the church the bats were folded deeply into hibernation and the air around them was still. There were heavy rains for a week that brought flooding down the river. Debris piled up against the footbridge by the tea rooms until the weight of it swept the footbridge away. After the storm the river keeper dragged out what was left and fenced the bridge off at either end. The river keeper worked for the Culshaw Estate, who owned the fishing rights, but there was always disagreement over who was responsible for the bridges and paths. The family who lived in Culshaw Hall were no longer Culshaws, and were generally felt to be out of their depth. It was a struggle to keep the building in one piece, never mind manage all the land. Most of their money went on the keepers, since shooting and fishing was all that brought in an income. The rest of it went on solicitors, to prove they had no obligation to pay for things the Culshaws once would have done. The sound of the reservoirs overtopping the dams for the first time in years was torrential and constant and swept through the valley. All month the church services were taken by visiting preachers and no one seemed to know where the vicar had gone. The churchwarden said she was on holiday, but this was understood not to mean that she'd gone away. The word stress was used, and when she came back no more was said. At the Hunter place there was a feeling of life being on hold. The bookings in the barn conversions had been cancelled for another year, and the place was quiet. Jess Hunter hadn't become friends with the girl's mother in the way she'd thought she might. It had become clear she wanted to stay around for the long term, even now her husband was mostly back in London, and Jess had tried to include her in family life. But perhaps having Sophie and Olivia around was difficult for her. They'd shared meals and sometimes a drink, but the woman was very closed. It was unclear how to respond. Jess prided herself on being a woman who knew how to get people to open up. Her daughters told her everything, which was more than could be said for her husband. He was away again this month, and Jess had only half an idea what for. Some high-level policy forum. Something about land management. The man was impossibly vague. She stood in the kitchen looking out across the courtyard towards the barn conversions. The girl's mother was on her doorstep, smoking a cigarette. Jess wondered if she could see into the kitchen from there. In the village questions were being asked about how long she would stay. People wanted the girl found so this could all be over. She might have got into one of the caves that burrowed deep under the hill. She might have curled up in a corner and still be down there now.

On Shrove Tuesday Miss Carter organised a pancake race in the school playground, once Jones had swept the snow and put down grit. There was a disagreement about how often the runners were supposed to flip their pancakes, and some of the children became distressed. Lucy Williamson had to be taken home with a bruised foot. Jackson's boys came down the road past the school and Simon asked Will if he wasn't going to drop in there with a

Valentine's card. Will said he'd no idea what they were talking about and then told them they'd best keep quiet because there was nothing to it. It was nothing serious. If people start talking it'll only complicate things with the boy's mother, he said. It wasn't clear when he'd started calling her the boy's mother instead of the girlfriend, or Claire. Probably about the time she went back to her mum's house. Which was meant to have been temporary but these things have a way of settling. His brothers were still laughing about his denials when they got down to the lower field and started hauling feed off the trailer. Will told them if they didn't knock it off he'd tell Jackson about the red diesel. They told him he wouldn't but they quietened down. The ewes gathered about as they tipped out the feed, knocking heavily into their legs. The brothers worked their way around, inspecting the fleeces and feet and arses and ears, and an easy concentration came suddenly over them as though there'd been no joking at all. They handled the animals firmly, quickly, muttering commentary to each other, and if their mother had happened to pass in the lane she would have seen much of their father in the way they held themselves and the way their young bodies moved under the heavy sky. In the after-noon the slush froze glassily again and was covered with another layer of late-falling snow. The night was cold. In the morning on the far side of the river Les Thompson led his herd across the yard to the milking parlour while the sky was still thick above the trees. The air was soon steaming with the press of bodies, Les moving among them while they got themselves into line. He was a big man, and the cows shifted easily to let him through. Dawn was a way off yet and wet when it arrived. Jackson had a stroke and was taken to hospital and for weeks it was assumed he wouldn't be coming home.

In the beech wood the foxes gave birth, earthed down in the dark and wet with pain, the blind cubs pressing against their mothers for warmth. The dog foxes went out fetching food. The primroses yellowed up in the woods and along the road. The reservoirs were a gleaming silver-grey, scuffed by the wind and lapping against the breakwater shores. In the evening a single runner came silently down the moor, steady and white against the darkening hill. Gordon Jackson drove back from a stock sale and saw a man by the side of the road, his arm held out as though asking for help. He wasn't wearing the charcoal-grey coat but it looked like the missing girl's father. He stopped and asked if the man needed a lift. The man looked at Gordon and didn't speak. At the parish council there were more apologies recorded than there were people in the room, and Brian Fletcher was minded to adjourn. But a decision needed reaching on the proposed public conveniences so they went ahead. There were hard winds in the evenings and the streetlights shook in the square. Late in the month Miss Carter brought her class to the Jacksons' farm for the lambing.

They crossed the road in pairs and pressed up against the line of hurdles in the open doorway of the lambing shed. Will had said he'd do the talking, and was waiting for them with the worst of the blood wiped from his overalls. His brothers weren't interested, and had all found something to do at the far end of the shed. Miss Carter thanked him again for letting them visit, and then Will found he didn't really know what to say. Most of the children had grown up in the area and knew more about lambing than Miss Carter. He asked her where she wanted him to start, and she asked whether any lambs had been born overnight. Just three, he said. We don't do much. We let the ewes get on with it as best we can. Check them over once the mother's finished cleaning them up, put a tag on, make sure they've started feeding okay. She asked if they could see any of the newborn lambs, and before he could answer he heard Gordon saying no from the far end of the shed. Will told her it was important not to move them away from their mothers in the first few days. She looked disappointed. She asked him to explain what would happen over the next weeks and months, and he talked about how soon they'd be out on the grass, which ewes had stayed out to lamb, the movement of the flock to ensure they had the best grass, the selection of the first lambs for processing towards the end of the summer. Processing? she asked. He didn't understand the question. One of the girls pulled at Miss Carter's sleeve and explained what processing was. Some of the boys were already picking up sheep pellets and flicking them at each other. Miss Carter handed out clipboards and asked them all to draw pictures and while they were busy she asked Will if he was planning to go to the Spring Dance at the village hall. The other teachers are talking about going, she said. Will said he hadn't really thought about it. He'd have to see what work was on. But those things are okay usually. Could be a good crack, he said. If you were thinking of asking I might give it some thought, she said. There was a look on her face that gave him something to think about. They heard the noise of a ewe in distress, and Gordon telling Will to scrub up if he was done. Will said he'd better get on. He said she might want to take the children back now. She told him she might see him at the dance. Right you are, he said.

In his studio Geoff Simmons washed his hands at the deep stone sink, the clear water dissolving the clay and running in a milky stream down the plughole and into the trap beneath. The wet pots on the tray were drying off and the kiln was just beginning to warm. In the hedge outside Mr Wilson's window a blackbird waited on its grassy bowl of blue-green eggs as the chicks chipped away at the shells. On the television there were pictures of floods across northern Europe: men in waterproofs pulling dinghies through the streets, collapsed bridges, drowned livestock. When the tea rooms opened for the season the footbridge hadn't yet been rebuilt. The parish council wrote to the Culshaw Hall Estate as a matter of urgency, and the estate said it was the job of the National Park. The National Park disagreed. The river keeper said he could only do what he was asked. The first small tortoiseshells began mating, flying after each other above the nettle beds until the females settled somewhere out of sight and waited for the males to follow. The National Park ranger from the visitor centre spent an enjoyable hour watching them, and making a record, and when he got back to the office he filed it carefully away. At Reservoir no. 11, the maintenance team went along the crest of the dam, looking for cracks in the surface or sinkholes. There were molehills on the grass bank to deal with. Along the river at dusk there were bats moving in number, coming down from their roosts to take the insects rising from the water. They moved in deft quietness and were gone by the time they were seen. The Spring Dance ended early when a fight between Liam Hooper and one of the boys from Cardwell spilled back in through the fire doors. It was soon broken up but by then there'd been damage and the Cardwell boys were asked to leave. Outside in the car park Will Jackson was again seen with Miss Carter from the school.

Martin Fowler was working behind the counter in the butcher's shop when the man from the bank came in and said it was time. You're talking about what now? Martin asked. He gave the man the kind of level stare that had once been enough to sort things.

The man from the bank had some files under his arm and he told Martin he would need the keys. There were two more men waiting at the door. Larger, these two. That's not going to happen, Martin said. There was a chain-metal rattle behind him and Ruth came through from the back, asking what was going on. The man from the bank repeated himself. But we've had no correspondence on this, Ruth said; nothing. She felt Martin go slack beside her, and the man from the bank looked sympathetic. All due process has been followed, he said. The documents were sent by recorded delivery, and signed for. It was the sympathy on his face riled her the most. There was no call for sympathy. She scooped the money from the till while his back was turned, and ushered Martin out with what little dignity she could find in him. The man from the bank had a new lock fitted by lunchtime, and notices put in the window. And that was that. They went home and they sat and she couldn't even find the energy to ask Martin for some kind of a bloody explanation. The sound of Sean Hooper dressing stone came from across the river, a steady clipped chime moving a beat behind the fall of his arm. The swallows were busy in and out of the barns. The well-dressing boards were brought out of storage and taken down to the river to be soaked. The girl's mother was still at the Hunter place and it was known that Jane Hughes visited sometimes. She was never there long, and no one thought to ask how the visits went. She'd have said nothing, of course. Sometimes she thought she'd like to be asked, even if only by her husband or by one of her colleagues in the wider church. But this was the job. She parked the car and went inside and a short time later she came out. The girl had been looked for. She'd been looked for at each of the reservoirs, around the breakwater rocks on the shore and up through the treeline and in all the boarded-up buildings and sheds. She could have fallen into the water and drowned. She could have been trapped in some kind of culvert or sluice deep under there. The divers had found nothing. People wanted to know. People felt involved.

When Jackson came home he was taken in a carry-chair from the ambulance to the motorised bed which had been installed in the front room. There'd been plenty of preparations to get to this point, but when the ambulance crew left Maisie felt a wave of panic at everything that had to be done. Gordon and Alex had been busy getting the room ready, but it was hard to tell whether Jackson was pleased. The weakness in his face had improved enough that he was now just about able to speak, but his fixed expression made emotions impossible to read. The bed had been turned to the window so he could see out down the street towards the church. There was a table to one side set with bedpans and medications, and a radio placed near the bed. There would be care-workers coming in, and nurses, and a physiotherapist, but there was still a long list of jobs they would need to do for him themselves. There was a row on the first evening when he made a fuss about being fed. There'd been no objection when it was nurses at the hospital but from his own wife it was too much. He managed to spill a bowl of soup with just a swift angry turn of his head, and when Maisie was done clearing up she asked Gordon to have a word. He didn't take long. If you'll not let us feed you you'll be dead in a week so think on, he said. In the morning Jackson took a bowl of scrambled eggs. Through the window he could just see Les Thompson walking his fields across the river, checking on the ripening grass. The heads would be forming and the leaves falling back. The cut was due. They would need a dry period soon if they were to get it in. There was talk about the survey stakes which had been found near the Stone Sisters. Cooper made enquiries at the planning office and ran a story in the *Echo* about plans for another quarry. The fieldfares were away in Scandinavia, building nests and laying eggs. A group of travellers moved into the old quarry down by the main road. Tony asked Martin if he'd ever heard anything more from Woods, and Martin said not. Tony asked if he'd not been a bit paranoid about the whole thing, and since it was almost a year now Martin admitted that might be the case. It was water under the bridge, he said.

————————

On the last day of term James and Liam and Deepak skipped school and took their bikes up the track above Reservoir no. 3. They had to push them most of the way up the hill. There was loose shale and deep ruts and the going was slow. At the top they took drinks and crisps from their backpacks. My dad's been offered a job in Newcastle, Deepak said. Newcastle, said James; how come? Newcastle's not bad, said Liam. I've been there. My uncle runs a sports shop there. I was helping in the shop once and Alan Shearer came in looking for football boots. He's been looking for a job for a while, Deepak said. It's my mum's idea. He was well fussy about the boots, said Liam. Your mum wants to move to Newcastle? Not really. She just wants to move somewhere else. Doesn't she like it here? She's been a bit weird about living here, ever since Becky, Deepak said. Funny thing about Alan Shearer, right, is he's got really tiny feet? Liam, shut up. Your uncle lives in Cardwell. No, that's my other uncle. You are so full of shit. Your mum's full of shit. James leant across and smacked the bag of crisps from Liam's hand. Liam scrambled on to his bike and set off down the hill. They watched him bump and skid down the track, the dust rising behind him. Wasn't it your mum's idea to move out here in the first place? Yeah. But she says it's changed now. You know. She says she wants to be somewhere closer to family. You got family in Newcastle? James asked. No, but. Is he going to take the job? I don't know. I don't think he wants to. But Mum's really unhappy. She keeps going on about it. Newcastle, fucking hell, James said. Yeah. They finished their crisps. James put on his backpack and picked up his bike. Are we doing this? Liam was almost at the bottom of the hill. He hadn't fallen yet. Deepak got on his bike, and looked at James. That summer. Did you actually get off with her, with Becky? James looked at him. I mean, no, not really, he said. Fuck it, Deepak; did you? No, Deepak said. I wanted to though. Are we riding down this hill or just talking about it or what? James said. Shut up about it. Let's go. They rattled down the track, their heads full of the noise of their bikes skidding in the ruts. At the bottom of the hill they came past Will Jackson, who was late collecting his boy from school. It was the last day of term and when he got to the classroom the other children had gone. He thought it might be a good moment to have a word with Miss Carter. Tom was full of questions about what they would do when they got home, and Miss Carter was busy clearing up, and so as he walked with Tom down the corridor it was now getting on for three months that nothing had been said. Probably there was nothing to say. She had texted him but he'd asked her not to. He hadn't wanted any complications. He wondered if complication had been the wrong word to use. Could be she would have taken offence. It wasn't always easy to know. He wondered what she'd done with his underwear; if she was saving it or if she would have thrown it away. It would have been no trouble to drop it in the post, but she hadn't. She'd asked him for the loan in the morning, pulling on the pair of blue-and-white-striped jockey shorts that looked a lot better on her than they'd ever looked on him. Snug, would be a word. Not something he'd heard discussed, how good a woman could look in a man's underwear. But there she'd been, standing at the foot of his bed, those blue and white stripes bending every which way, a mug of tea in each hand and a look on her face enough to blow anyone's fusebox. And later when she'd slipped out of the house, going the back way through the garden and into the woods so as not to be seen, he'd thought for a moment it could have been the start of something or other. The taste of her as he sat with a fresh mug of tea and didn't drink it. Will Jackson and Miss Carter from the school: it had a good sound but people would talk. And the boy's mother would turn it against him. There was no need for that. He could go elsewhere. But there was the give of the mattress beneath him as she'd clambered back into the bed. The force of her. He'd had to keep from bursting out the back door and chasing her down in the woods. And after those texts there'd been nothing. An awkward silence. A getting on with things. But she still had his underwear, and he thought perhaps that meant there was something to come. He should talk to her.

The National Park ranger, Graham Thorpe, organised a Butterfly Safari, and despite plenty of interest Sally Fletcher was the only one to attend. He muttered something about her probably having something better to do with her Sunday, but she told him she was keen. They walked along the river and through the quarries and up the hill behind Reservoir no. 8, and he showed her where to look for skippers, various fritillaries, coppers, tortoiseshells, and blues. They found half a dozen species but he seemed to be talking about two dozen more, describing their lifecycles, migrations, feeding habits, mating styles. He'd become very talkative, and Sally was enthralled. She'd had no idea there was so much to it. The two hours were over far too soon, and when she had dinner with Brian that evening she realised she didn't want to tell him anything about it. This would just be her thing now. At the edge of the beech wood and in the walls along the road the foxgloves were tall, and the bees crept in and out of the bright thimbled flowers. On a fence-post by the road a buzzard waited. The cricket team went over to Cardwell and although rain took out most of the day there were enough overs left for Cardwell to win. The bilberries came out on the heath beyond the Stone Sisters, and on the second Sunday in August a group went up from the village to pick them. The fruits grew sparsely and there was a need to keep moving and stooping across the ground. It felt less like a harvest than a search. The grouse shooting started. In the pens at the edge of the Culshaw Estate the pheasants could be seen ducking and scattering at the slightest noise. The days were long and still. There was a guilt in just walking the hills with the sun blazing down and some people worked harder than others to not let that guilt keep them away. It helped to avoid the path past the Hunter place, was a feeling. The girl's mother was still there. She was rarely seen but her presence was felt. The path climbing up round the back of the barn conversions had thickened with grasses, with so few feet trampling it down. The occasional photographer still crept up there in the early dew but they were soon spotted and brought down, their trousers wet with seed-heads and burrs. Always men, these ones. Nothing to arrest them for. It was usually Stuart Hunter who found them. He wasn't a man for confrontation but on this he would give no ground. They were never told twice. Jess Hunter wondered where he found this strength of purpose when it was often otherwise lacking. She wondered if he felt something towards the girl's mother beyond the responsibilities of a host. It seemed unlikely. He wasn't a man for something like that. Once he'd sent them away he would come back into the house pacing and breathless, and she sometimes had to hold him to calm him down. It reminded her of the adrenalised state he would get into after rowing events, at university. Sometimes the energy of it would carry them into the bedroom; but more often it would send him charging into his work, hammering through a day of spreadsheets and phone calls and heated conversations with staff. And still beyond the Hunter place there were reminders of the girl's disappearance all over the hill: the flowers at the visitor centre, the new fencing around the mineshafts, the barking of dogs along the road. Most people stayed away altogether, and took their walking to the reservoirs or the edge of the quarry or further to the deep limestone dales in the south where the butterflies rose like ash on the breeze and the ice-cream vans still appeared.

The summer had been low with cloud but in September the skies cleared and the days were berry-bright and the mud hardened into ridges in the lanes. At the allotments the main crop of potatoes was lifted, the black earth turned over and the fat yellow tubers tumbling into the light. It was Irene's turn to put together the Harvest Festival display at the church, so she and Winnie spent a week making sheaves of wheat at Irene's dining-room table. They'd been friends since Irene had first come to the village, but had only really spent time together like this since Ted's death seven years previously. Winnie still had the better eye for this type of thing. She was a few years older than Irene, was part of it. And she'd grown up here, whereas Irene had always kept a touch of the town about her. There was concentration in Winnie as well, which Irene was still trying to learn. Sometimes when she was with Winnie she felt like she might be talking too much. But there was so often just one more thing to say. When they were done they carried the arrangements down to the church, where they served as centrepieces to draw the eye away from the clutter of tins and packets the schoolchildren brought in, and people said it was one of the finest displays seen in years. The river slipped beneath the packhorse bridge and turned slow eddies along the shore. There were carers coming in to see Jackson once a day, washing and turning him and encouraging him out of bed. He could feed himself now, and his speech was better, but it still took the two of them just to hold him upright while he stood on his pale hairless legs. They were a help while they were there, but the rest of the time it was Maisie who had to fetch and empty his bedpans, and bring his food, and help him change into fresh pyjamas. She'd been told that if his mobility was going to improve it would mostly happen during these first months, and that he needed to be ready for physiotherapy as soon as it became available. Watching the way he worked the bed controls, the motors softly whining as it tilted up and down, she wasn't convinced he would have the fight. The boys were building a sun room at the back of the house, so that he'd have somewhere comfortable to spend the days and wouldn't just waste away in bed. It was taking some building. There were teenagers walking through the field behind the house, heading out to the beech wood for drinking no doubt. Will Jackson recognised the voice of the Broad boy, and the stone-mason's son, Liam Hooper. Girls as well. In the beech wood Deepak and the others settled into the den they'd built three years before. His family were moving out the next day. They'd brought blankets and Liam was lighting a fire. The cider was almost gone. The conversation had faltered. Lynsey and Sophie were sitting on a log with a blanket around their shoulders and James could see something in their eyes. They looked as though they had something to say and no intention of saying it out loud. They seemed pleased with themselves, and uncertain. James watched them and they were looking at Deepak. Liam was crouched by the fire, blowing into the kindling. The girls stood up and told Deepak they had a leaving present for him. Deepak looked pleased and confused. What is it? It's over here, Sophie said. Follow us. They strode away into the trees and Deepak looked back at James, shrugging. Liam sat up from the fire. Probably making him a virgin, Liam said. James laughed at him. You've got it back to front, he said. Liam blew into the fire again. Whatever, he said. Your mum gets it back to front. Lynsey came back first and she wouldn't look either of them in the eye. She pushed Liam out of the way and got the fire going properly. She kept touching her lips. Sophie was gone for longer and when she came back the two girls walked away quickly, holding hands. Deepak came through the trees and crouched by the fire and in the wavering light his eyes were dazed. The other two were looking at him. He grinned. You're not getting any off me so think on, he said, laughing as they both rolled him over on the ground. In the morning the embers were still smoking when the removal lorry arrived.

————————

In October the missing girl's mother was seen up at the Hunter place, loading a van with boxes and bags, including two large sacks of what Jess Hunter later told people were all the sympathy cards she'd been sent. The understanding was that she might not be seen again. There was embracing on the driveway with Jess and Stuart Hunter, and with Jane Hughes who had come along to see her off. The man who was with her started the engine of the small white van and they bumped their way down the track. The gate opened automatically as they approached, and they were out of sight before it jerked slowly closed and clanged against the frame. Jane Hughes talked to the Hunters for a few minutes more before driving down the track herself. On her way through the village she called in to see Jackson. Maisie had told her neither of them held much truck with praying. Jane had said she quite understood but she'd like to pop round all the same, and now she was in the kitchen, asking Maisie to call her Jane instead of Vicar, while they waited for the kettle to boil. She didn't say much, and instead let Maisie talk on about the running of the farm and the work her sons were doing and the plans they had for extending one of the buildings. Jane had the impression she was nervous about something. In a pause she asked how Jackson was doing. He won't see you, Maisie said. He doesn't want to see you. Jane told her that was fine, she quite understood. He's angry about things I think, Maisie said. He's angry but he's got no one to blame. Jane said she could understand that. And how are you doing? she asked Maisie.

We're getting by, Maisie said. We'll manage. We're getting some help. The boys were putting the ram out with the ewes for tupping. The ram wore a raddle and the ewes soon had swathes of colour across their backs. There was a racket in the field as the business went on. The mornings got darker again and in their flat above the converted stables Su Cooper was often up before dawn with the twins, lying them screaming on their playmats while she held the kettle under a tap and shoved the heel of her hand into her mouth to keep from screaming herself. She knew she should be stronger than this but some mornings she felt completely alone. Her parents were too far away. Her friends were too far away. She had no one in this village, no one she could count on. At night there were badgers fighting in the beech wood. The travellers moved out of the old quarry down by the main road, and although they took most of their rubbish with them they left a couple of broken-down cars behind. They were both burnt out within the week. Mischief Night came around and was busier than the year before, although nothing compared to what it once was. Irene stood in the square and watched the youngsters spraying each other with shaving-foam and asked Martin if she'd ever told him that as a lad her late husband had once managed to hide an entire dairy herd on Mischief Night. Animals were considered out of line after that, she said, proudly. Martin said he wasn't sure but he thought the story sounded familiar. The clocks went back and the nights overtook the short days.

In November the Cooper twins had their first birthday. The flat above the stables was too small for more than half a dozen people, so the party was held in the function room at the Gladstone. It was the first event held there since the police had stopped using it for press conferences, but Tony put up so many balloons and streamers that it was easy to forget those scenes: the rows of chairs, the police officers, the huge mounted photographs of the missing girl. The twins weren't walking yet, but were full of noise and thrived on the attention. They sat up on decorated high chairs at the head of a long table, and welcomed the food that kept coming their way. Su's parents were there, and some cousins from Manchester, and a dozen people from the village who Cooper had particularly wanted to ask for the sake of all the support they'd shown. It had been a long year. They were both exhausted. He didn't think it should be possible to survive on such little sleep, but they had. And the boys were so beautiful. He couldn't quite absorb the fact of their being his sons. Even when they threw their drinks on the floor, or cried when the birthday cakes were brought out, he was desperately proud of them. Of their appetite for life, and for change; of the way their brains and their personalities seemed to expand by the minute. And this wasn't supposed to have happened to him. He'd accepted that it wouldn't. He'd reached fifty with only two failed and distant relationships to show for it, and he'd trained himself to tolerate another way of life: friendships and acquaintances and independence. He'd taught himself to value the freedom to travel, to move around, to go out or stay in as the fancy took him. He hadn't travelled, in fact. Had always put it off, had never even owned a passport. But the opportunity was there. Being alone didn't need to mean being lonely. He'd managed to convince himself of this. And then Su. He didn't understand how it had happened. After a week she'd said they should have children, and when he'd laughed she'd told him no one was getting any younger. After a month she'd said they should marry, and taken him to Manchester to meet her parents. And he'd just kept saying yes. It had been such a simple pleasure, to keep saying yes. And for all those years when it seemed like they might not have children after all, he'd kept saying yes: yes, let's try this; yes, let's spend those savings; yes, this is worth another try. It had been difficult but they'd come through it together. The hard work of raising the boys was almost a reward. Su was going back to work soon, but the BBC had said she could start part-time and do some of that from home, so it felt as though they would manage. She was desperate to get back to work, some kind of work, he knew. He watched as she lifted Han Lee out of his high chair for the photos, and called him over to lift out Lu Sam. They stood close together, holding their boys, her family crowded around them while the photos were taken and everyone told them to smile.

———————

Jones the caretaker lived with his sister at the end of the unmade lane by the allotments, next to the old Tucker place. His age was uncertain but he'd worked at the school for thirty years. His sister was younger, and was never seen. She was understood to be troubled in some way. Most of the parents in the village had known him when they were at school. He had his own way of doing things, which pre-dated the other staff. There were locks in the school for which he had the only keys. The other staff were senior to him but he wouldn't be told and he worked to his own timetable. He had clear boundaries and some of these were known. The boilerhouse doubled as his staffroom and no one else went in. Through the doorway occasionally an armchair was seen; a radio, a kettle, a stack of fishing magazines. But the door was almost always closed. The boiler itself was often breaking down. In the middle of December it broke down again and Mrs Simpson went looking for Jones. She found him on the steep wooded bank behind the school, climbing up through the elder and hazel with a rubbish sack. He was reeling in a faded line of police cordon tape which was snagged through the trees. It took him some time and she watched. Two years already and it seemed like no time at all. He saw her and he climbed up the bank. Must have blown in from the lane, he said. Folk are careless. She peered at the coiled tape, and nodded. Boiler? he asked. I'm afraid so, she said. There's been no heat at all this morning. He headed over towards the bins and she walked with him. Inlets are probably clogged again, he said. Everything else all right? Yes, yes. Fine. He took out a pouch of tobacco and rolled a cigarette. She looked as though she had more to say. He nodded up at a bank of clouds over the moor, thickening. Weather, he said, and walked on. Mr Jones, she called after him. Will you let me get someone in? He stopped. It's a decent boiler, he said. I'll sort it. A goldcrest moved through the tall firs at the far end of the playground, picking quickly at the insects feeding between the needles. From the hills behind the allotments a thick band of rain was moving in. The reservoirs were a flat metallic grey. There was carol singing in the church with candles and children from the school playing their recorders and opening their mouths wide to sing. *Be near me, Lord Jesus.* The church was full. *I ask thee to stay.*

Richard Clark came home between Christmas and New Year, after his sisters had left, and on New Year's Eve he was seen going for a walk with Cathy Harris. They'd known each other at school, but had barely been in touch for years. They'd been as good as engaged, in fact, until he went to university and she didn't. By the time he graduated she'd married Patrick, who had grown up alongside them and been their closest friend. Things would have been different if she'd come away to university with him. He'd barely spoken to either of them again. Patrick had been dead five years now. Richard had been out of the country at the time. The mist hung low over the moor and the ground was frozen hard. It had rained long into the night and the air was cold and damp. It was no kind of a day to be walking up on the hills but they'd made an agreement. Richard pulled his scarf over his mouth and walked behind Cathy, watching where he put his feet. The climb to the first ridge was steeper than he remembered. He was sweating already. He stopped to undo his jacket. Cathy turned back, waiting for him. She didn't seem out of breath. She'd never left the village, and had kept the hill-fitness he'd lost. The mist was beginning to clear. They walked on. She asked how long he was home this time and he said he was flying out in the morning; that he was due for a meeting at lunchtime, local time. He asked how her two boys were and she said they were well. The oldest one was starting his A levels next year. Ben. Nathan was just starting secondary school. They had coped okay, in the end. He told her how sorry he was that he hadn't made it to Patrick's funeral. She shook her head and said she hadn't expected him to. It would have been a long way to come. She knew it was difficult. She changed the subject. She told him what it had been like coming up here with the search party, walking steadily across the ground, wanting to find something but dreading what it was they might find. Richard said he didn't think he'd walked up here since they'd been teenagers. She told him he was talking about ancient history, and laughed. They walked on. They were thinking different things. The missing girl's name was Rebecca, or Becky, or Bex. In the video which had recently been released the mother was using Bex. In the video the girl was laughing but it was difficult to hear what was said. It was strange to actually hear her voice. Some people said the video didn't look much like her. Her hair was longer than in the photograph, pulled back from her face in a thick plait which swung around her head as she sang and span towards the camera and pointed at whoever was doing the filming. The police were still treating the case as a missing-person inquiry.

3.

At midnight when the year turned there were fireworks going up from all across the village. The dance at the hall was crowded and hot and there was steam in the light of the doorway. In the morning there were spent rockets lying in the street and sparklers jammed into the planters in the square. There was rain for most of the day and snow on the higher ground. The tips of the new-growth heather could just be reached through the snow. Woodpigeons came into the gardens where feed was put out and were often chased away. A contractor came out to the Jackson place with the ultrasound tackle and Gordon Jackson took her out to the ewes. They spent most of the morning doing the scans and the two of them had to work closely. The proportion of twins was decent and there were fewer barrens than in most years. Gordon felt good about the way the morning had gone. The woman's name was Deborah and she knew how to handle the sheep. She had strong arms and a firm grip. He asked what she was doing at the weekend and she said she had family to see. There was an ambiguity in her use of the word family but he let it go. When he dropped her back at her van she left him with a smile that some would have taken for a dismissal. She stayed on his mind for some days. The parish council moved their meetings to the function room of the Gladstone, and there was an immediate improvement in attendance which Brian later told Sally reflected poorly on all concerned. Martin and Ruth Fowler separated, which was more of a surprise to him than it was to some others. He was heading for an interview at the job centre when Ruth stopped him by the door and said she was leaving. There was a winded feeling in his stomach but he didn't let on. Christ, Ruth, you couldn't have picked more of a moment? She held up her hands as though she was sorry and she told him there was never a good time, there was never the time to talk. He stood in the doorway and rubbed his face. There were words he wanted to say but they were muddled. If he started he would get there too late. He told her he'd got some good prospects for work, that things were on the mend. He stopped because there was no point. When Ruth made a decision. She touched the side of his face and he slapped her hand away. There were words but he couldn't get started. He was going to be late. He wanted things to be different but they weren't going to be different. Do what you feel like doing, he said. She stood in the doorway and watched him go. They had been married since they were twenty-two, a year after meeting each other at a Young Farmers' dance. Neither of them had been young farmers, but it was known as a place for meeting. He'd bought her a drink, and there was a bluntness in the way he spoke that she knew was a cover for being shy. He couldn't dance, but there was otherwise a grace in his gestures and especially in his hands which intrigued her. When they met for the second time he took her to see the butcher's shop he was taking over from his father. He gave her a tour, and as they stood behind the counter he kissed her and she leant back against the chopping block. For her this was when it was settled. The wood of the chopping block was bowled and smooth beneath her hands. When they married she moved into his house, and a few years after that, while she was pregnant with Bruce, his parents moved out to a sheltered housing complex in town. They were happy for a long time, or comfortable, and when that changed Ruth had been hard-pressed to explain why.

At the Ash Wednesday service Jane Hughes daubed the congregation's foreheads with a thumbprint of ash in a way that hadn't been done for years. There were only the very regulars there, and the service was short. But there was a hushed intimacy to it that made the ashy touch of Jane's thumb seem quite in keeping with the moment, and when they came out into the cold sunshine they were each caught by the same moment of self-consciousness, reaching towards their foreheads. In the churchyard a pair of blackbirds courted, fanning their tails and fluffing their rumps and watching each other bright-eyed. There'd been a break in the frost so Mr Wilson went up to the allotments and put some new rhubarb crowns in the ground. The place was busy as it hadn't been since autumn. Clive was potting up broad beans. Miriam Pearson was raking over a bed and sowing rows of early carrots. Jones was still digging. There was a short period in the afternoon when the heat of the work and the steady fall of the sun had people shrugging off coats and hats, hanging them on earthed shovels while they stretched their backs, but the chill soon returned to the day and the light faded and the ground began to steel. There was a new moon, thin and cold and high. In his studio Geoff Simmons wedged up balls of clay for the wheel, weighing them out and cutting each one with a wire. His studio was at the top of the lane behind the Jackson place, in a converted feed store he'd bought with an inheritance ten years before. The planning permission was for a workshop only but it was known he spent nights on a sofa in there. He had the front area set up as a shop but there weren't many who had yet beaten a path to his door. He sat at the wheel and soaked his hands in a bowl of water. The whippet lay curled on a rug beside the oil-heater. In the evening the teenagers were seen down by the weir, drinking. At the school there'd been talk that either James Broad or Liam, or both, had once slept with Becky Shaw. The talk seemed malicious and unlikely. Sophie and Lynsey wanted to know where the talk had come from and James told them he didn't want to fucking think about it. Sophie tried to give him a hug but he shook her off. Liam threw stones into the water. The girl had been looked for; in the beech wood, in the river, in the hollows at Black Bull Rocks. She had been looked for at the abandoned quarry, the storage containers broken open and the rotting freight wagons broken open and the doors left hanging as people moved on down the road. They had wanted to find her. They had wanted to know she was safe. They had felt involved, although they barely knew her.

The sound of the water over the weir came up to the village in staticky bursts, shifting and faltering on the wind as though the volume was being flicked up and down. Thompson's men led the first of the herd into the milking parlour, each cow finding her place and dropping her head to the feed-tray while the men worked along the line and cleaned the teats. By the river the keeper cut back a willow, and as he took off another branch he watched the trail of sawdust drift downstream. The curl into a back eddy. The drop and sweep across a shallow fall. There were footsteps on the path and he set to the next branch. There was always plenty of work. At school the police came and spoke to Liam and James and Lynsey about any involvement they'd had with the missing girl. New information had been provided regarding the family's stay at the Hunter place the summer before she'd disappeared. The interviews were handled sensitively, with the parents present at all times, but they led to trouble for the three of them at school. No further action was taken. They all three acknowledged spending some time with the girl that summer, but denied even knowing she was around over the Christmas period. They had no useful information to share. The police thanked them for their time and apologised for any distress which may have been caused. The clocks went forward and the evenings opened out. The buds on the branches were brightening. There were mattresses dumped in the old quarry and sometimes this was seen as a service by the couples who went there at night. Ruth Fowler moved away to Harefield. Neither she nor Martin had ever lived alone before. She found the adjustment easier than Martin. There was talk she was planning on opening a shop of her own. Organics. They went for that type of thing in Harefield. It was noticed that Martin was often away from the house. He was in the Gladstone or he was walking through the village, down the lane past Fletcher's orchard to the packhorse bridge. When he was home there were lights on through most of the night. In the mornings his car was sometimes seen idling outside the butcher's shop. Their daughter, Amy, was away at university when they separated. Ruth had offered to talk to her, and at first Martin was grateful but when Amy came and took her things over to Ruth's new place he realised what had happened. He knew she had to choose but he still felt snubbed. Bruce, their eldest, was in Manchester, the last anyone had heard. He could do what he wanted, was Martin's feeling. Martin didn't want to know.

At the school on the last day of term Miss Carter sat on her low chair in the reading corner with the whole class silent and looking up at her. Even Ryan Turner was quiet, for the first time since Miss Carter had known him. She was reading *Hansel and Gretel*, and when she came to the part where they found their bread-crumb trail had been eaten and they were lost in the forest she heard the children's attention deepen. She lowered her voice to a whisper. They seemed to lean in more closely, and were quieter. She could see herself in their faces now, when she was their age, and had gazed up at Mrs Bradshaw and dreamed of one day being that smooth-legged woman perching on the edge of a soft chair, reading aloud. The moment lasted only until Ryan Turner pulled a scab from his knee and started crying. In the long grass around the cricket field, the skipper larvae span their tiny tents of leaves together. There were cowslips under the hedges and beside the road, offering handfuls of yellow flowers to the longer days. The Spring Dance was held in aid of the newly re-formed playgroup, which Jane Hughes had been working on for some time. She was hoping to raise enough money for some outdoor play equipment to use in fine weather. The week after Easter her car broke down and Stuart Hunter drove her round for the Sunday services. She was doing three services before noon, with a five- or ten-mile drive between each. There were no more than a dozen people at any of the services, and Jane conceded Stuart's unspoken point about the inefficiency of the whole set-up. Two or more gathered in my name though, she said. Two or more. You won't tell anyone I used the same sermon, will you? My lips are sealed, Vicar, he said. He dropped her off at the vicarage in town and said that he wouldn't come in. And things are okay at your place? she asked. It's settling down, he said. We've not re-let that barn conversion yet. It doesn't feel right. Maybe you should come and exorcise it. He said this with a laugh, as though he wanted her to think he was joking, and as she got out of the car she told him to know that he and his family were remembered in her prayers. He had no way of laughing that off. There was rain in the evening of the sort it was pleasant to be in for a while, taking the dust from the air and leaving an exaggerated smell of early summer. In the beech wood the fox cubs were moved away from their dens.

Will Jackson called in to see his mother, and ended up helping the physiotherapist bring Jackson through from his bed and into the new sun room, one grudging step at a time. The effort of it exhausted Jackson, even with the two of them holding him up, and once they'd got him on to his special chair he was asleep before the television came on. Beside the chair there was a table of puzzles and toys so he could work on his motor skills. There were printouts of the exercises he was meant to be doing tacked up on the wall. The corners of the pages were curling in the sun. The physio said that people's rates of progress varied enormously, and that it was important to encourage him to be mobile as often as possible. When he left Maisie asked Will if he had time for a cup of tea, and he said yes if she wasn't going to talk about Claire again. She said she didn't want to interfere, she just wanted him to be happy. I'm doing fine, he told her. Things are settled. It was never my doing in the first place, but things are settled now. He looked at her impatiently. I've noticed the odd thing, she said, that's all. Mum, he said. I'm putting the kettle on and we're not talking about it. Fine, she said. They stood at opposite ends of the small, cluttered kitchen, listening to the wet sound of Jackson's breathing being drowned out by the gathering row of the kettle. There was rain and the river was high. The cow parsley was thick along the footpaths and the shade deepened under the trees. Stock was moved higher up the hills. The tea rooms by the millpond opened for the season, although business was slower than usual because the footbridge still hadn't been rebuilt and no one from the campsite could get across. The reservoirs filled. James Broad finally admitted to his parents how much time he'd spent with Becky Shaw. He'd met her that previous summer, he said, when she'd been down at the tea rooms with her parents one afternoon while he was mucking about on the bridge with Deepak and Lynsey. She'd come over and talked to them, and later in the week when she'd seen them swimming she'd asked if she could join them. The four of you swam together in the river? his mother asked. And you told the police none of this? We were scared, James said. It didn't seem important. We didn't want them asking more questions. So you all decided not to say anything, his father said. James nodded. It was, like, a pretty intense time, he said. There was all that talk. Of course there was talk, his father said. Why didn't you tell us everything? What were you thinking? He was raising his voice, and James was pulling back. His mother looked at him carefully. Is there something else? she asked. James? Christmas, he said. I saw her at Christmas as well. We met up a couple of times. On your own? He nodded. Just the two of you? He nodded again, and his parents looked at each other. James. Was there something going on between you? We were only thirteen, Mum. Come on. What would have been going on? James, his mother said. This is important. Did you see her the day she disappeared? He shook his head. He shook his head and he wouldn't say anything else. James's father had his hands over his face. Oh, Jesus Christ, give me strength, he said. James tried to ask if he was going to be in trouble but the words were whispered and cracked. His mother sat beside him. At fifteen his shoulders were as broad as an adult's. His whole body shook. James's father left the room. He heard James asking his mother whether the whole thing could really have been his fault.

Richard Clark's mother had her upstairs rooms redecorated. It was one of the first things she'd thought of after her husband's death, but it had taken almost a decade to get around to it. She'd wanted to redecorate before, but he'd always said it was squandering money. The rooms felt bigger when it was done, even after the Jackson boys had come over and put all the furniture back. When they'd finished, and she'd slipped them some pub money by way of thanks, she sat on the end of the bed and looked around at the changed room. The window was wide open to help shift the paint fumes, and she could hear people walking up to the square, the faint background whisper of the weir, the sound of Thompson's herd unsettled about something. The room felt brand new. She'd never felt so at home. The curtains blew in and out with the breeze. The river was high and roiled with rainfall and the new flies were hatching thickly in the afternoon. Ian Dowsett stood on the packhorse bridge and watched trout as thick as his forearm leaping clear of the water for the take. It was two days more until the season opened. His whole body rocked as he thought through the motions of whirling a line out across the water. On the television there were pictures of forests burning in Malaysia, whole hillsides stripped bare and the topsoil washing off into the rivers.

Early mornings in Thompson's cowshed the swallows were laying eggs, the males flying back and forth with food for their brooding mates. There was a hush up there in the roof after the shriek and dash of mating time. Jackson's boys, with Martin and Tony and a few of the older teenagers, went down to the packhorse bridge to lift the well-dressing boards out of the river. They were much heavier after a fortnight's soaking, and there was some grunting as they lifted them on to the back of a trailer, the cold water streaming down their arms. They rode on the trailer to the top of the hill and then carried the boards into the village hall. When they'd finished they had to put a chain on the trailer. Scrap metal had been going missing in the area for a while, and now they were taking the stuff that wasn't even scrap. Gates lifted off hinges, drainage gratings taken out of the roads. The thing was getting out of hand. There were blackbirds going in and out of the hedge in Jones's garden, yanking up earthworms and beetles and fetching them back. Jones's sister sat at the window a whole morning and watched them. She was waiting for Jones to come home and he was late. He was always gone longer than she liked. She hated it when they called him her carer. She could take care of herself but it was true she did need the company. The days were very long sometimes. She had ways of making the time pass but they weren't always enough.

––––––––––

In July the heat hung over the moor and the heather hummed with insect life. Sally Fletcher went with Graham, the National Park ranger, to do the official butterfly count. She'd learnt her identifications quickly, and Graham was able to rely on her sightings. They'd become quite the team, and Brian had asked if they were having some kind of affair. Laughing at the very idea. The reservoirs shone white beneath the high summer sun. There was a parish council meeting which was almost entirely taken up with the issue of the proposed public conveniences, and by the time they came to Any Other Business Tony wanted to close the bar. So there was a general shifting in seats when Frank Parker stood up and said he wished to raise the issue of verge maintenance. Brian asked Judith to check whether this had been raised before. Judith looked through the record and confirmed that it had. I think in that case, and in light of the time, we'll ask you to submit a written report to a future meeting, Brian said. Frank Parker experienced the brief turmoil of being offended and grateful at the same time. In the beech wood the fox cubs were doing their own foraging and the parents were spending longer away. In the night there were calls back and forth. The edges of the territory were understood. Around the deep pond at the far end of Thompson's land a ring of willow trees were in full leaf, shielding the pond as though something shameful had once happened there which needed keeping from view. There was a parents' evening at the school, and Will Jackson went down to see how Tom was getting on. Miss Carter showed him some of Tom's workbooks and told him that he seemed a contented little boy. She said she'd be starting at a new school in September and he said that was a shame. He said Tom would miss her. But Tom wouldn't be in my class in September, she pointed out. He looked embarrassed. But I just mean generally, about the place, he said. You'll be missed. She held his gaze for a moment. Generally about the place? He nodded. A look of realisation came into her eyes. Oh, Christ, Will, she said. You idiot. He stood up, holding Tom's report sheet, watching her watch him to the door. Afterwards he wondered whether she'd meant he should have asked. Later in the week there was a leaving assembly and when Mrs Simpson gave Miss Carter flowers the parents stood up and applauded so loudly that she didn't know what to say. At the river a heron stood and watched the water, its body angled and poised while the evening grew dark.

Claire had been seen spending time at the Jackson house, and Will Jackson was uneasy about why. After almost three years of living with her mother, keeping Tom half the week and barely saying a word when they met, she appeared to be softening. She'd been taking Tom to the Jackson house while Will was out working, spending time with Maisie and staying for tea when she was asked. Maisie seemed to brighten in Claire's company, as though they'd only just met and she was looking to make an impression. And Tom was happy to have both parents in the same room, looking from one to the other while he chattered about school, reassuring himself that they were both there. After one of these teas, Claire asked Maisie whether she wouldn't mind having Tom for the evening while she and Will went for a drink in town. Which was the first Will had heard of such a plan. Maisie said that would be fine. Tom jumped up and asked if he could read a bedtime story to Grandad. Will could feel the weather shift around him. He asked Claire what was going on as they walked out to the car, and she told him they were just going for a drink. He didn't think there was ever a just when Claire was involved. At the pub he bought the drinks without needing to ask what she was having. They sat opposite each other and talked about his father, his brothers, the farm. She talked about her work. He was watching her, waiting for something to happen. She seemed distracted. She couldn't keep still. It was like she had some kind of secret, and holding it back was more fun than telling it would be. He wondered if she had a new boyfriend. She asked if it was true he was going to be in that year's pantomime. He said he'd been asked. Well, you can't really turn it down, she said. She bought a second round of drinks. He had a half, on account of the driving. He'd expected they would run out of things to say, but they didn't. He'd forgotten how easy it was to talk to her, when they weren't arguing or keeping each other at bay. He'd known her as long as he'd known anyone – from playgroup, from school, from paddling in the river and running around the farm and long summer evenings swimming in the quarry – so it should never have been a surprise. Their falling into a relationship had been as obvious and easy as his working with his brothers on the farm. It was having the baby had been the problem. They were too young. Eighteen, and old enough for a council flat on the Close but nowhere near old enough for the responsibility of it. It had made serious people of them, and that had never been the plan. They'd had help to begin with, from both mothers and from people in the village, but it had all fallen away after a while. And then it had just been chores. Chores on the farm, chores at home, and nowhere to go for any time off. She'd got fed up with his long hours of working. After a while it had seemed like they only knew how to argue. And a while after that, she'd left. He'd taught himself how to live without her, and as nice as it was to sit with her now, he had no regrets about the way things had turned out. They finished their drinks and he offered another round and she said they should get on. They drove back in silence, the light thinning as they came through the head of the valley and round past the old quarry entrance where she asked him to stop and was kissing him before he'd even put the handbrake on. He pushed her carefully away. He asked what she was doing. We've had a nice evening, haven't we? she asked. And I know you'd like to. But I thought things were settled, he said. Her hands were moving up his thighs. I thought I'd unsettle them a bit, she said. He closed his eyes and rubbed his face. So you reckon you can just rock up and click your fingers, and that'll be that? Whistle and I'll come running? She sat back in her seat, looking at him. Yeah, she said. Pretty much. She got out of the car and walked into the quarry. She didn't even need to look back. He muttered to himself and shook his head and followed her into the quarry, quickening his step to catch up.

In September a soft rain no more than mist hung in the trees along the valley floor. The river turned over beneath the packhorse bridge and carried scraps of light to the weir. The missing girl was seen walking around the shore of the reservoir, hopping from one breakwater rock to another with seemingly not a care in the world. This was Irene's description. A public meeting was held in the village hall about the quarry company's plans to open a site close to the Stone Sisters, and there was a general air of opposition. There were crab apples and wild apples beside the freight line curving into the cement works, and on a Sunday morning when there were no trains Winnie walked carefully down there and filled four carrier bags, taking them home to cook up into a clear golden jam, flavoured with rosemary stems. There was a commotion at the Jones house, and an ambulance came to take his sister away. This had happened before. Nobody thought it appropriate to ask questions, and he didn't volunteer. He was seen in the week working at the school without interruption, and wherever she'd gone he didn't seem to be visiting. Evenings he was down at the millpond with his fishing tackle. The boatmen and skaters slid across the still surface and his mind was clear. He could feel the tension lift away as the fish began to rise. People had no idea. He watched the teenagers on the other side of the river following the footpath down to the weir. They carried bottles of white cider that Lynsey had bought in town, and sat on the benches outside the tea rooms to drink them. Sophie asked whether it was true that James's parents were going to split up. James said how was he supposed to know. It was none of his business. They hardly talked to him anyway. Not since. He stopped and lit a cigarette and tried to do a plank on the edge of the picnic bench. Liam asked not since what. James didn't answer. Liam asked was he fucking crying or what, and Sophie told him to leave it. Lynsey told Liam to walk with her, and when they looked back Sophie was sitting next to James, her arms curled around him and the side of his head pressed against her chest. His dad had taken him to the police, it turned out. He'd made him tell them about the time he'd spent with Becky Shaw. The detective they'd spoken to had been sharp with them both and said it was too late for the information to be of any use. He asked Sophie not to tell anyone this. The pigeons fought in the trees. The bats came out at dusk to feed low over the water, fattening up for the winter. There were wild pheasants in the pens at the edge of the Culshaw Estate, drawn in by the fresh water and feeders. After a fortnight Jones's sister came home and he put the fishing gear away.

In October the winds were high and in the mornings there were trees blocking the road. The sound of gunshots cracked down from the woods in pairs. There were more sightings of the missing girl's father, although some of them turned out to be false. It was known that he no longer wore the charcoal-grey anorak, and there was anyway no shortage of preoccupied men striding solitary through the hills. But there were enough sightings to give the impression of a man who couldn't keep away. There was talk that he and the girl's mother had divorced, and around that time the sightings increased. On the shore of the reservoir; around the edge of the quarry; down at the river by the packhorse bridge. Almost always seen from a distance, moving away. At the allotment the pumpkins fattened slowly, lifted from the damp soil on squares of glass, striped in the low autumn light. Jane Hughes walked back from the Hunter place and happened upon Jones beside the mill-pond. He was standing patiently with his hands behind his back, his shoulders hunched and his neck angled forward. She didn't want to interrupt, but as she walked past there was a softening in his posture which she understood as acknowledgement. She'd grown used to these cues. She stepped up beside him and looked at the water for a moment. Mr Jones, she said. Vicar, he replied. You've been keeping well? she asked. He nodded. And your sister? He didn't answer, but pointed in at the water, at some tiny change in the light she could barely see. Scared them all off now, he said. Really? I'm stood in the shadow of the tree, he explained; so I'm right. But you've come looming, so. She stepped away from the edge of the water apologetically. She looked at him. Are you fishing today? No, he said. But if I was. I'll remember that then. Sorry. There was the clatter of woodpigeons' wings in the trees overhead, and the sound of the water moving over the stones. Jones still had his hands behind his back. She's home again, he said. I gathered, yes. There's plenty of trout in there, he told her, if you don't bother them. We don't see her around much, Jane said, leaning out over the water as though watching for trout, giving him a chance to speak without being looked at. She doesn't go out, he said. She waited, but there was no more. That must be difficult for you, she said. Not really. She's no bother. Do you get any help? She felt him stiffen beside her, and his hands came round from behind his back, rearranging his jacket buttons, his cap. He turned away from the water. Weather, he said, nodding towards the hills. It looks like it's coming in, she agreed. Be seeing you then, he said, lighting a cigarette and setting off along the footpath towards the packhorse bridge. On the stubbled fields of Thompson's land a buzzard wandered, picking for worms.

———————

A fog rose early from the river and settled over the morning and the streets felt thick with sleep. On the bank at the top end of the beech wood the badger sett was quiet. There were tracks between the sett and the damp ground beneath the elder trees where the earthworms were mostly found, but the feeding trips were brief. There were dry leaves and grasses scattered up towards the sett. A settlement was reached over the footbridge, with the Culshaw Estate and the parish council and the National Park agreeing to split the cost. The Jacksons took the contract and had the job done in three days. On Bonfire Night the rain kept people indoors and although the bonfire had been covered it took a long time to light, smoking and spitting while a small crowd stood beneath umbrellas and cheered sarcastically. Later in the month Will Jackson took Tom out on the back of the quad bike to check on the ewes that hadn't yet been brought down to bye. While they were up there he explained that the three of them would be living together again soon. Tom was helping to check feet, and he concentrated very hard on the hoof he had jammed between his knees. Mum told me, he said, eventually. You're all right with it then? It's not up to me. No, but we want you to feel all right about it. Will found the first signs of scald on a ewe, and asked Tom to pass him the spray. Think it'll be easier than going backwards and forwards all the time? Can we talk about something else, Dad? Will looked at Tom and nodded, and they didn't say anything for a while, and once they'd checked the whole flock they sat on the edge of the trailer and looked down the hill.

A woman by the name of Susanna Wright moved into one of the three-bed houses on the Close with her children. Questions were asked as to how she'd been allocated when she wasn't known. Others had been on the list for longer. She was quick to introduce herself but vague about where she was from. Her accent was southern. She had a boy of fifteen and a girl of ten, Rohan and Ashleigh, who spent their first days in the village slouching about with the sullen expressions of children who've grown up in the city and feel threatened by people willing to say hello. There were questions about why she'd moved in at this time of year, and where the father might be, but nothing was said to her face. She was heard in the post office talking about a damp problem, and Gordon Jackson was soon round there offering to help. At the other end of the Close Claire moved back into the flat Will had managed to keep on since she'd left him the first time. There was no real ceremony to it; half her stuff had been left in the cupboards all along, and since that evening when they'd stopped off at the quarry she'd been leaving more of her things each time she stayed over. Tom wasn't sure he preferred the new arrangement. He wasn't surprised when he heard them arguing about curtains. He didn't think his dad had ever had an opinion about curtains before. He kept a bag of clothes and toiletries and schoolbooks tucked under his bed, just in case. A week before Christmas it snowed heavily overnight and in the morning people shovelled pathways from their doors, the village busy with the sound of metal scraping against stone and of car engines left running to warm up. Jackson's boys went out and put grit on the steeper roads but for the most part people had to drive slowly, their tyres squeaking on the compacted snow. In the evening there were carol singers going from door to door for the local hospice, and their voices trailed thinly through the still cold air.

Richard Clark came home just after Christmas, and for once his sisters were there when he arrived. When he sat down to eat with them he felt cornered. The husbands and children made for a crowded dinner table and he didn't have much to say. They were staying up at the Hunters' barn conversions, and on the doorstep when they left his sisters talked about their mother's health. There was talk about responsibility being shared. He couldn't be out of the country this much, he was told. He was the oldest of the three but it had never felt that way. He said he'd do what he could but it seemed that their mother was coping perfectly well. His work wasn't always predictable, he said. Your work's a total bloody enigma, Rachel said. You know what I do, he replied. He started to explain again about his consultancy business, but they made yawning noises and laughed and headed for their cars. The high street was busy. The pantomime was on in the village hall, and well attended again. It was *Aladdin* this year. Tony was Widow Twankey, and he made a good job of it. He delivered his lines in a loud deadpan which at times didn't look entirely deliberate, and he wore the heavy costume with a certain grace. Will Jackson was working backstage but had refused a part. When the audience headed out into the night the snow was falling thickly again. The next day Martin stopped off at Harefield to look at Ruth's new shop. She was surprised to see him. He was heading to his new job in town but this wasn't on his way. She asked how he was keeping and he said it was okay. There was a lot of fresh produce in wicker baskets, and sausages hanging in strings above the chiller counter, and a strong smell of coffee. There were many different types of olive. There were prices Martin found it difficult to believe people were actually paying, but when he asked how business was going Ruth said he'd be surprised. People had cut back on cars and foreign holidays, she told him, and they were spending what was left in shops like this. People liked to treat themselves to nice things. He wondered if this was a pointed remark but he let it settle. They'd had differences. It was done now. He was just glad to know things were going well. He drove into work fast enough that he almost lost grip on the last corner before town, and parked across two parking bays, and clocked on just before his shift was due. If he'd wanted a fucking economics lesson he would've asked.

4.

At midnight when the year turned there were fireworks from the Hunter place. The sound carried suddenly to the village hall and for a moment people wondered what it was. Irene was called out from the kitchen and asked to take Andrew home as he'd become agitated. At the next parish council the Hunters were asked not to repeat the display. When term started Rohan Wright caught the bus to the secondary school in town with Liam and James and Lynsey and Sophie. They'd seen him around the village but they hadn't yet spoken. There were nods and he told them his name. They asked where he'd moved from and he said south of London. Liam asked if his mum was the hippy who was going to run yoga classes, and the others told him to shut up. I'm not being funny, I'm just saying, he said. My mum's well into yoga. She knows Yuri Gagarin and everything. There were so many ways this didn't make sense that no one quite knew what to say. You know, he explained, incredulously. The spoon-bender! Your mum's a bender, Lynsey said, and James gave her a high-five. The bus turned on to the main road by her parents' farm-supplies place, and they asked Rohan questions about his old school all the way to town. Cathy Harris drove past the bus in the other direction, and when she got home she knocked on Mr Wilson's door and asked whether Nelson needed a walk. He said that would be a great help, and asked whether she'd have a cup of tea first. A routine of theirs, this, to make the arrangement seem temporary, when in fact Cathy had been walking Nelson most days for years. Mr Wilson's hip made it hard for him to get up the hill and as far as the shop, let alone the hour's brisk stride that Nelson hankered after all day. A cup of tea would be lovely, she said, bracing herself for the thud of Nelson jumping up against her. Mr Wilson closed the door and walked slowly to the kettle. The Millennium Millstones were pushed off their plinths, and Sean Hooper was contracted to repair them. By the packhorse bridge a heron paced through the mud at the river's edge, head bobbing, feet lifted awkwardly high. It stopped, and settled, and watched the water.

In February there was no snow but the frosts were hard. Ruth was sent a Valentine's card and knew that it came from Martin. The best response would be silence, she decided. At Reservoir no. 7, the maintenance team checked the upstream face of the dam, looking for erosion along the edge of the crest. There were cracks of ice in the shallow puddles along the path. Susanna Wright held her first yoga class in the village hall. There were only three people there, and because the room was too cold for safe stretching she spent the session talking about What Yoga Is and What Yoga Isn't. She said she'd speak to the caretaker about the heating, and then she asked who the caretaker was. The County sent someone to clear the old quarry down by the main road. The two burnt-out cars had been a beacon for every fly-tipper in the area, and it took three trucks to cart it away. Where's it all come from? Martin asked Tony, as they stood up on the cliff above the quarry, watching. Where's it all going is more the point, said Tony. They're only going to stick it in some other hole in the ground. Might as well leave it here. Wait while the quarry's full and then bury it all. Plant some fucking trees. Job done. There were gulls and crows circling overhead. Jones was with them but he had nothing to say. Martin headed off down the road to work. He'd taken a job on the meat counter in the new supermarket. He hadn't told people but they found out soon enough. They all shopped there, after all. It felt like the final humiliation, after Bruce, and the shop, and Ruth. But the hours were fine and although the pay wasn't great it was more in his pocket than he'd had when they were running the shop into the ground. They gave him a striped apron and a badge saying *Master Butcher*, but it wasn't butchery. The meat came in ready-jointed, and he was just there to hand it over. He didn't even have his good knives. They were locked in the shop, and the stroppy young bollock from the bank was refusing to let him have them back. He'd been in the job three months now, and his supervisor said there were no complaints as such but did he want to have a think about engaging with the customers a little more? Martin said he would certainly think about that, and went out to the loading bay for a smoke and a kick of the packing cases which were stacked there. The sun went down around half past four but it was already dark by then, the murky light blotted out by the high moors and the gathering clouds.

There was weather, and branches from the allotment sycamores blew on to the roof of the Tucker house next door to Jones. The place had been empty now for seven years. There was a dispute to be settled before it could be sold, but no one seemed to know what it was or who might be involved. Jones went up a ladder and took the branches down. He checked the slates. His sister watched from the front of the house. These things made her anxious. She would ask about them often until they were resolved. He told her the slates were fine and he put the ladder away. She went into the house. The woodpigeons built their nests in the trees by the river. The thin frame of sticks seemed barely enough to take the weight of one fat bird. But it was assumed they knew what they were doing. Cooper was seen working late on the magazine, hard up against the deadline once again. He enjoyed these last pressured hours. It reminded him of working on *The Times*, years back, before he'd come up here to do press for the National Park. There was that same sense of hurried exactitude, of getting one chance only to check everything through. There were differences, of course. The deadlines now were only a matter of his own pride, for one thing. And there was no one else in the office, which meant no one to go for drinks with once the issue was put to bed. The whole office was silent, in fact. He could hear the footsteps of the boys upstairs, hammering backwards and forwards, and Su's muffled voice as she tried to get their pyjamas on. She sounded exhausted, and part of him wanted to go up and take over. But he knew it wouldn't help, and that Su wouldn't thank him for it. She hadn't been in the mood for thanking him lately. He'd been getting things wrong, it seemed. Doing too much, or too little. She'd fallen behind on some projects at work, and been asked to take unpaid leave. A view had been taken about her home-working arrangements, and she seemed to hold him responsible in some way. It was stressful having young children. He understood this. It would pass. He printed off the final proof sheets, and leant over them with a poised red pen. Outside the wind was brisk through the trees. In the band of conifers above Reservoir no. 5 a pair of buzzards rebuilt their nest from the previous year, weaving in new sticks and lining the shallow bowl of it with fresh bracken and grass.

———

By April the first swallows were seen and the walkers were back on the hills. At the heronry high in the trees above the quarry there was a persistent unsettledness of wings. Night came down. At the allotments the water was turned back on for the year and Clive was the first to get his hose hooked up, the silvery water skidding across the ground before seeping into the cracks. There was blasting again at the quarry, and when the first siren came everyone ignored the long rising wail. The second siren came a few minutes later, and anyone with washing on the line was quick to bring it inside. The third siren went and the birds flung up from the trees in the quarry and scattered, and the air stilled for a moment before the deep thudding crack thundered out through the ground and was gone. At the first all-clear the birds settled in the trees. At the second the workers in the quarry went back. In the village the windows were kept closed for a few hours more until the dust had cleared. At the river the keeper dropped the cage of sample bottles into the water from the footbridge by the weir. Always the same spot, at the same time of day, on the same day of the month. Meanwhile there were two chaps who looked like they were scouting for fishing spots, and he wanted a word. He passed Irene on her way up to the church with two bags full of flowers. When she got there she heard singing from the vestry, and it kept on while she gathered the vases. She wasn't much of a judge but it was quite a piece of singing. Took a few moments to realise it was the vicar, because you didn't hear her singing like that in a morning service. She didn't recognise the tune and she could barely make out the words but there was something capturing about it. The high bright windows and the dust in the air and the smell of wood polish and Irene standing there with her arms full of flowers not wanting to move. Faintly another siren sounded at the quarry, and the singing stopped. Late in the month the Spring Dance was held in aid of Amnesty, which was controversial for those who thought politics should be kept out of it but was pushed through by Jane Hughes. It was agreed that no publicity material would be displayed as it could detract from the mood of the event. Some folk do find that manner of talk puts them off the hog roast, Clive told the meeting. His remark was carefully minuted. The police did a presentation on crime prevention at the Gladstone, and while everyone was in there someone took off with a stock trailer the Jacksons had left on Top Road. There were some who thought this story was funny when they told it but they were soon set straight.

In his studio Geoff Simmons threw a new batch of pots. Yesterday's were drying slowly at the back of the workshop, and the kiln was beginning to warm. He pressed a ball of clay on to the wet wheel and centred it off. The whippet slept in the sun. He palmed the spinning clay and drew it taller and fingered it into a vessel. The wall worked thinner in his hands. Throw lines formed on the surface and the water flowed out from the wheel. There were years of learnt discretion in these moves. It couldn't be shown. The pressure of his touch was exactly sufficient and this pot from the clay came to be. He slowed the wheel and shaped the brim. There was a bellying in and out that he liked to impose, and a curl at the lip. Customers sometimes asked if these were vases or jugs or drinking cups and he said only that they were vessels. He had been accused of being obtuse. On the rug the whippet kicked her back legs, dreaming of sprinting across fields. In the quarry by the main road the small coppers were mating again. There were swallows nesting high in the barns, the eggs glossy white and speckled red beneath the fluffed feathers of the mothers. In the woodland by the river the bluebells were massing. The clay for the well dressing was cut from the wet end of the Hunters' land, and carried up to the village hall. The men puddled it in a tin bath, stomping up and down while Irene kept adding water until she declared the consistency just right. When it was done Gordon Jackson went back to the Hunter place and asked Jess if she wanted to go for a drive. This had been mentioned. There'd been talk of wind turbines on the high ground overlooking Reservoir no. 9, and she wanted to get the lie of the land. She said she had some concerns. He thought there might be something else. Stuart Hunter was away. She'd been baking and she asked him to hang on while she got cleaned up. When she was ready she got into the Land Rover with him and they drove out past the visitor centre along the track leading up to the ridge. Gordon had a key for the gates. The track was deeply rutted and she bounced in her seat a few times and once there was a quick, embarrassed laugh and she reached out to grab at his arm. Eye contact, careful silence. There was a pattern but it was never routine. This had been developing for a time. At the top of the hill they stood against the Land Rover and he let her think the first kiss was her idea. He'd scrubbed his nails. She talked a lot and she had no shame about what they were doing. She wanted to be looked at and he took his time. Afterwards he wondered whether for once there might be something in it and he could see by the way she buttoned her blouse that there wouldn't. He was just catching his breath and she already wanted to leave. She offered him a smile that made him want to sit down. He wondered how much concrete they'd need for the wind-turbine foundations, and whether they would build a new road to bring it in.

Sophie Hunter and Lynsey Smith went to a party in town and made a mess of the arrangements for getting home. They had no money for a taxi so they decided to walk. It should only have been four miles but they took a wrong turn in the woods in the dark. It was funny for a time but then they were scared at the trouble they'd be in. You know what my dad's like about being late, Sophie said. He'll have already called the police. It's not just your dad,

Lynsey said, it's all of them. Lynsey was carrying her shoes and the mud was coming thick between her toes. They'd seen some car headlights and were heading down towards the road. I wouldn't mind but it was a shit party anyway, Sophie said. She tried to laugh but she heard Lynsey crying. She turned back and reached for her hand. She could barely see her face in the dark. It won't be far now, come on, you. Sophie, fucking hell, Sophie. They'll be so pleased to see us they'll forget to tell us off. Come on. I just wish. Lynsey, no. I just wish we knew what had happened to her. Lynsey; Jesus, again? Leave it out. They came out on the road by the cement works, and walked up the hill towards the village without speaking. The fourth car that came past was Mike Jackson and he gave them a lift. They were both kept home for a fortnight, and soon afterwards were given their own mobile phones, paid for by Sophie's parents and meant for emergency use only. Olivia immediately wanted one as well, but was told she was too young. Jess Hunter made Sophie help Irene with the cleaning work in the barn conversions for that fortnight, and Irene worked her hard. Irene took the work seriously. She was quick but she didn't take shortcuts. People employed her because they knew they wouldn't have to check. It was the same at home. One thing Ted had always said was she kept the place decent. If you knew Ted you knew that was high talk. He'd never been much help himself, bringing all that dust in on his clothes and his boots. And the bath, when he was done, at the end of a week in the quarry. Like someone had used it to mix cement. This had been how it was. He worked out of the house, she worked in the house. It was only fair. And that included Andrew. If the boy was up in the night it was only fair that she go to him. Ted was older than her by nearly a decade, and too old for that type of carry-on. She'd been close to forty herself when Andrew was born, and sometimes she didn't know where the energy came from. If the boy was having one of his fits then Ted was entitled to stay in his chair, the days he'd had. This wasn't something they'd negotiated. He liked the house to be quiet, and clean. It wasn't too much to ask. But now that he wasn't around she had more time to take on other cleaning work around the village. Cleaning was what she knew. She finished up and walked home the long way, cutting through the higher fields behind the Jackson place and the square. She had a little time before Andrew was back. The hard-baked footpath parted a way through the ripening grass. She felt the sun on her arms. She looked up to the moors. Years since the route of the Greystone Way had been moved and there were still deep ruts in the peat across the top of the moor, some of the walkers insisting on the original path, the eroded line widening steadily as people sidestepped the deepest mud. What was there to be done. The butterflies were out. The fieldfares were away, raising their young in the colder north.

———————

In July Will and Claire were married. The church was full of people who'd known them since childhood. Jackson was brought down in his wheelchair, dressed in a new suit he'd had bought for him on account of his changing size. There was food at the Gladstone, and dancing in the village hall. Gordon Jackson was seen dancing with Susanna Wright, but nothing seemed to come of it. Susanna and her children had become known about the place. She was volunteering at the playgroup in the village hall, and had kept going with the yoga class. She'd taken on an allotment, and put her name down for the pantomime. She was quick to talk to people, and even Irene had said it was likely she'd settle in. The boy Rohan had made a decent stab at his GCSEs despite the disruption, and had sparked up a romance with Lynsey Smith. They were seen walking together, down by the river or through the beech wood, but more often they were just in the bus shelter by the cricket ground, kissing until their faces were raw. There were jokes made in the Gladstone, and even Susanna wondered when they would find somewhere private. She'd long since put a condom in his wallet to be on the safe side, and happened to know it was still there. Ashleigh had made friends at school but there was only Olivia Hunter who was her age in the village. She spent a lot of time on the computer. At the allotments Martin sat on the bench at the top end of their plot. Ruth's plot now, although she'd raised no objection to him spending a little time there. She was making a better job of the place on her own than the two of them had done together. He didn't mind admitting that. It meant something. It said something about the two of them. Or perhaps she was getting help. From someone he didn't know about. It could be that. It could have been that all along. They could be looking at him now – Mr Wilson stooping over his asparagus beds, Clive forking out his compost – and pitying him for what he didn't know. This wasn't a line of thinking that helped, of course. He'd been advised. There were steps he could take, to steer around this line of thinking. He straightened his back and lifted his head and made himself a larger vessel for the difficult feelings. He looked outside himself and took other sensory information on board. He listed the plants he could see. Gooseberries and strawberries and currants; sweetcorn and courgettes and beans; nasturtiums and marigolds, sweet william, sweet peas; spinach, lettuce, kale. Nettles, cow parsley, thistles, bindweed. Plenty of bloody bindweed. Whoever the bugger was he wasn't much of a gardener after all, leaving all that weeding to be done. He opened the tap on the bottom of the water butt and set off down the hill. He had another go at being mindful but mostly he minded a drink. Tents were seen up at the Stone Sisters, and there was talk of an environmental group setting up a protest camp against the new quarry. Les Thompson walked his fields in the evening while the sun was still warm on the grass. The heads were up and the cut would come tomorrow. In the beech wood the fox cubs were taken away from their dens and taught to find food for themselves. A white hooded top was found in a clough on the top of the moor, oiled a deep peat-brown and fraying at the seams. The make and design were confirmed as a match by the missing girl's mother. The forensic tests took weeks and were inconclusive. Extensive searches were conducted where the top had been found but nothing further was unearthed.

Sophie Hunter and James Broad were known to be courting. This was the word Stuart Hunter used, without irony. Everyone had long assumed they would get together, but it was only a few weeks before they realised that something was wrong. They were in the cinema room at Sophie's house one afternoon while her parents were away, and she told him not to take this the wrong way but sometimes it felt like kissing her brother. James told her she didn't have a brother and she said that wasn't the point. He wasn't annoyed. He was almost relieved. He said that when he kissed her it didn't feel like kissing his sister but more like kissing her mum. She asked when he'd kissed her mother and he said often. She's a very liberated woman, he said, and she told him he was disgusting. It takes one to know one, he said. They were still holding each other, and although they knew where the conversation was going they were in no hurry to let go. He kissed her one more time, very softly, and shook his head. We used to run around naked together at playgroup, he said. It doesn't feel right seeing you naked now. People will be disappointed, she told him. Captain of the rugby team and the head prefect? We're supposed to be the dream team. This is it then? he asked. I guess it is, she said. That's okay, isn't it? He nodded. Mind you, she said, my parents aren't due back for hours. She watched him as she unbuttoned her top. Well, this is confusing, he said. He shifted on the sofa. But if you're going to be like that about it. She reached for the button of his jeans and they kissed again, quickly, and pulled off just enough clothes to have sex. He came quickly with a shout and a sigh and afterwards she stayed astride him for a moment, stroking the side of his face and telling him they would always be friends. And once they'd wriggled back into their clothes she told him, as though it was nothing, as though she'd only just thought of it, that actually Lynsey really liked him and he should think about that at some point. He shook his head and told her she was a disgrace. She asked him what the problem was. She wasn't even at playgroup with us, she said. It would be different. He buttoned his jeans and reached for the remote control. You can choose, he said. The cricket team went over to Cardwell for the annual match and found that Cardwell had only managed to get eight players together. There was some discussion over whether the game should go ahead, and when it did the result was a hard-fought draw. Martin disappeared for a week and when he came back he was limping and there were cigarette burns on the backs of his hands. Woods had a longer memory than expected, was all he would say when Tony asked.

Mr Wilson lived next door to Cathy Harris, in one of a row of old mill workers' cottages at the end of the lane by the cricket field. He'd moved to the area as a young man to work on the new reservoirs in the hills above the village. He and Jean had met in the drawing office, married within the year, and moved into the cottage together. When Cathy knocked on his door and asked if Nelson needed a walk, he invited her in for a cup of tea, as always. Nelson was running circles in the front room, and she reached down to knuckle him around the ears. He lifted his head and stilled for a moment, and Mr Wilson came through with the teas. He moved slowly now from age, and from his hip in particular, but Cathy remembered him as someone who'd always had an air of slow precision about him. She couldn't picture him ever having run for a bus. She didn't think he'd played in the village cricket team, although he'd been known to serve as umpire. He'd been an engineer with the water company until his retirement about five years ago, working on the reservoirs and the treatment plant for most of his career. He was proud of the project's technical achievements, and knowledgeable on their working detail. His opinions on bottled water were well known. He was a tall man, with long limbs which he always seemed to be arranging carefully as he spoke. She'd never seen him without a collar and tie, although lately he'd been favouring cardigans over the jackets he'd worn before. I've made some more of those date slices, he told her, sitting down and smoothing the creases of his trousers as he crossed his legs. In the garden a pair of blackbirds were feeding together on the hawthorn, their young long gone. There was weather and the days began to shorten. At the church it was Maisie Jackson's turn to put together the Harvest Festival display, and her decision to include a stack of unwashed fleeces alongside the more usual flowers and marrows and corn attracted remarks but nothing was said directly. There were blackthorn hedges on the track to Thompson's farm that were mostly left uncut. By late September they were heavy with sloes, the black fruits in the sharp air dusted blue. It was a popular spot, and most of them were picked early and frozen to sweeten off, rattling like ball-bearings as they were poured into demijohns and smothered in sugar and gin. Frank Parker submitted his report on verge maintenance to the parish council. It had taken him more than a year to prepare. He was thanked for his work, and his conclusion – that more regular attention needed to be paid to verge maintenance throughout the village – was duly noted. James Broad's parents finally separated, and his father moved out to a place in town. The swallows left for the year. There was some confusion at the first Workers' Educational Association meeting of the term when the book-keeping tutor turned up with a bag of protective clothing and a demonstration hive.

There were concerns about how Su Cooper was coping with the twins. She was seen arriving at the playgroup in the village hall one morning just as the toys were being packed away. She'd had to unbolt both doors to fit the double buggy through, wrestling it backwards up the step, and as she pulled it into the corner and turned to face the room it took her a few moments to understand that she was too late. Lee ran straight to the toy cupboard and started pulling out the cars, and she had to hurry after him and explain. Most of the other parents had already left. Susanna Wright went over and told Su it would be fine for the boys to play with a couple of cars while everything else was being packed away, and although Su tried to stop him Lee took this as a cue and dragged two cars out for him and Sam. Let me get you a coffee, Susanna said, resting her hand on Su's shoulder. Su hesitated, and moved away very slightly. Tea, she said. Susanna nodded, and Su followed her towards the kitchen, standing by the hatch and keeping an eye on the boys. They were driving the cars towards each other at great speed, crashing head-on and screaming. Susanna told Su she'd put some toast on. I'm guessing breakfast was a long time ago now, she said, smiling, and when Su didn't reply she went on to tell a long story about when Rohan had been a toddler and she'd left the house four times in one morning, only to be thwarted by a succession of dirty nappies, spilt food, and a broken buggy wheel. And when I finally got to the bus stop someone told me my dress was inside out and I burst into tears, she said, laughing, buttering the toast and passing it across the counter. Su smiled, thinly. It must have been hard for you, she said; by yourself. Oh, darling, no, I wasn't by myself then, Susanna said. Things were a lot easier once I was. The boys had started crashing their cars into the wall. It's always hard, Susanna said, softly. And it must be especially hard with twins. People understand that, you know. No one's judging you. Everyone knows what a great job you're doing, okay? She reached across the counter and put a hand on Su's arm, and again Su shifted slightly away. Her eyes were dry and her mouth was tight and there was a stiffness in the way she was standing. Please, she said.

On Bonfire Night Irene and Winnie put together a group from the Women's Institute and opened up the cricket pavilion to serve food. There were baked potatoes and chilli and some of the children poked marshmallows on very long sticks into the blaze. It was a dry night, and at one point the fire burned almost as high as the horse chestnut tree. Away from the crowd, Lynsey and Sophie were sharing a bottle of wine and being sarcastic about the fireworks. Sophie asked what had actually gone wrong with the whole Rohan thing, and Lynsey said it was hard to explain. She wasn't sure who had ended it, she said. There were arguments and then they just didn't see each other. But you liked him, Sophie said. Lynsey said yes, she liked him a lot, it was just that he got a

bit. She trailed off. In the firelight Lynsey looked at her expectantly. You know, she said. Attentive. He was always doing things
for me. Like, always. It was nice at first. It made a change from
the way things are at home. But it was like he thought I needed
protecting from everything. He was always asking what I was
doing. He always looked so fucking *concerned*, you know? She
made a frowning face of concern at Sophie, and Sophie laughed.
You can go off a wrinkly forehead, Lynsey said. Sophie asked if
she'd basically dumped him for having a wrinkly forehead, and
she said she hadn't dumped him. She'd tried talking to him but he
just hadn't got it. They had these arguments where he wouldn't
argue back. But anyway it was done now. It was over. Sophie
asked if he was all right about it and Lynsey said she thought so,
she wasn't sure. Sophie asked whether he might be in need of
consoling and Lynsey looked shocked. Don't do that, she said,
come on. He's cute though, Sophie said. She finished the wine.
He's got a lovely forehead. The two of them were heard shrieking
as they walked away towards the road. The bonfire was starting to
die down and the crowd was thinning out. The clouds were high
and the night was cold and the embers were still smoking in the
morning. On the eleventh a wreath of poppies was carried up to
the airmen's memorial, and words said. There were few in the
village now who could remember the heavy bomber thudding
into the moor, the roar of it carrying across the valley and the
awful explosions that followed and the smell of the peat burning

for days. The ribs of the fuselage shone silver in the heather, picked as clean as sheep bones by the wind and rain.

Jane Hughes had started calling in to see the Jacksons regularly, talking mostly with Maisie about the farming and her family and then putting her head round the door to say hello to Jackson. She'd never so much as tried to bring a bible into the house, Maisie told Irene. I think she just likes passing the time of day. Jackson's even started asking after her, though he doesn't say much when she's here. But she needn't think we're going to start watching *Songs of Praise*. She didn't tell Irene that last time Jane had been there Maisie thought she'd seen her place hands on Jackson's forehead and say some kind of prayer, and that Jackson's eyes had closed in what looked like appreciation, and that she'd wondered about all the things she didn't know were going on inside of that man's head. At the allotments there was little left to harvest, save the first tender buds of Brussels sprouts. The badger sett in the beech wood was quiet. In the deep sleeping chambers the badgers were keeping still, waiting for the winter to pass. There was low cloud and rain, the sodden fields churned up with the force of it and the sky staying dark for days. The river pushed under the packhorse bridge and carried its rising force to the weir. The reservoirs were high and the water poured over the rim of the spillways, cascading down the steps to the culverts which fed through the base of the dam. The missing girl's father hadn't been seen all year. There were reports in the newspapers that he'd been reunited with the girl's mother. It couldn't be said that his brooding presence was missed. Late in the month there was snow and the Jacksons went out on the hills looking for ewes. They carried sacks of feed on the back of the quad bikes and brought the flocks down to the lower fields. There were no losses yet but if this weather kept up it was likely. There was carol singing at the school on the last day of term, the hall hung with decorations and the words on a screen and the parents perching on tiny chairs to join in as the sky darkened outside and the weather closed in again. *While shepherds watched their flocks by night*, they sang, glancing up at the moors; *all seated on the ground.*

The missing girl's name was Rebecca, or Becky, or Bex. She would be seventeen by now, and the police published a computer-generated image of how she might look. There was something about this approximate-Becky that seemed too smooth. As though the Becky in the picture had been kept in a sterile room and was only now coming out, blinking, unsteady on her feet and with no more sense of the world than the thirteen-year-old child who had gone in. The police said they hoped the increased publicity surrounding the image's release would encourage people to rethink their movements at the time of the girl's disappearance.

There were dreams about her appearing on television again, gazing at the cameras as she was hurried from a car to a house in a London street, unable to talk about where she'd been. There were dreams about her crawling through the caves, her clothes smeared with mud and tar in the dark. There were dreams about her held captive, in basements and isolated barns, always with something across her mouth or her eyes. There never seemed any way to stop it. She had been looked for, everywhere, and she hadn't been found. She'd been looked for in every shed and greenhouse on the allotment, doors kicked in if the owners were away, old rolls of carpet and plastic matting lifted, torches shone in behind armchairs and stacks of peat and coils of hose. It wasn't known what more could have been done. The allotments were cold and bare, exposed on the high ground to the wind which came scouring up the valley. In his greenhouse Clive was laying out seed potatoes, half-listening to Susanna Wright, who was leaning in the doorway with a seed catalogue. She was telling him about the heritage varieties she was planning to order. It sounded quite the quantity. Her voice kept going up as though these were questions, but he didn't think she was asking advice. He wasn't going to offer if it wasn't called for. He did know that no one had successfully grown globe artichokes on this site yet. Through the iced greenhouse glass he could see the tops of the beech trees bending in the wind. There was Jones leaning over his spade, digging over his entire plot once again. The man had a love of bare soil that was hard to fathom. Jones was keeping his eye on the old Tucker place. He cut the ivy back from the windows and went up a ladder to clear the gutter. It would do no one any favours if the place went to ruin. His sister wanted to know where the Tuckers had gone and who would move in next. He said he didn't always have the answers. He asked her not to ask so many bloody questions, and when the tears came he said he was sorry. It went on like this. This was how it went on.

5.

At midnight when the year turned there were fireworks on the television in the pub and dancing in the street outside. The evening was mild and dry. The village hall had emptied out and when the bells were rung there was cheering for the first time in years. Richard Clark came home on New Year's Day, and when his mother opened the door he could see all her bedroom furniture crammed into the front room. Jackson's boys came and moved it for me, she said, as though that were an explanation. It was a shock, he told Cathy later, as they walked by the river with Mr Wilson's dog. He hadn't known how reduced his mother's mobility had become. His sisters had told him nothing. He wondered if they even knew how long it was taking her to get up out of her chair, to walk through to the kitchen and put the kettle on. He wondered how she was managing to get to the shops. There were people who helped, presumably. Neighbours. Irene.

Cathy didn't like to admit that she'd had no idea. She rested her hand on the wall as she squeezed through the gapstone stile, and stooped to let Nelson off the lead. She watched Richard squeeze through the gap. He thought there was something in the way she looked at him but it was probably nothing. That was all a long time ago. They'd both moved on. He understood that. They were different people now. He remembered how restless he'd been then, when they were seventeen and imagined they were in love. He'd been impatient for everything, and all they'd seemed to talk about was getting away from the village; going to university, travelling the world. He'd never disliked the place, or the people. It had just seemed natural to want to leave, and natural to want to talk about it even while they were undressing each other and learning what was possible with the scratch and yield of the heather beneath them. He wondered now whether Cathy really had talked about it in the same way, or whether she'd just let him rattle on. Patrick had never mentioned leaving. Richard remembered that much. He'd never talked about the future at all. There was no need. He just kept working in his father's timber yard after school, while his shoulders got broader, his hands rougher, his wallet fatter. Everyone knew he would inherit the yard once his father retired. It was the sort of certainty, Richard had realised later, that some people found attractive. He looked at Cathy now, walking on ahead, her stride long and effortless between the trees. He wondered if she was thinking about any of this. It seemed unlikely.

She looked back at him, slowing for a moment as she told him to keep up.

Martin told Tony he wouldn't send Ruth a Valentine's card. He knew it was over between them, he said, although he didn't fully understand what had actually gone wrong. She'd said nothing about the card the previous year. He knew that trying to fix things between them only gave her a chance to feel sorry for him. He definitely wouldn't send her a card. On the fourteenth he bought a card and posted it to her house, and on the back of the envelope he said he hoped she didn't mind it being late. The quarry was busy again for a time. They were working a new face, and blasting frequently. The trees along the road were all heavily dusted, and no one had hung washing outside for weeks. There was a want of rain to clear the air. If Andrew was home when the siren went Irene had to be sure to be with him. There was an anxiety it brought out in him that seemed more in keeping with the way the birds flew away or the sheep lunged over to the far side of the field. As a boy he'd just covered his ears and screamed. Now it was more of the headshaking and yelping to himself, but if she stood near him that seemed to be enough. She wondered if his head held the sound in the same place as it held his father. She wasn't sure what he remembered of his father. But it was never simple. What he knew and didn't know. People explained things to her, about what they said was his capacity, and often they turned out to be wrong. When the siren went at the quarry she wanted to hold him but he wouldn't be held. She could only stand nearby. He'd been strong enough to throw her off for years. Some days the siren sounded five or six times. From the eaves of the church the first bats were seen leaving at dusk, hungry from a long winter's sleep and listening for food.

On the moors the gamekeepers from the estate were burning off squares of heather. It was hot, vigilant work. They'd waited for a day when the heather was dry but the peat still damp, and for a low wind blowing downhill, and then they'd marked out their squares and were walking behind a line of fire, damping it down with flat rubber shovels, pushing the flame down the hill until it reached the break they'd already cut. The smell of the smoke carried down to the village. Cooper opened the windows in the flat above the converted stables and let it blow in. The place was empty. Su had taken the twins to her parents in Manchester. There'd been a lot of talk and when it finally happened she'd made the decision sound mutual. There were practical reasons. It would be temporary. She was exhausted and she needed the rest. Her parents would enjoy spending time with the boys. She had to commit to projects at the BBC before the door closed on her career for good, and this way her mother could have the boys while she worked. Austin was too busy with the village magazine, she knew that, he couldn't deny that. There wasn't room for him to stay with her parents as well. They could both do with some space. It would only be temporary. He wanted to believe her but he wasn't stupid. He stood in the empty flat. She had the boys' clothes, their nappies, their toys. It was difficult for him to take on board. The flat seemed much bigger. This didn't have to be about them, she'd said. She wasn't leaving him, she wanted to see him soon. She just needed a rest. She needed someone to look after her for a while. They would find a way through this. His first wife had said these same things, and she'd never come back. He wasn't going to let that happen all over again. He knew how much was at stake. He slept very little and in the morning he was outside the estate agent's office in town before nine o'clock, waiting for them to open.

After a week of rains there were warm still days and the plots at the allotment went wild. The nettles and cow parsley came up in swathes, the bindweed trumpeting through the hedges, and the regulars on the committee took note. In his greenhouse Clive potted courgettes and French beans, and watched Susanna Wright go at her plot with a pair of garden shears. Ashleigh was running round with a stick, scything the heads off the nettles and making more headway than her mother. Susanna stopped often to stretch her back, pulling her hair away from her face and tying it up. She had a very straight back, when she stretched like that. On one such occasion she caught sight of him and waved enthusiastically. He nodded. The greenhouse was hot in the long afternoon sun, and he gave the pots a good misting. Later she came over to say hello and talk about how much weeding she had to do. She was looking for sympathy, it seemed. Last time I was here there was nothing to worry about, she said. And look at it now, it's like a jungle. She was laughing, apparently with surprise. Clive nodded. Weeds will do that, he said. It'll not take long. It was two weeks since her last visit and what did she expect. She'd spent that whole afternoon painting a bench. So. Cooper was spending more time in the Gladstone, while Su and the twins were in Manchester. He'd been trying to downplay the situation, saying it was under-standable that she wanted to be with her mother at a difficult time, saying there was no doubt they'd be back soon enough, but it was generally understood that the man was in bits. He finally conceded to Tony at the bar one evening that he was finding things tough. There was a constant churning in his stomach, he said, a dread that things might stay like this. Martin asked if he'd tried Rennie's for the churning, and Tony told him to knock it off. I don't even know what it is, Cooper said. Adrenalin? I can't relax. I can't think of anything else. Have you tried yoga? Martin said, and Tony gave him a final-warning look. That's very good, Cooper said. Thank you. But really though. This is new to me. I never felt like this with my first wife. When she said she was leaving. I don't remember feeling like this. I know I just need to give her time, okay, people say that, give her time. But what if the time's not enough? What if she doesn't come back? What if she's already met someone else? Martin signalled to Tony to pour a whisky, and passed it along to Cooper. Get this down you, lad, he said. You think that's going to help, Cooper asked; honestly? Not really, Martin said. But it'll shut you up for a bit. There was some laughter, and Cooper tipped the whisky into his mouth, sitting in silence for a few minutes, rubbing at his churning stomach. In the evenings there were showers that came and went, flashing across the valley with the promise of bright sun always behind. There was the sound of a freight train, edging around the bend through the silver birch trees, the empty wagons clattering over the bridge.

The girl had been looked for at the flooded quarry. The fence had been checked for damage or signs of being climbed. The divers had roped up and slipped into the dark. She had been looked for in the caves along the river, and in those cramped spaces only cans and bottles and wadded tissues had been found. On the high embankment the river keeper cleared out a drainage ditch. Where it ran under the road someone had gone to the trouble of bagging up their rubbish before dumping it in. There was the usual mess of brambles to cut back. The rain was heavy and the work was wet, but the sound of the water passing through the pipes under the road was a welcome one. Come summer and the river would be in fine condition. The keeper wasn't a man for whistling while he worked but his mood was good. In the evening Susanna got the hall ready for yoga. It had taken a while but by now the classes were more popular than some had assumed they might be. She kept saying it was open to everyone, but whenever a man showed up he found himself the only one there and soon decided not to come back. Most of the women were regulars, and after a few months some of them were disappointed by how few poses they could hold. Susanna tried to tell them yoga wasn't about goals. There are no badges or certificates here, she said; it's all about finding your own point of stretch. Her voice always softened when she spoke like this, when she moved among them making small adjustments to their arms, their shoulders, their legs. Her touch was gentle and firm. To be adjusted by Susanna meant being the centre of her attention for a moment, and some of the women suspected the others of holding an incorrect posture on purpose. In the woodland by the river there were yellow pimpernels spreading along the banks, their glossy green leaves drinking in the shade and their small yellow flowers like spots of light. At the heronry there were new chicks high in the nests and a flap of parents fetching food back to the gaping mouths. Cooper had spent a lot of time in Manchester with Su while she stayed at her parents', and after two months of driving backwards and forwards he persuaded her to come home with the boys. From the way Su talked about it later it didn't sound as though he'd persuaded her so much as that he simply hadn't given up. Sometimes reliability can be very attractive, she told Cathy. And my mum was doing my nut in to be honest. They found a buyer for their flat almost immediately, but had trouble finding a place they could afford. In the end they went for an ex-council house on the Close, which had none of the character of the stables but did have an extra bedroom and a garden with a swing and a washing line and a gate opening into the woods. They borrowed money from her family to make up the difference, and Cooper moved the magazine office into a side room at the church. By the river the bright young leaves of the willows flashed with light.

James Broad finally told Rohan what had happened with Becky Shaw. They were up at Reservoir no. 9 in Sophie's car, hotboxing. James had driven and Sophie was already pale and shimmering in the back seat, and although she seemed half asleep she kept joining in with what he was saying. The car was milky with smoke. Lynsey was asleep beside her, but she kept waking up and talking about going to university. Rohan hadn't asked about Becky but James had decided it was time to tell. They'd all met her the summer before she disappeared, he said. Her family had come up for a fortnight and they'd started hanging out together. Not doing much. Kid stuff. Building dens. Swimming in the river. Going into the caves. She'd always wanted to do a bit more, push things further. She wasn't much older than they were but she'd seemed a lot more mature. She was so pretty, Sophie said, lighting the pipe again. Wasn't she pretty, James? James glanced at her in the rear-view mirror. Her eyes were closed and she was smiling. He looked at Rohan, and nodded. They'd all fancied her, he said, even if they hadn't admitted it at the time. There was something exciting about her, he said. She talked us into climbing the fence round the quarry, and she was the first one to jump off the rope-swing. She was hardcore. And she was smart, Sophie added, from the back seat. Lynsey sat up straight again. We should all go to the same uni, she said. Shouldn't we? We could live in the same halls and everything. James passed her the pipe, and they listened to the click and draw as she smoked it, the long pause before she sighed out the smoke. James and Sophie were both picturing Becky launching out from the rope-swing, this girl who none of them really knew, the light catching on her long bare legs as she fell through the air and something new stirred in them all. I was the only one who kept in touch with her, James said, after she went back to London. Emails, postcards, nothing much. I didn't have a phone and there was no Facebook in those days. But we kept in touch. We – fuck it. We liked each other, okay? We liked each other. He turned round and took the pipe from Lynsey, who was falling asleep again. He thumbed it full of skunk from the bag on the dashboard. Becky was the one who talked her parents into coming here again for New Year, is what she reckoned. He toked hard on the pipe, and coughed as he let the smoke go. So there's that for a start. Rohan took the pipe. And then when she was here we all met up and hung out for a bit, except it was cold and there wasn't really anywhere to hang out. It was nice seeing her though. We had a little bit of a connection or something. And she'd grown up a lot since the summer. He's talking about her being physically mature, Sophie said, sleepily. Don't be coy, James. You mean she had tits, yeah? Me and Lynsey were well jealous, weren't we, Lyns? Lynsey opened her eyes and looked at Sophie. Edinburgh, she said. We'll all go to Edinburgh. I'll do English, you guys do whatever. It's cheap up there. Sophie stroked her arm and said yes, we'll definitely all go to Edinburgh, we'll all go together, if we get in, we'll be a gang up there. Lynsey closed her eyes. I didn't just mean that, James said. But it was part of it, Sophie murmured. The car was quiet for a moment. When they talked about Becky now it was hard to actually picture her face. The photo on the news had never looked right, but it had replaced the image of her they'd held. She was being lost all over again. Outside the car the evening was still and the light was softening over the reservoir. Anyway, James said, we were all heading home one time and she held me back and we like kissed or whatever and then we arranged to meet up just the two of us, the next afternoon. Rohan looked at him. Sophie asked if she'd been a good kisser. James said he couldn't remember. That wasn't really the point. You mean no, then, Sophie said. Rohan asked what had happened, when they met, whether anything had happened. Sophie sat forward and put her hand on James's shoulder. She never turned up, James said. That was it. That was when she went missing. She must have been on her way over to meet me. Something must have happened. I was waiting for her at the old water-board buildings by Reservoir no. 7, and she never turned up. There was a silence in the car and then the long sigh of smoke streaming out of Rohan's lungs. The car was fogging and the windows were wet with condensation. Outside the wind was picking up and the rain was moving in. Sophie was turning her hand in front of her face, looking puzzled. I think we should go now, she whispered. Rohan lowered the window and the smoke poured out into the night and was gone.

Ashleigh Wright was seen up at her mother's allotment, hoeing along the rows the way Clive had shown her a few weeks earlier. When she was done she earthed up the potatoes, pulled slugs off the courgettes, and planted out some potted winter vegetables Clive had said were going spare. Afterwards she headed down to the cricket ground, nodding briefly at Clive on the way. Clive acknowledged, and went back to his watering. He hadn't wanted to meddle. But the girl had looked as though she'd listen. In the long margins around the cricket field a golden skipper worked her way down a stem of dead grass until she found an opening in which to lay her eggs. The young blackbirds had put on their adult feathers. Most days after school now Tom Jackson spent a couple of hours with his grandparents. Occasionally Maisie could persuade him to sit at the kitchen table and do some schoolwork, but most times he would chase after whatever she was doing, offering to help but just getting in the way, talking about school or television or the long games he'd been playing with his friends. He always included Jackson in these conversations, running in and out of the front room if Jackson was back in his bed. There'd been a time Jackson would have affected impatience with visits like these, but she was sure they were the highlight of his day. Hers too, if she was honest. Tom was one of the few people who could understand Jackson's halting, slurred speech, and just about the only person who could talk to him without making allowances. The speech had improved a lot over the last few years but he was reluctant to say much. His frustration at the way he sounded was obvious. But with Tom he seemed prepared to rabbit on, and she'd even heard him say things that sounded awfully close to bugger, or bollocks, which had Tom in fits of giggles. It even made Maisie smile, when she knew Tom wasn't looking. The thought of Jackson's reaction if he'd heard the boys say anything similar when they were young. So much discipline in the house, in those days. There'd had to be. Five of them in ten years, and the house not all that big. Five of them to be fed and cleaned and dressed and herded around. Five sets of clothes to be mended and patched and handed down. Ten muddy boots to be kept out of the house. Always so much noise. Jackson not thinking that what went on in the house was his business, unless one of the boys overstepped some mark or other. And her keeping them out of his line of fire and holding them together when they fell foul. Her back ached with the memory of it. She hoped Claire would have the sense to think one more was enough. She wondered whether it might be a girl. She wondered when they might tell anyone.

The last days of August were heavy with heat and the hedgerows turned brittle beneath it. The reservoir levels fell quickly and there was talk the flooded villages might be seen again. The cricket pitch was hard and cracked and made for some sharp bowling spells when Cardwell came over for the annual match. There were children from the campsite playing Pooh sticks on the footbridge by the tea rooms, and there was a fright when their parents couldn't be found. In the final innings of the cricket James Broad was placed out at long off. He was talking to Lynsey Smith, who was sitting just past the boundary rope with the last of a lunch-time's bottle of wine. Cardwell were settled in for a defensive spell and James had little to do beyond look like he was paying attention. I didn't think you were all that interested in cricket, he told Lynsey at one point, talking over his shoulder with his eyes on the bowling. I don't think I am, she said, and though he kept still a rush of alertness came through him as if he were diving for a catch. The game was lost, and in the evening the pair of them were seen leaving the pavilion early and walking through the square. Cooper ran a piece in the *Valley Echo* about the protest camp at the Stone Sisters. It had been there for a year now, and seemed well established. Word was they had their own compost toilet. It wasn't clear what they did up there all day, although drumming was sometimes heard. There were rumours of tunnels. The heather was thick with butterflies – skippers and fritillaries and coppers – and Sally Fletcher spent most of the afternoon making a count for the National Park. In the beech wood the foxes ran through the night. The cubs were now as big as the adults and were striking out on their own. They would soon be seen as competition. There was play but it took on a fierce edge and there were fights that ended in blood. The edges of the territory were understood. In the evenings now the noise of people talking outside the Gladstone was louder on account of the smoking ban, and no matter how many notices Tony put up he still had complaints from the parish council. Some people had no idea how their voices carried. There was a new woman working at the bar and Gordon had been talking to her. Her name was Philippa and she was only around for the summer. She was volunteering at the visitor centre to get some conservation experience. She was staying with a friend in the city and driving out each day. There was a tattoo of a kingfisher on her shoulder, the size of Gordon's thumb. On her lower back there was a finely drawn bluebell, placed in such a way that the bulb and root system could only be seen once her pants were down. He liked to look at it and she liked him to look at it and for a time this was enough. Each night when she drove back to the city Philippa assumed she would tell her friend about this man she'd met, and each time something stopped her. She wondered why she kept these things from people. Her friend didn't even know about the bluebell tattoo, nor about the man she'd been with when she had it done.

Cathy knocked on Mr Wilson's door and it took him a long time to answer. This had been happening more often. She could hear Nelson barking, thumping against the door, and she had a sudden glimpse of it one day happening like this, of her having to fetch someone to break down the door and of Nelson being in the way. Mr Wilson's hip was causing him real problems now, and his breathing was louder, and sometimes in the evenings she could hear him coughing up a storm through the wall. She'd had a suspicion, when he'd first asked her to walk Nelson, that he was overstating his own difficulties; that he thought it would be good for her to get out of the house and be forced into a routine. After Patrick's death. And she had in fact been touched by his thoughtfulness and the way he tried to hide it. The dog-walking hadn't made the least bit of difference to her sense of abandonment, of course. But it had got her out of the house. People stopped asking her how she was doing in herself. And sometimes she'd looked out of the window and seen Mr Wilson stride past with Nelson as though he'd never claimed to be having trouble with his hip. But recently the problem had been all too apparent, and was getting worse. He was on a waiting list for a hip replacement. And now there were days when it took him as long as this to answer the door, and there would be a day when he didn't answer at all, and she wasn't ready for that. Nelson's barking shifted up a pitch, and the door shook as he clattered against it, and then Mr Wilson opened up with a smile. By the packhorse bridge a heron paced through the mud at the river's edge, head bobbing, feet lifted awkwardly high. It stopped, and settled, and watched the water. The fieldfares wouldn't be back for another month or two, once autumn began to collapse. The weather on the hills was fine for September, and the scoured stacks of gritstone that made up Black Bull Rocks were warm to the touch. In a hollow deep between the stones, James and Lynsey had found a comfortable spot and were making up for lost time. They had been kissing for a while and then Lynsey had pulled James's trousers to his ankles and crouched between his thighs. They had tried this a couple of times but now James thought it might be going to work. He wanted to say something encouraging but found he couldn't speak. He fell back on to his elbows and looked to one side and saw a butterfly folding

125

and opening its wings on a flat rock beside him. He wanted to tell Lynsey and then he felt himself give way, hugely, the breath drawn out of him. It was like slipping into the reservoir in the middle of summer, the ice-cold water against his hot skin and all the sudden silence. He went way below the surface, into the dark, down to the silt and the stone foundations of the flooded villages, down to the unrelenting pull of the sluice. He couldn't breathe. The sun was everywhere. He opened his eyes and Lynsey was looking down at him with a smile that was half-puzzled. But he was astonished. She asked why he was shivering. Afterwards she wanted to talk but he couldn't. She wanted him to kiss her but he felt embarrassed. When he'd got his breath back they walked down the hill together. She wondered if she'd done something wrong. He wanted to tell her how good he felt but he could only punch her gently on the arm and say nice one, mate. They had to walk separately from there to the village, in case anyone saw them. Rohan didn't yet know. They didn't think it worth telling him until they knew what it was themselves.

It was a good year for sweet chestnuts, and in the woods on the estate the spiny husks spread open underfoot. The beaters opened the release pens at the edge of the woods and drove the pheasants towards the guns. At Reservoir no. 5, the maintenance team put on wetsuits and went down the slipway to take a drowned sheep out. There was a weight to it with the sodden wool and the smell was something hard to take. At the school there were UCAS sessions and James and Rohan and Lynsey and Sophie started talking about moving away. They all said how much they'd miss each other but there was no more talk of applying to the same university. Lynsey had trouble at home when she talked about applying at all. Her father asked who would do his laundry if she left home, and then acted as though that was a joke. Her brothers asked why she would go all the way to Edinburgh to study English when they didn't hardly speak it up there. Her mother asked, gently, whether she couldn't at least think about a science. You're enjoying the biology, aren't you? she asked. There's prospects there. Your father would understand that. He's not going to put money into you going up there to read books. Lynsey knew that. And she knew that when she left home her mother would be faced with all the housework she'd been doing. And she knew she couldn't talk to the others about this, because they would have no idea. In the woods and by the river at night the bats were mating, feeding heavily to build up fat as the year began to slow. The clocks went back and the nights overtook the short days. Les Thompson was in church on a Sunday for once, and was heard after the service asking Jane whether she might stop off by the farm one day. She knew not to prolong the conversation, and told him that Tuesday late afternoon would suit. Just before milking? He nodded, and left, and on Tuesday her car was seen bumping slowly along the track on the far side of the river which led round to Thompson's place. He'd lived there his whole life as far as she knew, and this was the first time she'd made a call. His sister had lived there until fifteen years ago, and since then he'd worked the farm by himself. When he opened the door she could tell he'd made an effort. There was a clean shirt, and a shaving nick, and his fingernails had been scrubbed. Vicar, he said, nodding. His voice was deep, and always sounded as though it came from a great distance. He gave off the air of a man shouting, but without any of the volume. She waited. Shall I come in? she asked. He went through to the kitchen, and she followed. She was in there for almost an hour, while Les tried to say that his sister was dying and he didn't know what he'd do without her. They talked on the phone most evenings and he was over to see her most Sundays, and it was going to be different. It took him a while to be out with it, and the cows were making a racket in the shed by the time he was done. She chatted to him a bit longer while he worked, and he turned down her offer of help. She collected these confidences from people, and carried them around. It was like piling rocks into the boot of a car, she told her dean once, and sooner or later there are too many rocks and the suspension bottoms out each time you hit a bump in the road. He smiled and told her he knew it was difficult. He prayed with her, and she kept carrying the rocks around.

———

Irene walked down to the church from the bus stop and let herself in to do the flowers. The vases had been emptied and washed, and the new flowers were keeping fresh in the sink. Plenty of ferny greens, lots of yellow and white. She spread the stems out across the table and began working up arrangements. Tried not to worry about Andrew. There'd been something off about him this morning. Something agitating him. They'd get to the bottom of it at the school, whatever it was. No good worrying all day. She'd learnt not to worry once he was elsewhere. Took enough energy worrying when she was with him. People didn't know. They thought they could imagine but they had no idea. Didn't even know what it was with him, really. When he'd been born there was no sign of anything wrong. Not wrong. Wrong was a word they were discouraged from using. The parents. At the day centre, at the school. Different was the word preferred. But either way there'd been no sign. He'd been bright-eyed and howling the same as any newborn. Beautiful. Even Ted had been soft with the sight of him. It had only been later she'd started to wonder. When he wasn't playing the way other babies were. When he didn't reach out and hold things. When it became impossible to hold his gaze. When he started to bite. The boy's not right, Ted had taken to saying, and she'd told him to hush. Hadn't questioned him like that before and he didn't like it. The boy needs discipline, Ted had said; you're spoiling him. There were times she'd had to stand in his way and catch what was coming. But when he was four years old and not yet speaking there were trips to the doctor, to the hospital. There were tests and observations and support groups. She didn't take much benefit from the support groups. The other mothers were younger than her and she felt out of place. But she began to learn a new language. Learnt a different way of being a mother, to a child who had a different way of being in the world. Tried not to think what was lost. Did a lot of praying but learnt not to pray for him to be normal. Not to say things like normal. Ted took no part. He thought there was something wilful or malicious about the boy. Was impatient with the mollycoddling. Resented the money being spent. Resented not having a son who could kick a ball, or go snaring rabbits. She thought she'd caught him weeping over it once but she couldn't be sure. He wasn't one for doing his emotions that way. It was the drinking and the shouting and the slamming doors, usually. And the rest. Andrew was seven when Ted died. Coughed his lungs to bits and no one could say whether it was the smoking or the quarry dust that had done it. He always said he smoked so much to keep the dust down. Halfway through his fifties and people kept telling her it was a tragedy. The one thing she couldn't admit was feeling something like relief. It made her feel wicked. But things did change once he was in the ground. Things were quieter. She packed out the last vase and left them all on the table for Winnie to place around the church. She took a half-dozen stems that hadn't fitted in the arrangements and carried them out to Ted's grave.

———

Richard Clark came home for Christmas. As he drove through the village he saw Cathy outside the post office, and stopped to ask if she wouldn't come round for a cup of tea. She was surprised but said yes, and climbed into the hire car for the short drive. His mother's front door was unlocked and they walked in together. His mother was lying on the kitchen floor. She smiled up at them both, and asked if he'd had a good journey. It took the two of them to pick her up and get her into a chair. You needn't look so worried, she said. I would have got myself up in a moment, only I heard you coming in through the door. Thought I'd save myself the effort. Richard asked if this had happened before and she told him to put the kettle on. You'll stay for a tea, Cathy? Cathy had backed away a little, towards the door, as though not wanting to intrude. Her hand was hovering over the zip of her coat. I will, Mrs Clark. That would be nice. It's been a while, hasn't it, Richard's mother said. It has, Cathy agreed, and Richard heard the rustle of her coat being slipped from her shoulders. It was daft but something stirred in him. A fog came in and lay heavy for a week and even at noon the only colour in the street was the buttery light spilling from house windows, held behind curtains that people kept closed. These weren't days for working outdoors if it could be helped. The sloe gin from the year before was sampled. The allotments were bare but for the odd row of kale or leek. There was carol singing in the church with candles and the familiar smells of cut yew and polish and damp coats. The numbers were down but the sound still rang out against the cold stone.

Jane Hughes held a service at the church to mark five years since the girl had gone missing, and this time the mother managed to attend. Care was taken not to call it a memorial service, although there were few in the village who thought she could still be alive. It was announced as a Service of Prayer for Rebecca Shaw and her family, and that seemed to be open enough. There were reports in the newspapers that both parents had gone back to work, and her mother certainly had more colour than the last time she'd been seen. But she didn't speak during the service, and when people came up to her afterwards she only shook their hands briefly, and said thank you for their concern. The girl's father was seen walking up the hill behind the visitor centre, heading towards Black Bull Rocks. Cathy Harris asked Richard to call round in the morning before he left for the airport. He'd only been back for a few days, and had barely left his mother's house. Come round for a coffee or something, she'd said, standing on his mother's doorstep, zipping up her coat. We should talk. He wondered if she wanted to make him feel guilty about his mother, or if she might find some other reason to persuade him to stay. He loaded up the hire car and drove down her lane before the sun was up. He could see her in the kitchen as he parked the car, standing over the table while her sons ate breakfast. The room was a bright square against the dark silhouette of the house. He watched her lean across them to take a piece of toast. He watched the relentless way the boys were eating, talking and laughing while they crammed food into their mouths. He looked at their broad shoulders, their expansive gestures. They made the room look full. Complete. He saw Cathy shush the boys, and turn up the volume on the radio. They were probably listening to the news. He turned it on in the car. He watched Cathy, with her back to him, lift her hair in both hands and twist it into a knot. He remembered her doing the same thing years ago. He tried not to think about it. That was a long time ago. Her marriage had been a happy one, he assumed, and he'd had some good relationships himself. He wanted to tell her this: that there had been relationships, that he hadn't been lonely. Perhaps she knew, or assumed. Perhaps it didn't need saying. When she turned to the window there was a hairband pinched between her lips, as he'd known there would be. On the radio they were talking about the girl. The police were appealing for further information. There were no new leads. The investigation remained open, despite the passage of time.

6.

At midnight when the year turned there were fireworks going up all across the village but from the hill they looked faint and the sound failed to carry. James and Lynsey had walked up earlier in the night with blankets and torches and a bottle of vodka and by now they'd run out of things to say. Each of them was already worried that it was getting more serious between them than they'd expected, but neither of them knew how to bring it up. It wasn't that she wanted it to stop, Lynsey had said to Sophie, it was only that she hadn't wanted anything so serious this time. James hadn't talked to anyone, but was carrying some kind of confusion around. He felt bad about Rohan. But he liked the things they were doing together and he thought that should be enough. When the fireworks were done they turned to each other and kissed without indecision, and James tried not to think about Becky Shaw. She could have walked high over the moor and stumbled into a flooded clough. She could have fallen anywhere and be lying there still. In the beech wood the foxes were ready to mate. There had been scent-marking and fighting and now the pairs were established. The dogs followed their vixens around for days. When the coupling came it was joyous and loud. Les Thompson's sister died and there was a funeral. It was the first funeral Jane Hughes had taken where the burial was in the churchyard outside. Mostly these days it was crematoria. Thompson's sister hadn't lived in the area for years so there weren't many people at the service; a dozen at most pressed around the grave afterwards while the undertaker's men lowered the coffin into the ground. Les Thompson was a man of few words at the best of times but today he was completely silent. He'd been into town for a new suit, and had found one that fitted beautifully, given his proportions. He carried himself slowly. He nodded when people spoke to him, and his handshakes were heavy and warm. The snowdrops were up and the crows flew overhead and the wind moved through the trees. Jane had to keep herself from smiling.

The winds changed and came from the north, pulling a bog-sweet smell of damp down from the hills. After dark two of the older badgers snuck out of the sett at the top end of the beech wood, sniffing at the air before foraging across the wet soil around the edge of the abandoned lead pits, looking for the earthworms that had always been there. Will and Claire came back from hospital with a baby daughter, and went straight to the Jackson house to introduce her to Tom. They were calling her Molly, and when they laid her on Tom's lap he looked terrified. Will's brothers laughed, and Jackson was able to smile. On the television there were pictures of an earthquake's aftermath; people walking down a road covered in dust, collapsed bridges, rescuers kneeling in the rubble to reach down into dark spaces. In the evening on Valentine's Day Ruth drove over from Harefield to find Martin and return the card he'd sent. He looked at her holding it out but he didn't take it back. I didn't send that, he said. Martin, she said. This has to stop now. I'm not here to be won back. He was shaking his head. I'm telling you, he said, I didn't send that. There was a softening in his expression. He felt as though he had the upper hand for once. She looked at him and she didn't know what to believe. They were standing outside the Gladstone, and again she held out the card. The streetlights were on already. They both looked at it. The handwriting inside was obviously disguised. She looked around, feeling suddenly watched. I didn't send it, he said again, and he seemed proud of the fact. He turned and went back into the pub, and there was a sway of warm chatter as the door swung closed behind him. She got back into the car. She felt the world expand around her. In the distance by the motorway the lights on the television masts blinked red.

———————

The clocks went forward and the evenings opened up and the days stood a little straighter on their feet. The catkins came out on the willows by the river and swung wildly in the wind. The allotment sycamores dropped a branch on the old Tucker place and took off a dozen slates. The rain got in and soon afterwards a For Sale sign went up. In her back garden Su Cooper drank a coffee while the boys kicked a ball. They kept asking if they could go through the gate and into the woods, and she was telling them to just please wait until she'd finished her drink. She let the coffee sit cold in her mug. We won't go far, Lee said. We'll stay where you can see us. Just wait, she asked them again. Always asking them to wait, it felt like. Just a few minutes more. Let me finish my coffee. She was holding a trowel in one hand; she'd come out planning to deal with the plants that had been sitting around since she'd brought them back from the garden centre a fortnight ago. But really she needed to get on her laptop and answer a string of emails about the series proposal that was due in the next day. The early feed-back hadn't been great and the project felt sketchy. The idea of tracing the origins of urban dialect words was a good one, but they were lacking a narrative drive. She needed time to talk to her colleagues and develop the proposal further, but Austin would be out until after the boys were in bed. They'd been restless all morn-ing, and had got into a fight when she'd tried to take ten minutes at the laptop. She'd have to work on it after they were asleep, and hope her colleagues would still be available to talk to by then. She needed a fresh coffee. The boys were opening the gate to the woods, and shouting something about wolves, looking back at her. She put the trowel down and ran towards them, howling and raising her hands like claws. They shrieked, and scattered into the trees, and she had to choose quickly which one to chase down and devour. There were fresh elections to the parish council, and Brian Fletcher was re-elected chair. Janice Green continued as secretary. Miriam Pearson stood down, and as usual was replaced by her husband, William. The lambing was coming to an end and the Jackson boys were worn out. There had been talk of bringing in help but there was no way of making it pay. These later ewes were all lambing outdoors and when the weather was fine there was some pleasure in watching them take care of themselves. The way one would circle and paw and take herself off to a corner of the field, the way the new lambs stood and looked about in surprise. But there were others who needed all manner of helping. They kept their sleeves rolled and the lubricant to hand.

In April the first swallows were seen and the walkers were back on the hills. Richard Clark's mother had another fall while he was staying with her. He'd only been back for a few hours, and was upstairs writing an email. The woman he was seeing had wanted to come with him and meet his mother. This wasn't how he saw things between them. There'd been some discontent and she'd sent another email. He was trying to straighten it out when he heard a thump from the kitchen. His mother was already picking herself up by the time he got downstairs, levering herself to her knees and pausing for breath, a toppled chair beside her. Oh, would you look at me, she said. Too much haste, rushing about. No harm done. Richard righted the chair and helped her into it, and asked if she'd been to the doctor about this. There's no medicine for tripping over, she laughed, lightly. But do you feel dizzy? he asked. Faint? It's nothing a cup of tea won't fix, she insisted. Richard got her settled in the front room and took her some tea and cake. He texted his sister to tell her what had happened, and she texted back to say she couldn't talk just then. He stood in the doorway, texting a reply, and looked at his mother. He wondered why none of them had yet moved back to live with her, to give her the care she needed. This wasn't how she'd brought them up. Later he saw Cathy and they went walking through the woods with Mr Wilson's dog. He apologised to her again for not going to Patrick's funeral, and she stopped. There was an expression on her face that was halfway between laughter and irritation. Richard, she said. Why are you talking about this again? What are you trying to fix? I don't know, he said. It's just that I feel bad about it. I know I should have done something. But Richard, this is water under the bridge, you know that, don't you? It was just impossible, he said, with work. They walked on through a clearing, and it took a moment for their eyes to adjust to the light. She didn't understand where he was going with this. Patrick was a good man, he said; I never held a grudge. You could have written, she told him, and he nodded. We coped though, she said, if that's what you're worried about? I actually managed, can you believe it? I kept busy. There was plenty to deal with. Paperwork. Finances. People who came around wanting to make things better. I was Stuart Hunter's new best friend for a while there. He was after the timber yard. I wanted to hang on to it. I thought the boys might be interested in taking it on once they were done at university, but they really weren't. And it needed someone to keep it working straight off. Stuart offered us a good price. I've never liked the man, to be honest. But it was a good price. Nelson had got left behind somewhere, and when they called him he didn't come back. Cathy went back to look for him, and found him fussing over an old walking jacket or body-warmer, navy blue, with the lining ripped and the stuffing spilling out. She pulled him away, and went to catch up with Richard.

At dusk the men from Culshaw Hall were out shooting pigeons. They'd been taking feed from the pheasant pens and were well up in number. Each time the shots cracked through the evening the pigeons in Mr Wilson's garden spilled into the air. The areas of moorland that had been burnt back in February were already flush with new growth, green squares in the patchwork of heather.

A full moon rose over the reservoirs and flooded them with pale light. The nights were warm and slow and the bats fed for hours on the flushed crops of insects which came up from the water. The female bats moved away from their winter roosts and gathered together to breed. The days started brightly and the village was humming with life. In the churchyard yew a male goldcrest sang with the urgency demanded by spring. Rohan Wright found out about Lynsey and James. He told them he understood but he didn't. Neither of them saw him around for a while. He put a band together with some friends from town, and was using the village hall for rehearsals. There were complaints about the noise, but the committee felt strongly that the young people were entitled to make use of the facilities. They were asked to refrain from rehearsing any songs with language. Jackson hadn't got much better, but nor was he getting any worse. A care nurse came in three times a week to help him do his exercises, and either his speech had improved or his family had got better at understanding what he wanted to say. He was able to take himself to the downstairs bathroom, and only needed a little help getting dressed. But he had to use the wheelchair if he wanted to go further than the yard, and that wasn't often. Maisie had Molly at home two days a week to give Claire a break, and Jackson's eyes always shone when she was in the room. At the village hall the puddled clay was pressed into the dressing boards, resting on trestles in the centre of the room, while everyone stood by with the mosses and petals and bark they'd been gathering all week. There was an expectant atmosphere, of people looking forward to a job they knew would be hard and long. There was a morning mist, milky and thick, burning off as the sun poured into the valley. From the river by the weir a heron hoisted itself upwards, its feet dragging limply behind. It climbed quickly over the trees towards the quarry. Along the roads and in the uncut edges of fields the first wildflowers were thriving.

In June there was a party at the Hunter place for the end of Sophie's A-level exams. There was a marquee and a band and candles in glass jars lining the driveway. There were cars parked along both verges on the road and they did some damage. The noise of the party carried down to the village. Sophie's parents were there but they mostly kept their distance, and made sure Olivia stayed away from the punch. In the morning Jess made Sophie a hot drink and brought her out into the fresh air. They sat up in the folly, Sophie wrapped in a duvet, looking down over the wildflower meadow and the orchard and the courtyard. There were a lot of empty bottles about the place. There were young men sleeping on the grass beside the ornamental lake. I don't want anyone driving home until they've had a proper breakfast, Jess said. They'll be pickled in alcohol. Sophie nodded. Her eyes were red. Jess put an arm around her. Harry didn't work out then? I should have known better, Sophie said. It's my own stupid fault. Jess turned Sophie's face towards her and looked her in the eyes. Really? she said. Because you were the one putting yourself around? Sophie looked down. No, but still. I should have done more to keep his interest. Sophie Hunter, Jess said; that is not how I brought you up. I'll let you off this time because you seem a little fragile, but remember this: where a boy puts his John Thomas is not your responsibility. It's his. Okay? Jess asked who the girl was. Someone called Jasmine, Sophie said, from Cardwell. Jess couldn't help spluttering at the mention of the place, and Sophie laughed faintly. Exactly, she said. And what kind of a name is Jasmine anyway? Jizzmin is more like what I heard. Jess put up a hand and told Sophie to hold back. Come on, Mum, I'm allowed to be childish about it. I'm not worried about childish, Jess said. But don't go blaming your sisters for men's behaviour. Mum! She's not my sister. We're all sisters, sweetheart. Oh, Mum, please; this isn't the 80s. There was a splash and a shout and two boys emerged from the lake fully clothed, draped in weeds and shouting with either hysteria or fury. Sophie said she thought she was going to be sick, and her mother helped her over towards the bushes, gathering her hair away from her face and stroking her back.

———

In July the first fledgling swallows were seen tumbling from their high nests and breaking into flight, and were soon sweeping across the meadow grasses in search of food. In the morning the sun angled over the hillside as Les Thompson led the last of his cows from the parlour towards the day's grazing. Les closed the gate behind them and headed back to the parlour for washdown. There was paperwork to sort and he didn't fully understand it. Since his sister had passed the numbers weren't adding up. In the old quarry by the main road the larvae of small coppers were feeding on the sorrel plants where they'd hatched, carving deep grooves in the leaves where they could hide while the sunlight shone through. A Facebook account was discovered in the name of the missing girl, claiming that she was travelling in Thailand and Goa. There were photos of a young woman matching the computer-generated images of Rebecca Shaw the police had put out a year or so before: on the beach, in a bar, sharing a hammock with a friend. It was quickly shown to be a hoax, and the student behind it had issued an apology through her family's solicitor before she even got back to the UK, but afterwards there were people who thought there might have been something to it. Mrs Simpson held an open afternoon at the school for the children who'd be starting in September. There were only the Cooper boys and a girl from the new housing-association flats, so there was plenty of time to talk. She showed them around the school, and later while the children played in the corner of Miss Dale's room she made hot drinks for the parents and answered their questions. She was surprised by how many questions Su Cooper had; she'd always thought of Su as being rather quiet. Austin Cooper didn't look surprised at all. Su asked about the curriculum, and opportunities for creative play, and about the use of outdoor space. She also asked what diversity training the staff had received, and Mrs Simpson was confused for a moment. There was no need to worry about that, she told Su; everyone at the school was always treated equally. We like to think we're more or less colour-blind, she said, smiling. I mean, until you mentioned it I wasn't even really thinking of you or the boys as being, you know, ethnic or anything. You're just Su to all of us, aren't you? There was a look on Su's face that Austin recognised but which Mrs Simpson appeared not to notice at all. The other mother asked about school uniform.

August was hot and slow. The seed-heads of cow parsley and thistle blackened in the field margins, collapsing in the early dew. The river was clear and slow and the sun struck it hard. There were brown trout teeming thickly through the water. In the evening Ian Dowsett set up in the shade of a beech tree and tried dropping a few different mayflies but nothing was right for the rise. He could hear voices from someone's back garden at the top of the steep bank and the air was still. In Cardwell the cricket was drawn for the second time in three years and some of the younger players started to talk confidently about a turn in the tide. In Fletcher's orchard the blackbirds were fattening on the early windfalls, lazy about territory and forgetting to sing. Sally watched them from the kitchen window while she made an omelette for dinner. She folded half of it on to a plate for Brian to have later. He'd left a note on the table to say he'd be late back from the parish council. When she'd eaten she left a note saying she'd be up early for a walk so please not to wake her. She drew a smile and a kiss at the bottom of the sheet of paper. She wondered if they'd counted would there have been more kisses in writing than in real life. She didn't suppose it mattered too much. Later when he came in she heard the front door close so gently it barely clicked. She reached over and turned out the light, so that he wouldn't see it on the way to his room and think he'd kept her waiting up. There were springtails in the old hay at the back of the lambing shed, feeding and laying eggs and hatching out, and at the end of a long stem a single male sat poised with his tail hooked to his belly, ready to spring into the air for the first time in his life. There was a moment's hesitation. Overnight the heat broke into heavy rain but by late morning the ground was dry. In his studio Geoff Simmons turned the new pots on the wheel, using a narrow knife to cut a bevelled edge at the base and a leather to work the rough patches smooth. There was a customer looking at the pots on display and he was trying to judge whether to speak. When she'd come in he'd acknowledged but he knew people preferred to browse. He knew they liked seeing him work. But she was the first customer all week and he couldn't afford for her to just leave. She was on her own which might mean she had intent. She was holding a pot well and letting it sit in her hand. She had a good eye. It was back on the shelf and she had glanced at the door. This was where she would decide. He took his foot from the pedal and let the wheel slow. He glanced up and let himself look surprised that she was there. The missing girl's mother was seen at the tea rooms. The girl who served her had no idea who she was, and wasn't much interested when she was told. That was a long way back now though weren't it, she asked, and the woman working alongside her conceded that maybe it was.

The missing girl was seen camping with the protesters at the Stone Sisters site, her hair in thick plaits and her face smudged with woodsmoke, and the police had to go and verify the girl's real identity. The numbers at the camp had dwindled since it became clear that no excavation was imminent. There was an altercation between one of Jackson's boys and the handful of protesters who were left. Traditionally the Jacksons had used the area for grazing, and they were of the opinion that it was time the camp cleared out. But they had no legal right to the grazing, and the Culshaw Estate didn't want the expense of an eviction. So the Jackson sheep went elsewhere, and the protesters stayed. The Tucker place had been sold for a while but there was no sign of anyone moving in. The roof had been repaired but nothing else. The abandonment seemed to offend people more than an empty holiday cottage would. The Tucker descendants weren't known and so couldn't be pressed. The night before leaving for university, James and the others went for a drink together in town. There was talk of how much they'd miss each other, but there was no real regret that they were heading different ways. There were complications, after all. Lynsey and James had had a confusing conversation in which they'd agreed that they weren't breaking up exactly but that they shouldn't be tied, they should be free to see other people, they should see where things stood at Christmas, or next summer. They'd all keep in touch; of course they would. They'd visit. This had all been said already, and so by the time they were sitting in the beer garden by the river they had nothing in particular left to say. They talked about the packing they hadn't finished, and the routes they'd be taking the next day. They drank quickly, to fill the gaps in the conversation. Lynsey was driving, and was first to say she wanted to get back. She was parked in the car park on the other side of the river, and the bridge was a quarter of a mile down the road. James was already taking off his socks and shoes. One last time, he said. Sophie finished her drink and slipped off her sandals. Lynsey rolled her eyes. Really? Rohan was still smoking a cigarette. He held it in his mouth while he took off his shoes and socks, and the smoke curled up through his fringe. Lynsey looked impatient but she leant down and slipped off her shoes as well. I definitely won't be doing this when we're back at Christmas, she said. Why, will you be mature by then? asked James. She gave him a look which was less playful than he'd been expecting. They all held their shoes out on the table. It was dark now and the light from the pub spilled out across the grass. They banged their shoes on the table and counted to three before running to the end of the garden and hopping into the water. The river ran shallow across a bed of shale and they were only wading up to their shins. This had been a tradition for as long as they'd been coming to the pub, but when they got into the cold water Rohan still bellowed with surprise, and Lynsey shrieked until she laughed. There were gasps and the slamming of car doors. Rohan's cigarette smouldered in the ashtray, the smoke turning in the air and their empty glasses catching the light from Lynsey's headlights as she swung round the car park and drove away.

Sophie Hunter was at the university for a day and a half before she phoned her parents. They'd been trying not to watch their phones, because there was nothing to worry about; all the way down the motorway, with the back of the car empty and quiet, they had told each other there was nothing to worry about, that Sophie would be absolutely fine. But when the phone rang they both jumped, and Stuart stood by while Jess talked to her. The conversation started lightly but Jess thought something was wrong. Are you meeting people? she asked. Are you making friends? Sophie said she was meeting lots of people, yes, and some of them seemed nice. But the trouble was that as soon as she mentioned where she was from they all wanted to talk about the missing girl. I don't want to talk about it any more, Mum. How come they even remember? Jess reminded her how big a news story it had been, at the time. People remember that sort of thing, she said. Later, via Facebook, Rohan and Lynsey and James reported the same experiences. Rohan called it The Curse of the Missing Girl, and Lynsey told him not to be cheap about it. In the village Mischief Night had become more or less the same as Hallowe'en, and for the first year doors were actually knocked on and the phrase *trick or treat* was used. Toilet paper also featured for the first time, draped across trees and bushes in people's front gardens, and it was a hell of a job cleaning up the next day. Ashleigh Wright and Olivia Hunter were found to have been mostly responsible. They were coming into themselves now their older siblings had left home, was the feeling. Pumpkins were stolen from people's front steps, and dumped in the walled orchard at the end of the Fletchers' garden, which was overgrown and failing. The fruit hadn't been harvested for years and the trees were thickly gnarled. He'd been told there were grants to restore it but he seemed in no hurry. Inefficiency was a point of pride with Brian Fletcher, a man known for being late to his own wedding despite living opposite the church. The reservoirs were high and the river thickened with silt from the hills and plumed across the weirs. A decision was taken to lay a second line of flagstones across the top of the moor, to limit the erosion caused by walkers, and a helicopter was brought in to drop them at intervals along the route. The flagstones came mostly from derelict mills in Manchester, cut a few centuries earlier and deeply rutted by the clogs of the workers going in and out for their shifts. At the school Jones had another argument with Mrs Simpson. The boiler had broken down again and an inspection had recommended replacing the system altogether. The boilerhouse would be demolished. He wasn't having that. The boiler was fine. It just needed some work.

When they'd left for university, James and Lynsey had said that of course they would keep in touch. They all had. Lynsey had texted the others a few times, but keeping in touch turned out to mean reading the updates on Facebook. Halfway through the term she took a coach to Newcastle, where James was studying, and only texted him for directions when she got there. She thought it would be cool to surprise him, she told Sophie. But then he introduced her to Holly, his girlfriend, and offered her Holly's room to sleep in since she wasn't using it at the moment. It wasn't quite what Lynsey had planned. They'd left things open between them but she'd thought they could pick up again. There were things she wanted to talk about. There were possibilities she'd had in mind, such as sharing his bed. Instead of which she drank most of a bottle of vodka and was sick into Holly's bedroom sink. When she woke in the early morning the sink was still full of it, and she left without saying goodbye. She caught the first coach back to Edinburgh. The coach drove through flat arable land and she felt a long way from home. She wanted to message Sophie but she had no signal. When she slept the bumps in the road became hills and she dreamt she was driving into the village, where the stems of coppiced willow stools on the Hunters' land gleamed red and gold in the narrow winter light. The foxes were lying low. Martin Fowler was working at the meat counter in the supermarket when Bruce came through with his new partner. Dad; this is Hugh. Martin nodded, concentrating on the back bacon he was cutting. The slices fell thinly away as the blade whined and rolled to a halt. He fanned them out on a layer of waxed paper in the display chiller, and then looked up at Hugh, who seemed more embarrassed than he did. He nodded. Hugh; how do. He didn't know what else to say so he turned back to Bruce and asked whether they'd been to see his mother. We're heading there now, Bruce said. Martin nodded. She expecting both of you? Yes, Dad. She's expecting us both. She's met Hugh before, you know? Martin nodded, and from the corner of his eye he saw his supervisor step towards him. I should get on. Good seeing you. Pop over some time? Bruce nodded. Yes, Dad. I'll do that. Some time. As they were leaving, Bruce told Hugh that he'd never heard his father say how do like that before, it wasn't something he said, he must have come over all flustered. Hugh just wanted to get back to the car. Martin's supervisor said he could have an extra break if he wanted, go for coffee in the store restaurant or something, and Martin said, thanks, no, but he was fine for coffee.

Jackson stopped using the sun room, and it gradually filled up with boxes and rolls of sheeting and sacks of feed. Tom had started making a Guy Fawkes, and left it unfinished in the reclining chair. Mike was in there looking for some waterproofs and from the kitchen the others heard him yelp and drop something heavy, and then shout something that sounded like *shit up my arse*. Nobody looked him in the eye when he came back in the room, and they were quiet as he filled the kettle. That was a lot of work we put in to build a fucking storeroom, he said. What was the bloody point of that? Is he never going to use it? Maisie told him they should be patient, that their father was feeling more tired than usual at the moment and wasn't able to get out of bed. The doctor said there'd be ups and downs, she said. Mike made himself a tea and headed outside. Shit up my arse? Simon asked. Fuck off, Mike said, and slammed the door. At Reservoir no. 9, the maintenance team were unblocking the spillway screens, clearing out the weeds and rubbish in anticipation of heavy rains to come. At the allotments the Brussels sprouts stood tall, their leaves wilted and holed and the sprouts knuckled tight against the frost. The allotment committee asked Susanna Wright to give up her plot for lack of cultivation. She knew they had a point but it stung. She hadn't realised what time would be involved. Folk never do, said Clive. Takes a retired or a nut-job to work an allotment properly. Well, I'm not yet either of those, Susanna said, giving him the key. On the estate the laying pheasants were taken in for winter feeding, and new stock delivered. In the woods the wild pheasants clustered together and fed on the spilt feed left in the pens. On a Friday after school Jones set to repairing a sash window in Miss Dale's classroom. He had the casement down and was halfway through singing the second verse of 'Fernando' before he realised that Miss Dale was in the reading corner. When he saw her she caught his eye and kept an absolutely straight face. He nodded, and went back to scraping the paintwork and grease from the casement channels. After a few moments he thought he heard Miss Dale singing the next verse very quietly, but when he looked he couldn't see her moving her lips. It took an hour to get the casement back up, and when he was done she was still working on her papers. He packed up his tools and said goodnight. Goodnight, Mr Jones, she said, smiling. There was rain through most of the month and more floods and the debris jammed up against the footbridge again but this time the footbridge didn't fail. There was carol singing in the pub, and when the sheets were handed round there was a lack of enthusiasm. But by the time they got to the 'Calypso Carol' the singing could be heard from the square and people had started crowding in from the main bar. *Oh now carry me to Bethlehem.*

On Boxing Day James and Rohan met at the Gladstone and compared notes on university. They saw Liam for the first time in years, and had bought him a drink before it became clear how little they had to talk about. He'd taken on the stone work with his father. His hands were swollen with bruises and pinched little cuts. There's years of learning in it yet, he said, but it's a good trade. We're working on a demonstration wall at the visitor centre if you want to look? Rohan said probably they would. James was texting Sophie to get her and Lynsey to come down. A storm came and blew snow sideways across the valley, and when it had passed the trees were edged with white. The Jacksons had losses in the hills. Richard Clark came home just before New Year. His sisters had given their mother a mobile phone for Christmas, and when he got there it was still in its box. Rachel told me it would make it easier to keep in touch, she said, waving at the thing. Richard asked if she wanted him to show her how to use it. I've a perfectly good telephone right there. She can leave me a message if I'm out when she calls. Says she's too busy for chatting on the phone, but it only takes five minutes. Richard gave her a look.

Five or ten, she said. Ten at the most. She gave him a look in return which meant not to push it any further. Richard was fiddling with his own phone even as they spoke. I think the thing is, Mum, Rachel thought it could be useful in an emergency. What kind of emergency? Just, if you were out somewhere, if you needed to call for help. Or even if you were upstairs and couldn't get to the landline. Landline? This wasn't going well. He resented that he was the one having to do this, when it had been Rachel's idea. Just let me get it charged up and turned on for you, he said. You can send the grandchildren texts, that would be nice, wouldn't it? She picked up the box. It was awfully big and heavy. It didn't seem very mobile at all. On New Year's Eve there was another hard snowfall and drifts on the roadside by evening. A pale light moved slowly across the moor. The weather stayed cold and there was snow on the ground for another week.

7.

At midnight when the year turned there were fireworks on the big screen in the village hall and the sound of 'Auld Lang Syne' along the street. The Cooper twins were out for their first New Year, watching the fireworks from the Hunter place, their mother hurrying them back to bed as soon as the last rocket fell to earth. In the morning the snow was ankle-deep but by noon a hard rain had washed it away. The change came quickly, thick piles of snow falling in on themselves and hurtling away down drains and run-offs to the river, the river bright and loud with it and the streets left scrubbed and darkly gleaming and everywhere the first green tips of snowdrops nosing out of the soil. After the rain there was a quiet, and the melting of roof-snow down drainpipes, and the calling of birds on thawing ground, and the whine of a chainsaw up in Hunter's wood. On the television there were pictures of an overturned ship, helicopters hovering, life jackets floating in the water. In the fields south of the church there were wild pheasants feeding, their dashed brown feathers muddled in amongst the tall dead grass. A line of parsnips were lifted at the allotments, the creamy heft of them shrugging free of the frost-black soil. At night there were foxes shrieking in the woods, and everyone who had stock on the hills sat up and bristled, listening. When the doctor came for Jackson's check-up, Maisie admitted how little he'd been getting out of bed at all. She said she was worried there could be something affecting his energy levels, but that the physio hadn't thought there was anything to worry about. The doctor examined him, and afterwards she told Maisie that she thought Jackson was depressed. Maisie laughed and said she didn't think so. Jacksons don't get depressed, she said. We don't have the time. She'd heard it said so often that it just came out without thinking. She stopped and the doctor smiled gently. I think time might be his problem, she said. But there are steps we can take. He'll not take happy pills, Maisie said. Well, that needn't be our starting point. But we should look at something. A late-afternoon fog came in before dusk, and when the bus dropped off the secondary-school children their voices along the high street were muffled and lost.

———

In the pub before opening hours Irene was cleaning the floor. She was quick but she was thorough. Tony was talking about his plans for expanding the food offer, and she could have done without the distraction. He was talking about a pizza oven. She didn't have an opinion. It wasn't her money. On the television they said something about a missing girl in the south of England. Tony came around the bar to turn the sound up and Irene told him sharply to mind her wet floors. He stepped back and they both looked up at the screen. The news reporter said there would be a reconstruction. Irene carried the mop bucket through to the kitchen and told Tony to keep off until it was dry. A thirteen-year-old girl had been taken from a holiday cottage, and for a time it seemed there might be a connection with the disappearance of Becky Shaw. But her body was discovered, and a suspect arrested, and he was found to have been out of the country when Becky had disappeared. These things just kept happening, it seemed. The Tucker place was rewired and replastered and a new damp-proof course put in. There was talk the man who'd bought it was from Birmingham way and recently widowed. There were no signs of him moving in. Tony put a pancake dinner on at the Gladstone, and made the mistake of calling it All-You-Can-Eat. People could eat a lot of pancakes, as it turned out. The kitchen ran out of batter, and not everyone was understanding. On the bank at the far end of the beech wood the badger sett was quiet. Twenty feet in from the entrance, past dead-ends and leaf-lined sleeping nooks, the first cubs of the year were being born, spilling blind into a dark world of grassy warmth and milk. The days started with a cold mist that didn't lift until lunchtime and then only seemed to get snagged in the tops of the trees. The butcher's shop was empty. The chopping block had been left behind the counter, the bowled wood darkening with the years. There were fat spoony leaves of corn salad for those who knew where to look, under hedgerows and around the edges of the old quarries. At the school on the weekend Jones came in to buff the floors, the polishing machine humming softly as he pushed it back and forth. It took two hours to get all the way round, and he stacked the chairs and turned off the lights as he went. In Miss Dale's class the socket for the machine was by the display of children's artwork. There was a game he had of guessing whose names would be on which pictures. He was good at it. This was something people would be surprised about. He plugged the machine in and buffed the floor until it shone. He would have to be getting back. His sister would be restless. It couldn't always be helped.

Richard was back in the village to see to his mother, and on a quiet afternoon he and Cathy went for a walk on the moor. They'd found they could talk again about almost anything, and they talked a lot. As they came down the far side of the hill, dropping towards Reservoir no. 7, he asked if she'd been seeing anyone since

Patrick's death, and she asked about his relationships, and a conversation he'd been hoping would tilt towards a particular possibility became instead a kind of confessional. It felt like a mistake but there seemed no way of stopping it. In particular, having listened to Richard's list of short-lived pairings, Cathy made the mistake of telling him about Gordon Jackson, years back. Richard was surprised, but he tried to sound understanding. Grief does things to a person, he said, and Cathy held herself back from asking how he would know. She told him that in fact it had happened before Patrick's death. About six months before, she said. And regularly, for a time. I was with him when they called me to the hospital. It stopped after that. I could have carried on, but Gordon didn't want to. She could see Richard was shocked now, although he claimed not to be, and she told him that relationships were more complicated than perhaps he realised; more complicated than it sounded like he wanted them to be. She felt something like irritation or resentment as she said this, and wasn't sure why. He said that perhaps she was right but he was willing to learn. They followed the access track around the reservoir. The ground was dry. There'd been no rain and the water levels were low. They headed back towards the village. Afterwards it felt as though they'd had an argument. When she thought about Gordon, as she allowed herself to do once she got back home, it was only with a quiet relief that it had happened at all, long past the point of thinking she should be allowed those kinds of joys again. The first time had been rough and shambolic, and the only time risks were taken, but after that there were careful arrangements and they made sure not to hurry. They were such straightforward pleasures; lasting satisfactions that she carried around with her for days afterwards and couldn't shake off. One of the many surprises was how soft Gordon's skin had been; even his hands, which by rights should have been more weathered. How gentle he also was, and how strongly felt his need. When she saw him in the village now she sometimes wondered about the softness of his skin. She thought about Richard and smiled at the timidity he hadn't been able to grow out of. She had never decided whether it was something she found attractive. She heard Nelson barking, and went to knock on Mr Wilson's door. Jackson's boys were busy with lambing. There were some early losses but on the whole it went well. The nights were long and they took turns sleeping a few hours each. In his studio Geoff Simmons worked on handles, pulling each one down from a fist of clay, thinning it through his finger and thumb before slicing it off and laying it out to dry with the others. The whippet walked slow circles around him, waiting. In the beech wood the first fox cubs were seen above ground.

———

By April there'd been no proper rain for four weeks and there was a lack of good grass for the stock. The new month brought a warm wind from the south and by mid-morning the village was hung with wet washing. Susanna came in from her run through the woods and rushed to pour herself a glass of water, gulping it down before she'd got her breath back and feeling the cold shock of it wind down through her chest. The Spring Dance was held in support of Water Aid, at the insistence of Mr Wilson, who said that if they thought they were having a hard time with this so-called drought then he could tell them a few things to think on. His thoughts on the matter were known, and the decision was approved without him needing to hand out the information sheets he'd brought with him. Jim Stephenson from the high school brought his brass band for the dance. Rather than the more traditional pieces, they played arrangements of disco classics: Stevie Wonder, Donna Summer, Sly and the Family Stone. When he'd first introduced these pieces to the band Jim had needed to listen to them on CD in order to familiarise himself; but by now, with the performances confident and smooth, he found himself conducting with a movement that was close to dancing. Jim Stephenson was not a young man. Afterwards at the bar Miriam Pearson asked what had been going on with his hips. Some people watching had been amused but Miriam's response was something else. Slightly flushed but not at all embarrassed, he told her that the music left him unable to keep still. That's where you feel it when the rhythm's doing the right job, he said, and Miriam smiled. That's very true, Mr Stephenson, she said, as he wiped at his bald head with a large white handkerchief. There were St George's mushrooms up on the bark chippings by the timber yard, and as far as Jones could tell no one else knew they were there. He took pleasure in fetching them since the yard had been sold to the Hunters. Was like taking something that belonged to Stuart Hunter, and he'd never liked the man. One of the protesters up at the camp broke his leg and had to be carried down the hill by the mountain-rescue team. He'd been trying to leap from stone to stone; something which was talked about as an ancient rite of passage but which was clearly impossible when the gaps between the stones were looked at in the cold light of day. The missing girl's mother was seen with a man no one recognised, walking through the village. In the evening they were in the lounge bar of the Gladstone, sitting closely together and sharing a bottle of wine. She seemed to make a point of meeting the gaze of anyone who looked for too long, and holding the gaze until it was moved away. At one point in the evening they were seen to be holding hands.

In May the days broke open with light. Breakfast was eaten under the spell of clear sunlight, and tea prepared to the sound of children playing outside. In the horse chestnut tree by the cricket ground the woodpigeons were fighting, rearing up at each other with rattling wings. It wasn't always clear what kept them from falling out of the tree. The noise of it could be heard as far down the road as the church. Early before school Jones was out at the allotments earthing up potatoes. Clive was on his plot putting out the courgettes from his greenhouse, but Jones didn't see him and soon headed home, his tools over his shoulder. Later Clive saw Miriam Pearson carrying trays of plants to her plot from a car. She'd bought them in the garden centre, he took it. They'd need a whole lot of water before they even got into the ground would be his suggestion but he wouldn't give it unwarranted. Her path edges were looking neat. At the parish council Janice Green read a letter from the bus company which threatened to remove the service unless there was an improvement in the car-parking situation. There was general objection to the letter's tone but it was conceded that they had a point. A discussion about enforcement and pinch points ensued, and when everyone seemed to have finished William Pearson said that really what they were talking about at the end of the day was Martin Fowler constantly parking like a cunt. A number of those present actually turned their faces away. Judith was asked not to minute that last remark, and William was asked to leave, at which time it became clear that the coffee he'd been pouring from a flask all evening had been mainly whisky. Once the door was finally closed behind him it was noted that he did have a point about Martin's parking habits, and it was suggested that words would be had. In the conifers above Reservoir no. 5, a buzzard sat warmly on her eggs while the wind pulled through the trees. There was rain in the evenings of the sort it was pleasant to be in for a while, taking the dust from the air. Ashleigh Wright friended her father on Facebook. He had found her and sent a message and she was excited to be in touch. She knew not to tell him where they were living, but there was enough in her posts for him to work it out. He dropped the name of the village into conversation and she had a bad feeling she couldn't tell anyone about. Richard and Cathy took Mr Wilson's dog in her car up to Reservoir no. 13 for a change of scenery. It was high ground, and the wind cut straight off the edge of the moor, pushing the water in dark furrows towards the top of the dam. They walked along the track around the shore, leaning into the wind and raising their voices as he told her he was thinking about moving into his mother's house for the long term. He could take on contracts that didn't require him to travel. He told her he'd enjoyed spending time in the village after so many years away. It had been good reconnecting with people. He asked what she thought and she said he should think about all his options carefully. She asked how his mother was doing, whether she'd had any more falls, and he felt her nudging the conversation away from what he wanted her to say. He let himself be nudged. He said she seemed fine but they were keeping a close eye on her. They reached the head of the reservoir, where the track came to an unsatisfactory end. When they turned and headed down to the car the wind at their backs gave them a sprung posture, their knees braced slightly to keep from running.

In June the widower moved in to the old Tucker place. He came up the lane one morning in a hired van, and from his allotment Clive could see him unloading boxes and bags and chairs. It was obvious he was going to need help. Clive waited until he saw the man sitting on his wall for a rest and then went up the lane to offer. There was a sofa and a bed and a couple of long wooden packing cases in the van. The carrying didn't take long. The widower was polite in his gratitude but there were no introductions and Clive wasn't invited inside. The weather brightened again and in the sunlight the river was like glass beneath the packhorse bridge, breaking only when it fell over the weir. The keeper went out checking licences. It was known he was thorough so there was rarely anyone fishing without. But the holidaymakers sometimes knew no better. Les Thompson towed the mower around the first of the fields, cutting from the outside in, lifting and dropping the mower at each turn and leaving a broad swathe of grass to wilt in a haymaker's sun. Brian Fletcher brought a mug of tea and a plate of toast outside and balanced them on the low wall beside his car. Sally had been up and out before he woke, leaving a note on the kitchen table to say she was off for a walk through the old quarries. Butterflies, again. This was her thing now. It was hard for him to see the difference a lot of the time, or to get close enough to tell. A flash of colour, gone in a moment. It was hard for him to take an interest. But she didn't expect him to, just as he didn't expect her to take an interest in his cars. No doubt she couldn't tell the difference either. She probably hadn't noticed that this was a new one. A 1968 Citroën DS with swivel headlights. He'd been after one for some time. It had taken some discussion before the man would sell. The emails had gone back and forth. But he'd been patient. He had a way with words, he liked to think. He had a way of judging what to say, and when to say it. The whole thing had been reminiscent of when he and Sally had first conversed. The emails that had gone back and forth before they'd even met. He looked at the clean lines of the body-work, the elegance of the silhouette. He finished his tea and his toast, and went to lift the bonnet. In their nest in the conifers the first buzzard chicks were hatching. The long days raised the hedges high. Down by the river the walkers had already left a network of flatted paths in the meadows. Winnie worked on the well-dressing designs, the sheets of greaseproof paper spread across her dining-room table. She started with the framing and arches, moved on to the lettering, lined out the sky and clouds and sun and hills, and finally detailed the figures and animals in the foreground. As always, she doubted it was sufficient for the committee's purposes; as always they assured her effusively that it was. Three young blackbirds appeared on Mr Wilson's lawn, plump and bristle-feathered, and were taken by crows. In their colonies the bats gave birth and held their pups in the folds of their wings. There was a nightly shift and murmur as the young bats fed and the movement was like a breeze through the trees.

At the end of his first year of university, James Broad drove his things back to the village and put them in the bedroom that had once been his. He'd been told he needed to do sorting out in preparation for the move. Neither of his parents could afford to buy the other out of the house, so they were selling up altogether. His mother was buying an ex-council flat at the end of the Close, and his father was moving away. James didn't know what he would do. They'd told him he was free to choose. Sophie Hunter had failed her end-of-year exams, and come home unsure of what she needed to do to even qualify for her second year. Her mother told her she'd be able to resit them, surely, but that it wouldn't be the end of the world to retake the year. Her father said that no matter what happened they were proud of her and they loved her. It was the obvious effort it took to say these things that stayed with Sophie. She felt as though she was the one who needed to make them feel better. Her mother was under the impression that a year of wild partying had got in the way of studying, but the truth was she had just found the work too hard. I do understand that this is a time for discovering yourself, her mother said; and if you can't party out when you're young then when can you? Sophie told her it wasn't like that. There aren't even that many parties, she said. I am doing the work, I'm just doing it badly. Her mother dropped her voice, and asked if Sophie was using protection. Sophie held up a hand and asked her to stop. It's not like it was in my day. Just so long as you stay true to yourself. Sophie put her fingers in her ears and told her loudly that she couldn't hear. Jess Hunter smiled fondly at her daughter. She could remember doing exactly the same thing to her own mother when she was that age. At the top of the meadows by the river the ox-eye daisies were thick through the knee-high grass. In the long grass around the cricket field the first skippers were emerging from their pupae and unfolding their wet wings. There were second clutches of swallows successfully fledged and their white flashing underbellies curved through the evening. The Workers' Educational Association group took an IT-skills course. There was some awkwardness when a question was anonymously submitted about how to avoid stumbling on sites with excessively adult content. Brian Fletcher asked what the hell was meant by excessively adult, and nobody wanted to explain.

———

Susanna Wright opened a shop in the old Tucker hardware place, selling crafts and gifts and greetings cards. She stocked a good range of pottery and Geoff Simmons was known to have taken offence. His studio shop was further out of the village and he was always struggling for trade. Susanna offered to stock his work but he declined. His reasons were mumbled but she heard him say *knick-knacks* and took offence of her own. He wasn't invited to the opening party and he wouldn't have gone if he was. There was sparkling wine and bunting in the street, and a man in a waistcoat who stood outside playing an accordion and trying to catch someone's eye. People took pleasure in a new business being opened, although it was assumed that only tourists would buy the manner of thing she was selling. Cooper took a picture of Susanna with Rohan and Ashleigh outside the shop, the accordion man leaning in to the shot and all of them raising their glasses. The picture went on the front cover of the *Valley Echo*, and Ashleigh posted it on her Facebook page. In the morning the sun was high by the time Thompson's men had finished the milking and washed out the parlour. They scraped out the muck and hosed down the surfaces, the water running greenish-brown and then clear into the drains outside. They went back to the house for breakfast. They'd been up three hours already. There'd be more money in pouring the milk straight down the drain. If the prices didn't pick up soon it would be impossible to carry on. But there was nothing else. The reservoirs were like beaten pewter. A caravan appeared in Brian Fletcher's orchard, wedged between the brambles by the gateway. There was moss in the window frames and silver tape across a crack in the panelling. It wasn't known what Fletcher had in mind. At the heronry the nests were almost abandoned and the ground was littered with fallen sticks. The heather was in full bloom and the purple of it spread across the hills. There was rain for a week before the cricket match and no chance of play but the Cardwell team were entertained at the Gladstone all the same. A darts match was played to settle the trophy, which Cardwell carried comfortably home yet again. Mike Jackson told his family he was planning to emigrate. This place is never going to split five ways, he said. Maisie waved at him to quieten down and Simon slipped through to the sun room to turn up the TV. Any normal family would have settled this by now, but we're supposed to just hang on and see what surprises Dad's got in his will? He thinks he can sit in there and run the farm by remote control, but he hasn't got a clue. You know that. We should have diversified years ago, expanded, taken on loans. Maisie was watching him talk but she couldn't really hear. She was thinking about how far Australia was, and the certainty that she'd never go. It's just for a while then, is it? she asked. They're crying out for experienced men down there, Mike said. It's good money. You can save up enough to come back and set yourself up then, in a year or two? There's cheap land in the northern territories, he said. Grants and everything. But it'll just be temporary? Mike looked at her. He was her youngest. He was the last. It's only Australia, Mum. It's not the moon.

The summer had been wet but in September the skies cleared and the mud in the lanes was baked into thick-edged ruts. There were springtails under the beech trees behind the Close, burrowing and feeding on the fragments of fallen leaves, and somewhere deep in the pile a male laid a ring of sperm. A blackbird's nest was blown from the elder tree at the entrance to the Hunter place, the mud mortar crumbled and the grasses scattered as chaff. Tony produced an arrangement of hops for the Harvest Festival display, and it was certainly striking but there were some who felt the pungent smell was out of place in a church. Jones's sister was seen at the post office, buying packaging paper and string, and this was understood as some kind of a breakthrough. Irene sometimes told people that Jones's sister had been at her wedding, and had been the very life and soul. Such a shame, what happened, she would say. As though anyone actually knew. On Sunday in the evening Brian and Sally Fletcher ate a meal together. Brian grilled lamb chops and boiled potatoes while Sally made a salad. It was a rule they had, to make sure they did this. For most of the week they kept different hours, and communicated through notes on the kitchen table. This suited them both. They had come to marriage late, and were each comfortable in their own company. But they'd decided they should always eat together on a Sunday night. I don't want to go forgetting what you look like, Brian had said. A meal, and a conversation, and then settling down together to watch whatever was on television. It was something about a murder, on the whole. At the allotments Ruth was seen working alone, pulling handfuls of beans down from the overloaded canes. The leaves were covered in blackfly but this late in the season she wasn't concerned. It was food for the ladybirds at least. She was letting the courgettes mature to marrows because even if no one really liked cooking them they did look good in baskets outside the shop. They made people think of harvest festivals, and that made them come into the shop and spend money. The blackberries were thick on the brambles growing up around the greenhouse, and she thumbed a few into her mouth each time she went past. There had been words with the allotment committee about the brambles. The matter was not yet settled. Her phone beeped, and when she read the text a smile opened on her face that she found herself hiding behind a berry-stained hand. She sat on the bench for a moment, watching the shadows lengthen across the valley and feeling the warmth and thinking carefully about her reply.

On Mischief Night there were stink bombs down every side street and passageway until the supplies ran out. Irene was heard grumbling that if they thought that was mischief they were leading very sheltered lives indeed. She asked if she'd ever told the story about her late husband hiding an entire dairy herd, and was told that indeed she had. There were costumes from popular horror films, and pumpkins with carved, glowing faces. Few turnips now. The stubbled fields on the south side of the church were thick with fieldfares feeding. In the pub while Irene was cleaning there was talk of a Bond film the cinema club was putting on. Someone said it wasn't one of the better Bonds, and Irene said if it was the one with Daniel Craig in then it was the best. Now there's a man, she said. I'd pay good money to watch that man in a documentary about paint drying. She had expected laughter but there was silence. She carried on mopping, and told them to lift their feet. She didn't know why she'd said anything. People were surprised. Thought if you were sleeping alone that your blood had stopped circulating. Thought if you were not capable of exciting a man's attention there was no excitement left in you. People were surprised by the most obvious things sometimes, it seemed. You only live twice, Tony said, from behind the bar. Classic Connery, Martin chipped in. There was a debate. Irene put the mop bucket away. At the school there was a row when Mrs Simpson brought in some heating engineers to inspect the boilerhouse and Jones refused them access. You can't do this kind of thing without notice, he said. It's not your boilerhouse, Mr Jones. I'll not be pushed, he told her, and the engineers said they'd come back another day.

———

Cathy knocked on Mr Wilson's door and asked whether Nelson needed a walk, and he told her the kettle was already on. Nelson paced backwards and forwards while they sat in the front room, his tail crashing against the coffee table. Mr Wilson had been baking cakes again. They were really very good, but she knew there was no point asking why he never donated cakes to village events. That's more of a ladies' thing, isn't it? he'd said, the one time she had asked. She'd told him this was nonsense, but knew he wouldn't change his mind. She couldn't remember him doing any baking while his wife was alive. But that was a long time ago now. She probably wouldn't have noticed if he had. Jean had died fifteen years before, or more, when Cathy's boys weren't yet at school, and it was all Cathy could have done then to know what day it was. She remembered standing behind the front door with them and counting to ten, regaining her composure, so that she could walk through the village without it being apparent that she'd had to physically wrestle them into their clothes, and clean food off the walls, and scream into a pile of cushions. And then straighten clothes, smile, open door. Be ready to say good morning, be ready to listen to advice from anyone who passed in the street. Mr Wilson hadn't been elderly then at all, she realised. He possibly hadn't even retired. And yet she'd always thought of him as that, as elderly. Unconscious association with the word widower, perhaps. Or the distance of youth. Although she hadn't been as young as all that, and had felt older, so much older all of a sudden, tired all the time. Smile, breathe, straighten clothes, open door. Be ready to agree what a delight the two boys were, to agree that yes they were a handful sometimes but it was worth it in the end, with a chuckle. Always the fucking chuckles, in those days. And keeping it together all the way down the lane because Mr Wilson was so often outside his house, doing something with the flowers or mucking about with his dog – it wasn't Nelson then, this was a pointer, Franklin – and then collapsing through the front door but not stopping because she couldn't stop, she could never stop, the boys always needed something else or were breaking something else and the tea needed making and the boys needed putting to bed, please, finally, and Patrick needed something when he got home. She finished her tea, and thanked Mr Wilson for the cake, and went to fetch Nelson's lead. The sound of a truck came from way up in Hunter's wood, dragging out timber, the engine over-revving with the strain on the heavy ground. The first snows of the winter fell at the end of the month but they were wet and they didn't settle.

The Christmas decorations went up in the square and Tony put up a sign saying he was taking bookings for Christmas dinners. There was carol singing on the radio in the tractor shed, and when Gordon Jackson heard Will singing along to 'Silent Night' he wouldn't give over about it for days. He kept breaking into

Shepherds quake at the sight every time Will came into the room. Susanna's ex-husband opened the shop door one afternoon and said hello as though he'd been invited. He seemed relaxed and open-handed, but there was something about the way he shut the door behind him. Susanna, he said. Here you are. Smiling broadly. He was a small man. He was. She nodded. She didn't trust herself to speak. She looked past him through the window and there was no one outside. People tended not to pass through on this street. He stayed between her and the door and he asked how she'd been. Her phone was on the shelf beside the till, and he was in the way of that as well. It was a small shop. She wanted to ask him to leave but it didn't feel safe. She felt all her placatory instincts rushing back. Her passive defences. But she kept her posture tall. She tightened her core. She told him she was well and asked what had brought him here. Susanna, relax. You seem tense. Come on. I'm not here to stir anything up. Sorry to disappoint you, but I'm not here to win you back. She breathed through the rush of irritation. She shook her head very slightly and he stepped towards her. I'm just here to see Ashleigh. It's been long enough. She needs a father. She shook her head again. Ashleigh's at school, she said. I can wait, he replied. This isn't what we agreed, she told him. You're not supposed to be here. He took another step towards her, but with his palms held out as though this would make it look like he was stepping back. Susanna, we didn't agree anything. The way he said the word *agree*. She stood very still. Her phone was out of reach. The shop was small. She heard his breathing quicken as he stepped towards her.

The pantomime was *Goldilocks and the Three Bears*. Andrew was cast as Baby Bear. He was too old for this but he went along with it because he knew his mother would be happy. He could feel his speech thickening with the anxiety of being on stage, and it was muffled further by the costume's fluffy head. When he found Olivia Hunter sleeping in his bed, her long blonde plaits trailing over the pillow, he gave up trying to make himself understood and just watched over her. This felt like the right thing to do. There was something peaceful in it, he thought. Jess Hunter was dressed as Mummy Bear and she came rushing on stage to talk. Who's that sleeping in *your* bed, Baby Bear? she asked, and even with the fixed features of the bear costume Andrew managed to look baffled. He left the stage sooner than the script required, and afterwards couldn't be found for a time. Richard Clark came home for New Year's Eve and his sisters were talking again about their mother moving into a home. The conversations were whispered and fraught and she cottoned on. I'll be going nowhere, she said. You needn't worry about that. You'll have to carry me out in a box. Don't upset yourself, Mum, Rachel said, raising her voice as though hearing or lack of understanding was one of Mrs Clark's problems. We just want you to be somewhere you can be a bit more comfortable, Sarah added. Somewhere you can forget about me, you mean. Somewhere we don't need to be worrying about you every five minutes, Mum, yes. Come on now. Don't take on. Richard watched the conversation as if he had no part to play. It was as though they were following a script. The decision would be made without him, either way. He had to leave early to get back for a meeting, and when he left they were still discussing it. There were lights seen in the caravan in Fletcher's orchard, and someone moving around. The brambles began to be cleared. Mike Jackson sorted all the paperwork for his trip to Australia, and was starting to pack a bag. Maisie refused to help him or to even discuss it. You're breaking your father's heart, she told him, and he was more or less sure this wasn't true. He's just putting on a brave face, Maisie said. The missing girl's name was Rebecca, or Becky, or Bex. In the photo her face was half-turned away from the camera as though she didn't want to be seen, as though she wanted to be somewhere else. She would be twenty years old by now but she was always spoken of as a girl. It had been seven years, and there was talk that now she would legally have to be declared dead. This turned out to have no basis in law, according to a statement released by the police. Any such declaration would always depend on the circumstances. The girl's parents had never stopped looking and the police statement confirmed that the case remained open. In the village people looked up to the hills and felt that they'd long known. She could have walked high over the moor and stumbled into a flooded clough and sunk cold and deep in the wet peat before the dogs and thermal cameras came anywhere near, her skin tanned leather-brown and soft and her hair coiled neatly around her. She could have fallen anywhere and be lying there still.

8.

At midnight when the year turned there were fireworks in the rain, and thunder in the next valley. The rain broke over the hill like a wave and blew straight into people's faces. The river was high and thick and there were grayling in number feeding on the caddis larvae and shrimps. In the morning Ian Dowsett was out with a new box of flies and having a job to keep his footing in the current as he dropped the weighted nymphs into the water. Susanna's ex-husband appeared again, and this time the altercation was seen. The police were called, and he was arrested. There was a new injunction. Susanna was embarrassed and she didn't want to talk about it but in the end the story came out. When she'd first moved to the village it had been to get away from him. She'd been living in a refuge with the children, but he'd found out where they were. His threats hadn't been enough to have him charged, but there was an injunction. She was offered support to move away from the area. She knew about this village because an aunt had once lived here, and it had seemed as good as any. She'd planned to keep this information to herself. She thought that part of building a new life involved not thinking about what had happened. She'd thought she could leave it behind. But now he'd shown up, and everyone knew. This came out in conversation with Cathy Harris one evening, when Cathy was helping clear up after yoga. Cathy had a way of waiting that made you want to say more, Susanna had found. When she nodded it was as though she already knew what Susanna was going to say. Few people, seeing her husband, had thought him capable of that sort of violence. He didn't have the build for it; he didn't seem the type. She'd heard people say this, even after they'd known some of what he was doing. There'd been a time when this had made her think it was her fault; that there must have been something she was doing to provoke such a well-mannered man into behaviour he wasn't otherwise prone to. That there must have been something she could do to protect him from the storm of his own rages. He was always so apologetic afterwards. Careful to explain just what had gone wrong and what he wanted her to do differently in order to help him not do it again. He had always talked in terms of this loss of control, and yet he was so careful not to leave marks on her face. He had twice broken her arm, and once dislocated her shoulder. She had lied about these injuries at the hospital. He had told her she'd be nothing without him, that people thought she was brash and loud and awkward. He'd told her she needed to lose weight, build strength, dress differently, laugh less loudly, not eat in public, have different friends, be a better mother. When Rohan had asked why they didn't leave it had been the first time such a thing had even felt possible. He was twelve at the time. He seemed to understand what was happening before she did. She'd told him that his father loved them and was just having a difficult time at work and things would be better soon, and he went and printed out an information sheet about domestic violence and the refuge network. When they left there'd been no relief, and no certainty that she'd done the right thing. Those feelings had only come gradually. But in the village she'd found herself ready for something new. She'd found herself standing taller. Straighter. The yoga had helped.

In February it snowed solidly for a week, and on the hills the drifts were eight feet deep. The road between the village and the town was ploughed, high banks of snow heaped on either side, but beyond the village it was blocked. Jackson's boys had to go up on foot to pull out as many sheep as they could. Most of them were easy enough to find, pressed in the lee of a drystone wall or huddled around a tree, but the losses were high. On the estate the pheasants were moved from their winter enclosures to the smaller laying pens and their feed was enriched. At the allotment the last of the leeks were yellow against the snow, fat-bodied and toppling, their papery skins peeling away. By the river a willow came down in a storm and carried on growing as though nothing had changed, the branches all bending slowly towards the sky. Molly Jackson had her second birthday. At the party Maisie watched Will and Claire carefully, and afterwards she had questions Will didn't want to answer. She knew things were going badly again and there was nothing she could do but look out for the children. Shrove Tuesday fell on the fourteenth, and in the kitchen at the Gladstone Olivia Hunter was having a hard time making heart-shaped pancakes. It had been Tony's idea, and she didn't think he'd tried it out himself. He'd given her a cookie-cutter to use as a mould, which was fine until it came time to flip them over. She kept burning the tips of her fingers. In the lounge there were jokes made about broken hearts, and Tony was careful to relay these to her when he came into the kitchen. It was a long evening. The next day there were only three people at the Ash Wednesday service, and one of those was Jane Hughes. She suggested they sit together in a circle by the altar, and she ran through the liturgy in a soft murmur that wouldn't have carried much past the first row of pews. At the close she daubed Irene's and Brian's foreheads with ash, and asked Irene to daub hers, and they sat there with the cold marks on their faces. Outside in the late-winter sunlight Sally Fletcher was seen bringing down two mugs of tea from the house and talking to the man who'd been staying in the caravan. He was her brother, it turned out. He'd made a good job with the brambles and the general clearance and was starting to work on the trees. Brian Fletcher had told him to take out the dead wood first and they'd see where to go after that. It wasn't clear what arrangement they had with the man, but there was an impression he never went into the house. He was sometimes seen standing in the doorway of the caravan, smoking. He had a sullen look about him. There were tattoos.

The widower was settling in at the old Tucker place. He'd done a lot of work in the garden. He'd taken out the paving and planted fruit trees and built up a number of raised beds. It looked more like an allotment than a front garden and there were some who thought words should be had. But under the circumstances it was felt he should be left alone. He'd not been much seen in the village and it was understood that his quietness might be part of the grieving. There was little known about the family he was said to have lost, and nobody wanted to ask. At the allotments Jones planted onions. His rows were straight and there would be no weeds. When he was done he carried his tools back to the house. At the school, heating engineers had gained access to the boilerhouse and condemned the boiler. There was talk of a modern system in the main building. Mrs Simpson told Jones he could still use the boilerhouse as a storeroom and he said nothing in reply. The clocks went forward and the evenings opened out. The buds on the branches were brightening. Irene was having trouble with Andrew. She'd tried talking to the vicar but it was never the right time. There were support groups at the day centre but they weren't for her. They were for the parents who wanted things to be different, who wanted things fixed. She knew there was no fixing to be done. Just wanted a way of managing. A way of being safe in her house. That was putting it a bit strong, maybe. But he was a big lad now. And he had tempers that came on quick. Like his father. He'd called her terrible names. She didn't know where he was learning these words. From the computer, it must be. No idea what he was doing on that computer most of the time. Only that when he sat there he was absorbed. Still. But there were days when he wouldn't move away from it. Days he didn't get dressed, wouldn't come to the bus stop. There were dangers on the internet, she knew that; but she didn't rightly know what they were. She was worried but she didn't know what she was supposed to be worrying about. She could talk to Cooper. He knew computers. And she could always unplug the thing, if anything bad started happening. Although what would Andrew do then. He was a big lad now. At Reservoir no. 3 the maintenance team worked across the steep face of the embankment, looking for burrows or soggy ground or unexpected vegetation. So far they'd found nothing but they kept looking. The levels were falling quicker than they should be. There were losses that couldn't be explained. There was a storm in the night and the rain came hard against the windows like gravel.

As the dusk deepened over the badger sett at the far end of the woods, a rag-eared boar called out a sow, pacing around the entrances until she emerged with a soft circling whine and was taken. The woods were thick with the stink of wild garlic and the leaves gleamed darkly along the paths. Jackson's boys went out to the fields and checked over the sheep. Most of the lambs were on grass now and growing fast. The mothers had lost condition and some were marked out for extra feed. The morning was warm and there was a heady tang of nutrition coming up from the land. The lambs were electric with life and jolting around each other. There was a rare chance to sit on the trailer for a smoke while they watched them. At the weekend Cooper took the twins out for an early walk to give Su a chance to catch up on sleep. She'd been working a lot recently, and coming to bed late. He filled their backpacks with snacks and drinks, and they headed out through the garden into the woods. They were excited, running on ahead and swiping at the nettles with sticks. He let them choose the way when they came to junctions in the path, but managed to steer them towards the visitor centre and the track leading up to Reservoir no. 3. It was further than the pair of them had managed before. At one point they passed the locked access hatch to a cave entrance, and were bursting with questions. He explained about the lead mines, and about the natural caves, and told them that yes, there were people who went down there to explore. They asked if it was safe and he said not for them it wasn't, laughing and walking on as though that would be the end of their interest. They were flagging by the time they crested the hill, so he decided to stop there. They sat on a flat rock and ate their snacks, and Sam asked if it was true that there were houses under the water. Lee called him an idiot for even thinking this, and Cooper explained that there had once been villages down there, that all the reservoirs had been made by flooding the valleys. They looked at him, waiting to see if he was joking. The world didn't always sound right when it was first explained. There were a few in the village still who could remember the river spilling its banks behind the newly built dams, a slow seeping over that didn't seem capable of filling the valley in the way the engineers had promised, each day a little higher, the outlines of the demolished villages being lapped over by the waves and the dam making more and more sense until by the time the Duke came to ceremonially open the sluice the water was pouring over the top of the wall. Business at Susanna Wright's shop wasn't keeping pace with the projections she'd shown her small-business adviser. She stayed open late and picked up sales from people in the village who needed last-minute birthday cards or gifts, but the walkers who came through mostly had no interest in the candles and crafts she was selling. Ashleigh sometimes worked with her after school but it took some effort to look busy. Geoff Simmons walked past most days with his whippet but he never came in. At the Spring Dance Irene found herself being asked by Gordon Jackson. She couldn't remember all the steps but found herself falling into them easily enough. She hoped no one was looking. She could feel the thickness of his body beneath his shirt, and found no reason not to think about that. He was holding her as though he might lift her into the air. Twice she felt his legs against her, and the stiffness of his thigh muscles was the memory she carried with her afterwards. He said something she didn't catch and smiled down at her and for a moment she felt as though he didn't know anyone else was in the room. This was a talent, she understood. Ted had never looked at her in that way. She had long suspected that Gordon had a reputation and now she understood why that might be. The dance finished and she went to sit down. Gordon was startled by the unwanted possibilities he'd felt stirring in himself. He wouldn't pursue them but he was worried they'd even arisen. Some people would call it a problem, he knew. He looked around for Susanna Wright.

In May the reservoirs were low and the river slowly carried a scrim of weed to the weirs. The sun was higher in the sky. The days filled out and the long nights of winter were distant. Les Thompson walked his fields and waited for the first heading of the grass. The stems were starting to stiffen and at the base the leaves were dying back. The cut was days away. In the conifer plantation the gold-crest nests were thickly packed with eggs the size of babies' thumbs. There were sheep bones by the side of the tracks on the moor, picked clean and beginning to brittle. The sound of a lorry missing the cement-works entrance was heard, climbing the hill to the village and the engine rising suddenly in pitch before cutting out entirely as the driver dropped another gear. In the beech wood the fox cubs were weaned. By their den entrances they fell about each other or sat waiting for their mothers to return. There was trouble at the Jacksons' when Simon told his mother he'd be going to Australia with Mike. A second man was seen in the orchard with Sally's brother, and although he was known to be staying in the caravan it wasn't clear that he was welcome. He didn't appear to be doing any work. Richard Clark called round to see Cathy. They'd agreed to go for a walk, but when he knocked on the door one of her sons answered and said she was out. Richard waited for more information but none was offered. He asked if she'd be back soon and the boy said did he want to wait. Hardly a boy in fact; a young man now, already done with university and filling the house with his lumbering uncertainties. Thanks, Nathan, he said, guessing at the name; I will, if that's okay. Nathan shrugged and left the door open. Richard went through to the kitchen and checked his phone. Probably he shouldn't text her. She'd be driving back from somewhere. Held up in traffic, or by a conversation at the market, or wherever she'd gone. He looked at the photos and notes stuck on the fridge. REMEMBER JOBSKILLS INTERVIEW WEDS, in Cathy's handwriting. And a photo of Patrick amongst the ones of the boys at university, and of people who were presumably cousins and grandparents. So much that he didn't know. So much that he'd missed. Nathan came into the room and slapped out a kind of drum roll on the worktop and asked if he wanted tea. Thanks, Richard said; yes please. Nathan put the kettle on and reached over a mug. I was at school with your father, Richard said, tapping the picture on the fridge. Nathan either knew this already or wasn't interested. The three of us were very close friends, he went on; your mother and Patrick and I. We did everything together. Nathan had his back turned, fishing the teabag from the mug. Milk's in the fridge yeah? he said, edging out through the door. From somewhere in the house, Richard heard a television turning on. He waited long enough to drink the tea and then let himself out. When he texted Cathy later to ask if there'd been a mix-up she said she was sorry but she'd had to go to Manchester and had forgotten to let him know.

At the bus stop Andrew waited with his mother. There was something happening way up on the hill. There were vehicles moving on the access road. The first phase of a construction project. He could search the planning records online when he got to the day centre. Now that he'd seen the activity he would find it hard to get through the day without finding out. For now he just watched, and his mother watched him. She had no idea what was going on in his head most of the time. He was old enough not to need walking to the bus stop, but she preferred seeing him off. If she let him just walk away from the house she wasn't going to stop worrying. But if she saw him going up the steps and sitting in the seat behind the driver she could switch off for a few hours. Which was half the purpose of the day centre. Respite. His quietness was a relief now. It had been a noisy morning. He wasn't what anyone would call dressed appropriately. But he was dressed. She felt his hand pulling at hers, and holding it. He tipped his head down towards her, still looking up at the hill. He mumbled something that sounded like Mummy, and laughed. He said it again. Who knew what he was thinking. The bus came round the corner and he dropped her hand like a hot coal. She watched him climb the steps and when the bus drove away she didn't know where to go. She didn't feel ready to go to the post office as she'd planned. She didn't quite know what had happened. She went and sat in the churchyard, in sight of Ted's grave but not too near. He wouldn't have had a clue, of course. That man. What had she expected, really. She'd been young but she should have known better. She sat for a few minutes, moving on before anyone could see her and think they should ask. She could do without the asking. In the village hall the well dressers were pressing strips of bark into the wet clay where the design had been pricked out, and it was late in the afternoon before this first stage was complete. In their nest in the conifers the first buzzard chicks were hatching. There were hot days and one afternoon the Cooper boys ran back and forth from their house, filling water pistols and balloons and tracking water through the hallway until no one in the Close was safe from a soaking. Some people took it in good heart. At midsummer the protest camp held a full-moon party, and some of the younger villagers went and joined in. The drumming was heard for most of the night. There was talk of nudity, although this was never confirmed. The missing girl's father did a long walk for charity, from his London home to the top of the moors above the village. There was a lot of publicity about it in the papers, and a website published updates of how far he'd got. He mostly followed canals on his route north, as he said that was the best way of not getting lost. He also made lengthy remarks about following the psychic energy of the water right back to the reservoirs, but most of the papers chose not to publish those. He came north at a surprising pace, and when he arrived there was a crowd of reporters waiting to meet him in the village. He said he was proud to have raised so much money for the missing-persons' charity. He asked for some privacy to go up to the hill and the photos in the newspapers were mostly of him walking away on his own. The evening before Mike and Simon left for Australia, the Jackson boys all went into town for a few drinks. Claire was with them for a rare night out. They'd left Tom and Molly with Maisie. At the start of the evening Claire was talking quickly and making a point of pacing the brothers for drinks, and then at some point she was no longer there. She'd been in the pool room when Simon had last seen her, and Mike thought she'd gone out in the yard for a smoke, and when they made Will phone her to see where she'd gone there was no answer. She'll have gone home and be asleep already, he told them. It's what she does. Simon started to argue but Gordon gave him a look to leave it, and while he was at the bar he phoned Susanna and asked her to check. None of them thought it worth asking why this seemed like something that had happened any number of times before.

The long days of July were hot and the heat rose from the heather in waves. In the mornings the air outside the Jacksons' lambing shed was dashed with swallows. James Broad finished his second year of university, and didn't come back to the village at all. His mother had prepared the small guest room in her new flat for him, but from his Facebook page she learnt he was travelling in Thailand with someone called Saoirse. The girl looks pretty enough, his mother told Susanna. But I don't even know how to pronounce her name. There was a day of action at the protest camp. Some of the villagers went up there to join in, but most people just listened to the noise of drumming drift down the hill. The first excavations started a week later. Su Cooper found a post-office book for a savings account of Austin's that she knew nothing about. There was close to five thousand pounds. When she challenged him about it he said it was meant to be a surprise. Bloody well is a surprise you've got five grand I didn't know about, she said. What else is there, a second mobile phone? What are you, Austin, some kind of a drug dealer? Or are you having an affair? She giggled when she said this, at the outlandishness of it, but she was furious enough not to regret the hurt on his face. He told her he'd been saving up for a big family holiday, that he'd been planning to surprise her. He wanted to take them all to China, he said. China? she asked. He thought the boys would appreciate learning about their roots, he told her. Their roots? Their *roots*, Austin? Their roots are in bloody Chorlton, man. What are you talking about, roots? I thought it would be important for them, he said. She shook her head. You haven't even got a passport, she reminded him. What do you know about travelling? Do you know how big China is? Where would we go? I thought we could talk to your parents, he said. I thought they'd have ideas. I wondered if they might want to come with us, show us around? Su covered her mouth in shock, her eyes widening. She leant back in her chair and looked up at the ceiling. Really, Austin? But my parents fled China, remember? They actually *fled*. Do you know what that word means? Do you have any idea?

Things have changed now though, he said. It's not the same place they left. She looked at him, shaking her head again. She loved him but he could be such a prat sometimes. We're not going to China, she said. This conversation is finished. You can keep the money for something else. You can spend it on your mistress if you like. She smiled at him in exasperation. She held on to the savings book and put it with the rest of their papers. Martin Fowler was seen talking to that pair in the caravan in Fletcher's orchard, and sometimes even sitting at their fire, drinking cans of lager and looking out of place while they muttered jokes he didn't understand. Ruth sometimes asked after him, and was told he was doing okay. Cathy Harris and Richard had lunch together in town, and she told him that she'd signed up to an online dating agency. He kept his voice casual and asked how that was going. She said there'd been a few misfires but that she was seeing some-one regularly now. He could feel her watching his face for a reac-tion. I wanted you to know, she said. He shrugged, and said that was nice, and then he asked the man's name. Anthony, she said. He works in Manchester. Is it serious? he asked. I'm not sure yet. But it's nice. I'm having a good time. It felt strange not telling you, that's all. He said he appreciated that. He talked about the next project he would be working on, and when she wondered whether they might have any dessert he said he should really be going.

———

In August the weather kept up. For a week there were mists rolling down from the hills, burning off as the sun rose sufficiently high. In the heat people broke down the fence around the flooded quarry and swam, despite everything that was known. Notices were put up but people were still seen swinging from the rope and leaping into the shockingly cold, deep water, screaming as they fell, cheered on by others spread out on the baking rocks around the water's edge. The river crept beneath the packhorse bridge and seeped into the gravelled shore. In the woods and along the shaded riverbank the ragged robin was still in flower. The cricket team went over to Cardwell, and the match was lost again. There was talk the second man in Fletcher's orchard was an associate of Woods. The talk was unfounded but he looked the type. He had a rough strength that was nothing to do with the gym, and a ropy tension in his arms. His eyes were always moving and he spoke in a type of low mutter. There was something of the prison yard about him. Man's name was Ray, according to Martin, who'd stopped by on his way down to the river one morning and ended up making some suggestions about the pruning. The other one went by Flint. Martin said they weren't friendly as such but they made for passing company. Ray had a good supply of cheap tobacco, and Flint knew a thing or two about knives. When he found out Martin had once run the butcher's he asked if those were Martin's knives up behind the counter. Martin said they'd been his father's. Flint said they looked like they were worth a bob or two. Sheffield, Martin said. Back when they knew what they were doing in Sheffield. You'd have to go to Japan to find work like that now. Japs know about blades, Ray muttered. Truth. He spat into the fire and went off to the caravan. He never took much part in the conversations. Martin wondered if he might be a bit remedial, although he knew it wasn't called that any more. He noticed that Flint sometimes kept an eye on him while they were talking, the way you'd keep an eye on a dog that was liable to upset the furniture. When he went into the caravan he always put the radio on and a distraction came over Flint while he talked. There was something between them that Martin couldn't rightly describe. Not a gay thing but some hold they had over each other. At least he didn't think it was a gay thing but who really knew these days. Martin felt like he was intruding, some evenings. Took his leave without sitting down and carried on along the lane to the packhorse bridge.

The widower was known as a man with secrets, so there was no real surprise when he turned out not to be a widower at all. His children came and spent the end of the summer with him, dropped off by a woman who was understood to be his ex-wife. It wasn't clear how the misunderstanding had started but some people felt cheated. The children were three teenagers or almost-teenagers, who seemed to spend most of their time at the playground or along by the river. In the first week they were seen setting off from the visitor centre with their father leading the way, returning an hour later in the sort of glowering silence that follows a difference of views. They weren't known to go walking again. The missing girl's father had been causing more concern. Since his charity walk he'd returned to the area repeatedly, always on foot, and been found on private land and in farm buildings and in restricted areas around the reservoirs. Eventually he was arrested and questioned at length, and although there were rumours he was being reconsidered as a suspect he was again released without charge. The first fieldfares were seen, gathered on a single hawthorn and chattering into the wind. It was a good year for hazelnuts. There were few in the village now who went to the trouble, but for those who did there was good gathering. There were thick stands of hazel growing along the high ground between the flooded quarry and the beech wood, and it was possible to pick bagloads at a time. Winnie took her share, of course, and lately Ruth had been coming along to take a few baskets for selling in the shop. Very popular they were, she told Winnie. People will pay a good price. It was Mr Wilson's turn to put together the Harvest Festival display at the church. He told Reverend Hughes that he was planning to raise awareness of unexploded ordnance for a charity he supported by making an arrangement of model landmines and mortars and calling it 'Bitter Harvest'. She told him she understood how strongly he felt about the issue, and she shared his concerns, but perhaps a poster next to the bookstall at the back of the church would be more appropriate? There was a break-in at the old butcher's shop and the knives were taken from the wall. Later they came into Martin's possession and he asked no questions. The smallest one was missing and he thought that was reasonable. Boards were put up over the shop doorway. The rosehips were out, and Su Cooper took the twins along the river path to collect a bagful. Winnie had told her how to make the syrup, and promised it would keep the boys free from colds through the winter. It was only once they were heading home that all three of them noticed how badly they'd scratched their arms. You look like you've been fighting with a sack of cats, Austin said to her later, holding Su's arm up to the light in bed. He kissed each scratch, and she winced and drew him closer. In the night she went downstairs and checked on the faint red syrup slipping through the muslin she'd hung over the preserving pan. It didn't smell as pretty as it looked. She wondered if the boys would even take it.

Martin Fowler was working at the meat counter in the new supermarket when those two from the caravan showed up. They met him round at the loading bay on his cigarette break, and a few nights later they all went hunting together. It didn't go well. There was some disagreement about which way they should head, and what they were after, and in general there was too much talking for Martin's comfort. He wouldn't have come if it hadn't been for the knives. He owed them something. The evening was clear and still. They set off around midnight, down over the packhorse bridge and across the hill towards the high moorland beyond the Stone Sisters. There had been drinking. Martin had been careful to pace himself but he wasn't sure about the others. They were carrying a backpack each, and a lamp, and Ray had a gun in a long black bag. They'd asked him along to do the dressing. This one made a right bloody mess of it last time, Flint said, and Ray had nodded cheerfully. Fair cop, he said. Not my thing. I'm a shooter. There'd been a moment, in the caravan, when Martin had realised there was no licence for the gun. This could have been a moment to leave, but he'd stayed. It took an hour to get beyond the Stone Sisters, and another hour to reach the first clough at the edge of the moor, which Flint had insisted would be the best place to start. They were after a deer, apparently, although Ray had said that if that didn't work out they could just go for rabbits or hares or grouse. Basically, he'd said, if it moves, we kill it. Martin was fairly sure they weren't going to see anything with the noise they were making. This was partly his justification for coming along; that no harm was likely to arise. His evenings were long sometimes. It was good to have something to do. The three of them sat in surprising silence for half an hour, the ramshackle incoherence of the evening transformed into concentration and poise, and when Flint finally turned on the lamp Martin wasn't completely surprised to see a small group of deer standing a hundred yards away. They had a look of interruption. They'd been grazing on the heather and were now staring into the light, blankly curious. Martin held his breath. He heard a rustle as Ray brought the gun to his shoulder. Five of the six deer scattered. The sixth turned its head and tensed to run and was knocked from its feet by the first of Ray's shots. Martin had been too close to Ray when the gun went off, so he didn't hear what was said as Flint started running towards the deer, which was even now lunging to its feet, a piece of its foreshoulder torn away. The light swung wildly as Flint raced across the heather and then the gun went off again, closer yet to Martin's head, and the light went dark as Flint threw himself to the ground. In the whistling silence Martin could just make out the deer, careering lopsidedly towards the lower end of the clough, and Ray bending over Flint to shout something before hurtling in a high-stepped gallop across the heather, his gun held over his head. Martin sat and watched while Flint got to his feet and brushed himself off, uplit by the grounded lamp. There was a ringing sound as his hearing came back. Flint appeared to be checking himself for blood. Somewhere over the hill they heard another shot. Martin headed home. At the weir a heron speared suddenly into the water, its body wriggling on long straight legs, and came up empty-beaked. It shook its head, twice, and resumed waiting. There were springtails in the compost heap in Mr

Wilson's garden, and in the morning Nelson sat watching while they leapt and popped from the surface. A steady rain began to fall and fell unchanging through the day. At the quarry great pieces of limestone slab were being craned into trucks and driven out to the main road, dozens of loads a day, the truck engines grinding under the strain. Somewhere a lot of building was being done.

In November it rained for so long that the cricket field turned into a bog and the bonfire display was called off. The fieldfares retreated from the fields beside the church and fed beneath the hawthorn hedges. At midday Jones left the school and fetched two pies from the shop. At home his sister was waiting for him behind the front door and she told him the police had been round. They took the computer, she said. She was doing that thing with her hands, as though rubbing some dirt away. I was halfway through doing an online survey and they wouldn't let me finish, she said. He asked if she'd made the tea and she said of course. She asked why they'd taken the computer and he told her they would just check it was all working okay. He told her it would be returned soon. Nothing to worry about, he said. But will they read my Facebook? I don't want them reading my Facebook. Stephanie was so cross with those comments I made on her hiking pictures. Do you think she reported me? Do you think

I'm in trouble? He told her he didn't think she was in trouble. He told her not to worry. He said he might have to go away for a few days. He took the newspaper through to the toilet and when he came back she'd warmed the pies and laid out their lunches on trays. They carried them through to the lounge and sat in front of the television. There were pictures of bush fires in Australia. What will they do with the computer? she asked. They'll just check it, love. He ate his lunch and carried his tray through to the kitchen, and when he was done he said he was heading back to the school. He asked if she'd be all right. She nodded. He asked if she had anyone coming round and she looked up at him suddenly, and asked why would she have. She was frightened. No reason, he said, I just wondered. What do you think happened to that missing girl? Christ, Susan, who knows? What? Anything could have happened. It was years ago. Poor kid. They're not going to find her now. Why are you asking about her? This has got nothing to do with the missing girl. What's got nothing to do with the girl? she asked. What is this? Susan, it's nothing. There was nothing. He put his boots back on and as he opened the door she called his name. She had that voice again. He asked what she wanted. She said she was scared. He told her it was okay. He told her he'd be home in time for tea. He heard her crying as he closed the door. There were days he could pull the place down with his bare hands. But what would she do. He was to play the cards he'd been dealt. Promises had been made. He walked quickly along the main street to the school, and when he got there two detectives in plain clothes asked if they could search the boilerhouse. He nodded, and rolled a cigarette. They took his laptop computer away. Late the next day Cathy Harris went to the Clarks' with an early Christmas card for Richard, before he went away for work again. She wanted him to know what affection remained. He was pleased to see her and he couldn't bear to see her, and as she hovered on the doorstep his mother called her in. The three of them stood in the kitchen and his mother said what a delight it was to see Cathy again. It had been too long, she said; Cathy should come over for dinner. Richard filled the kettle and fetched down the tea mugs. He didn't know what he could do to make things the way he wanted them to be. He didn't know why he was even thinking about this when he was seeing someone else. Cathy was going to spend Christmas in Manchester, with Anthony. He didn't understand why she wanted him to know. His mother had a small television on the kitchen counter, and on the local news there was a report of a man in court on child-pornography charges. The reporter mentioned the missing girl, and from the corner of his eye Richard saw Cathy put a hand on his mother's arm. A police officer was shown saying the case was unconnected to the missing girl. There was a shot of a man being led into the court building, and the sweater pulled over his head wasn't enough to keep them from seeing that the man was Jones.

———

The Jackson boys helped out at the school while Jones was away. This was the term people were using: away. There was a discomfort in discussing the matter. Arrangements were made to look in on Jones's sister, and she was soon found another place to stay. She had questions that no one wanted to answer. At the school some of the children asked if they could make cards to send Mr Jones, wishing him well and hoping he would come back soon. In the staffroom this was discussed at length and it was hard to know what to do. By lunchtime the word *paedo* was heard in the playground and any idea of making cards was dropped. In the afternoon there were difficult conversations. It's a word that means someone who hurts children, or thinks about hurting children, or touches children in a way they don't like. We don't know if Mr Jones has hurt anyone. The police are trying to find out. If any of you are worried about anything that's happened you can come and talk to me by yourself. It's okay to ask questions. Sometimes we just don't have the answers. On the television in the evening there were pictures of starving children, and men with guns and knives, and women hiding their faces, and later the same shots of Jones going into court were shown. The woodpigeons got under the netting on Clive's allotment and stripped out his Brussels sprouts and kale. The bats were folded snugly into hibernation, their breathing slow, hanging together in leathery clusters from the eaves of the church. Cathy knocked on Mr Wilson's door and asked whether Nelson wanted a walk. They had tea and cake and then she took Nelson quickly up the lane to the church, down past the orchard to the packhorse bridge and along the river. Always the same route, and Nelson didn't need to be told the way. At Hunter's wood she squeezed through the gapstone stile and followed the river up through the narrowing gorge, the path climbing away from the water, even Nelson beginning to slow as he lumbered up the steps to the visitor centre. She stopped to catch her breath for a moment, then turned down the road towards the beech wood and the allotments and the village. The Millennium Millstones had been pushed off their plinths again, and when Sean Hooper came up to repair them he said the structure was basically unsound. The strength it must have been taking, it was hard to know why anyone would go to the trouble. There was carol singing in the square, but the weather was wet and not many people showed up.

Brian Fletcher had someone in to advise on the orchard restoration, and coloured strings were tied where the pruning was to be done. Sally's brother and the second man, Ray, were busy for a week with stepladders and pruning saws, and the two of them were seen looking proud of their work. The cut branches were heaped up and burnt, and in the evenings their voices carried down the valley with the wet spitting smoke. People knew this was Sally's brother now, but they didn't know the other man. They didn't know what the arrangements were. It seemed unorthodox, but that was par for the course with the Fletchers. Their marriage was little understood. There was some speculation but most felt it was no concern of theirs. The twenty-year age gap was one thing, but it was clear they knew how to get on. Brian's family had lived in the area for years and there was some connection with the original Culshaws. But Sally was from somewhere else entirely, and his family didn't approve. He went ahead and they cut him out altogether. The wedding had been a quiet affair. Neither of them enjoyed the fuss. It was known their introduction had been arranged online but this was never acknowledged. There was heavy snow and it settled. Irene and Winnie went to the sales in the city, as they'd done every year they'd known each other. It took a bus and a train to get there and the crowds never got easier to face. But it was worth it for the prices to be found. Martin happened by Cooper's office while he was working on the new issue, and they fell into conversation about computers. Martin was thinking of selling his, he said, but he wanted to be sure the memory was properly wiped. Passwords, bank details, all that. You'll get a more or less clean drive if you reformat it, Cooper told him. But the only way to be sure is to physically destroy it. A hammer works well. A hammer? Martin asked. Won't that affect the resale value? It will tend to, Martin, yes. There is that.

9.

At midnight when the year turned Rohan found Lynsey on the dance floor at the village hall and kissed her while 'Auld Lang Syne' was sung. Rohan said later that they'd both been as surprised as each other, but in truth he'd been hoping that something would happen again for a while. Lynsey went home by herself soon afterwards, but in the morning she was seen leaving Rohan's house. There'd been no snowfall since the previous week but neither had there been a real thaw. The streets were cobbled with frozen slush. Someone falling at the top of the lane by the church could have slid right down to the packhorse bridge. The Cooper twins spent an afternoon proving this, until Lee turned his ankle and had to be carried home. At the school when term started there was a sickness bug that went round. Jackson's boys were kept busy with the sawdust and bleach. By the end of the week the staff had gone down with it too and the school had to be closed for a time. There was talk of the kitchen being at fault but nothing was ever proved. The pantomime was *Snow White*, and in the absence of seven small enough actors in the area the parts of the dwarfs had been taken by the tallest and broadest men the production committee could find. It was meant to be funny but not everyone got the joke. Irene in particular could be heard trying to whisper objections. She wasn't good at whispering. Andrew took his role of Bashful very seriously, and delivered his lines clearly. When he knelt beside Ashleigh, who was playing Snow White, and promised to watch over her, the laughter quite abruptly subsided. There was a hesitation which was either a dramatic pause or Andrew forgetting his line and then Irene whispered that she still didn't see why they couldn't have just used children and the spell was broken. Late in the month Martin drove out to the disused quarry and took a sledgehammer to his desktop computer, kicking the pieces beneath the chassis of a burnt-out car.

Sally drove her brother to his hospital appointment. This was the first chance she'd had to talk to him since Ray had turned up. He told her he'd felt some of the old ways coming back. She told him she'd been worried, that Ray wasn't good for him and couldn't he understand that? We've seen some times together, sister, he said, with the enigmatic tone he'd been attempting for a few years now. She asked what he meant, and he told her they had an understanding. They were stuck behind a cement lorry and running late. She was tense on the pedals and she kept checking the mirror. She asked what kind of a hold Ray had over him. She called him Phil and he corrected her to Flint. She told him he was only ever in trouble when Ray was around. He doesn't look out for you, she said. He doesn't care about you. Undertakings have been made, he said. She pulled across the road to see if there was space to overtake. There wasn't. She told him Ray was going to get them both in trouble again, that he was mixed up in all sorts. Flint looked at her steadily. When freedom is outlawed only the outlaws will be free, he said. She told him to grow up. She called him Phil and again he corrected her to Flint. She said that had never been his name before. The road straightened, but a delivery van swept past from behind her just as she started pulling out. She swerved back and swore, and Flint smiled patiently. She asked whether he'd got the name from Ray; whether Ray also told him what to eat, what to drink, when to go to bed and get up in the morning. Undertakings have been given, Flint said again. She told him to stop saying that. She told him their mother had never trusted Ray, that she'd had good reason not to let him into the house when they were younger. He stiffened, and told her not to talk about their mother. She was a good judge of people, Sally told him. Stop it, he said. The traffic slowed as they approached the town, and then stopped altogether. Brian's not happy with the situation, she said. Are you kicking me out again? he muttered. He understands you need somewhere to be safe, she said, turning to him. But not in the house, he said. Don't let the freak in the house. It's not that, she said, almost managing to keep the impatience out of her voice; he's just not happy with Ray. He doesn't trust him. People have had words. There are suspicions. Flint wanted to know what sort of words, what sort of suspicions, and she said only that people had reason to worry. People don't know anything, he said. Loose lips sink ships. She asked him to calm down and listen, and told him that Ray couldn't stay any longer. I can't make him leave, Flint said. He can't stay, she told him. He won't listen to me, he said. She told him they needed to do something. Brian had had enough. He asked what kind of hold Brian had over her, and she told him not to be clever. It doesn't suit you, she said.

By March the wild pheasants were fat from their winter feeding and ready for spring. At the top of the beech wood a male pheasant walked amongst a group of females and lifted his plumage expectantly. In the late-afternoon light the burning heather flickered against the hill. The protesters got in to the new quarry site and stopped operations for the day. They were arrested, and charged with aggravated trespass. Some of the older people in the village were more sympathetic towards them after that. We've a history of trespass around here, Mr Wilson told one of them at the post office. You just let us know if there's anything you need.

Su Cooper had a group of friends over from Manchester for dinner. This was happening more often now she was full-time at the BBC again. They were work friends mostly, but also people in Manchester she'd known growing up. Sometimes she stayed after work to have a drink or a meal with them, and sometimes they came down to the village. They were friendly enough but Austin didn't have much to say. One of them was talking about a mutual friend who had lost funding for a documentary project she'd been working on for ten years. He cleared the plates and said he was just popping upstairs to finish something off for the *Echo*. From the way the laughter carried on he didn't think they seemed to mind. Later when they left Su was bursting with talk, bouncing on her toes as they loaded the dishwasher together and retelling some of the stories he'd missed. He liked seeing her like this but he didn't feel a part of it. Under the ash trees the first new ferns unfurled from the cold black soil. Rohan was home to see his mother for the weekend and he wouldn't tell her what was wrong. Whenever he texted Lynsey she always took longer than he hoped to reply. He tried a couple of times to arrange a visit but in the end he realised he had to stop. He was surprised by how much more it hurt the second time around. From their caravan in the orchard Ray and Flint took a walk past the Stone Sisters and on through the far valley to Cardwell. It was a long walk but it was worth it. They came to a bungalow Ray had clocked previously and knocked on the door, and when the old lady answered Flint told her they'd been walking all day and were a little lost and could they possibly trouble her for a glass of water. She took them into the kitchen. She moved slowly and Flint told her to take her time. She poured them each a drink and then her eyes went to a biscuit tin on a shelf. It was like she was telling them it was okay. There were no biscuits in the tin but there was money. When it was done they saw themselves out.

Cathy knocked on Mr Wilson's door and asked whether Nelson needed a walk, and he said he hoped she wouldn't mind him coming along. You've no need to be asking permission, Mr Wilson, she said. He stepped out with his shoes on already and his coat folded over his arm. Is it warm? he asked. Not as warm as it looks, she said. He put on his coat, turning as his arm got caught in the sleeve so she could help him without anyone acknowledging. They were slow up the lane and they crossed over to get out of the shade. She walked with her arm part-offered and once or twice he took it. Nelson got stuck nosing around in the long grass where the lane joined the road, and Cathy asked what had brought him out of the house. He didn't answer immediately, and Cathy realised just how out of breath he was. He told her it was the anniversary of Jean's death and he was taking flowers. He asked whether she minded them stopping off at the churchyard. She asked if he realised he wasn't carrying any flowers. He made a show of looking at his exasperated hands and then smiled. One of the consolations of a death in springtime, he told her, lifting a pair of kitchen scissors partway from his pocket for her to see. Nelson pulled hard on the lead and she had to walk on ahead, and by the time she was able to turn and wait he was carrying a thick bunch of fresh daffodils. She couldn't see where he'd got them from, and thought it best not to ask. He led the way through the churchyard to Jean's grave. He was walking quicker now, and the catch of his hip was more pronounced. And then he was talking to her, to Jean, which was something she'd never been able to do at Patrick's grave. He stooped to lay the flowers down. He had to push against the headstone to lever himself upright, and this time when she offered her arm he took it. She looked away from him, up at the clouds blowing over the hills behind Jackson's farm, and the tears came. They didn't come often. Mr Wilson gave her a neatly folded handkerchief, and they sat on the bench by the churchyard gate. When she was finished, she said she'd wash the handkerchief before she gave it back. He didn't argue. They sat for a moment while her breathing steadied, and then she asked if it ever got easier. He didn't answer straight away. He told her that not long after they'd married, Jean had insisted he stop smoking. Cathy wasn't sure this was an answer. This was in the 1960s, he said. Nobody was giving up smoking in those days. I enjoyed my cigarettes, as it happened. But she was very insistent. She could be an insistent lady, you'll probably remember. And she told me it was making me stink, making the house stink, all that. And she said she'd read about it making you sick; cancer and whatnot. I don't think she ever said it was her or the cigs, but I wasn't about to take any chances. Anyroad, I did it. Knocked it on the head. No nicotine patches or none of that. Sometimes I'd just go down the pub and breathe in deep to make up for it. But that was that. She was grateful, but I don't think she understood what it meant. And then she asked me, near the end, when she was very ill, if I'd ever missed my cigarettes. She got to thinking about all sorts, near the end. Not often, Jean, I told her. Only after meals. Cathy turned and Mr Wilson was laughing, silently. Only after meals, he said, again, the laugh turning into a hacking cough. She looked at him. It's a bloody metaphor, Cathy, he said. She nodded. I got that, Mr Wilson. She patted his knee. Very good. Nelson stretched at the lead, and Cathy asked if they should walk on. You go ahead, Mr Wilson said. I'll stop here. Take you all day to get around with this hip holding you back. She asked if he'd be all right getting home and he said he'd be fine. I'll just rest up here a bit longer, he said. He watched as she strode down the lane past the orchard, and he waited until she was out of sight before taking out a pouch of tobacco and rolling himself a cigarette.

————————

By May the reservoirs were as low as they'd been in forty years, the ruins of the old village buildings dry above the waterline and people walking down to picnic where the churchyard had once been. There were hosepipe bans over four counties; the hills were drying out. Will and Claire Jackson separated again, and Claire went to live with her mother while she looked for a flat. Tom stayed in the village with Will. Martin stood for election as chair of the parish council, on a vague platform of being what he referred to as a new broom. It was the first time anyone could remember the chairship being contested. It was noted that there was a difference between being a new broom and never having attended a meeting of the council, and Brian Fletcher was voted back in. In the village hall the well dressers were into their third day of pressing in the petals and mosses, and tempers were running short. Some of the newer dressers were lacking for technique, and Irene had to be clear when sections weren't up to scratch. She even had to explain that the petals were meant to overlap in the manner of roof slates, so that any rainwater could run off. It boggled the mind how someone could live in a well-dressing village and not know that. At the badger sett in the beech wood after dark the first cubs of the year came out. They stayed close to the adults, watching their mothers find food. There was a cacophony of smells. They marked a path back and forth between the adults and the sett entrance, scratching and shuffling and keeping the way clear. The Jacksons moved their sheep up on to the moors. The lower fields needed time to recover. The sheep made a ruckus as they bunched together up the lane but they soon settled down. A police officer was seen going down to Fletcher's orchard, and as he stepped through the gate he saw a man urinating against the dry-stone wall. This was Flint, who turned and nodded, wiping his hands on his trousers. The police officer said he was making enquiries about a theft. Flint shrugged, and the police officer asked about his place of residence, his line of work, his recent whereabouts. He explained that these were routine questions. Flint gave him routine answers. There were noises from inside the caravan. The door opened, and Ray came out. He nodded at the police officer, and at Flint, and went to urinate against the dry-stone wall. The police officer asked were there any objections to his having a look around. Flint shrugged again, and the police officer poked around in the nettles under the caravan, and into the gap between the caravan and the wall. Ray and Flint looked at each other. The police officer stepped into the caravan and started opening the cupboards and drawers. Ray adjusted his trousers, and Flint held out a hand to steady him back. The police officer stepped down from the caravan and thanked them for their time. Flint said he thought they were entitled to see a search warrant for that type of thing, and the police officer said he just wanted to exhaust all the avenues of possibility. Ray said he could exhaust some more avenues of possibility for him if he liked, but he waited while the police officer was halfway up the lane before he said it.

———

At dawn on Midsummer's Day the sun fell into line with the two pairs of fallen stones at either end of the Stone Sisters. The drumming could be heard from down in the village. The bracken was up but was browning already. Ashleigh Wright was found to have been missing days at school. There was a phone call to Susanna and a meeting with the head of year, Ms Bowman. Ashleigh was at the meeting but she couldn't be brought into the conversation. She slumped low in the chair and her hair hung over her face and she wouldn't be drawn. Was there bullying. Was she finding the lessons too difficult, or too easy. Where was she going when she wasn't in school. Was she meeting anyone. If there was a problem they wanted to work with her to resolve it. But she couldn't go on like this. She kept shrinking into her chair, and when Susanna put a hand to her shoulder she jerked away. It was difficult to ask questions into that sullen vacuum without becoming frustrated. Susanna and Ms Bowman fell silent. It was a small room and warm and there was condensation on the window. Outside there were shouts as the younger year groups took their morning break. There was a stack of books on Ms Bowman's desk that needed marking by the end of the day and she tried to keep her eyes from it. Susanna's hand was still smarting from the way Ashleigh had pulled back. This was new. Or not new, in fact. It was the same way she'd retreated when they were with the children's father. Susanna hadn't seen it for a long time. There had been a kind of strength in it then, she knew, the kind of strength a child shouldn't need. But she wondered what was happening now to make her retreat in that same way. Ms Bowman was watching the two of them. She knew there was a history. There'd been little concern with the brother but this one seemed more troubled. Probably they would need to talk separately. There might be a referral, if the mother would accept that. But now time was short and the poor girl just wanted leaving alone. She smiled at Susanna and gestured that she would call her later. Susanna stood to leave and Ashleigh was already heading through the door. In the corridor Ashleigh walked away without saying anything and Susanna watched her go. Her spine was all twisted and her shoulders hunched and her feet were dragging as she walked. Her posture was doing her no favours but she wouldn't want to hear that. Susanna was feeling pretty tense around the clavicles herself. She'd go for a run when she got home. All those things that had happened. When she thought they were passed they kept coming back. She lifted her head and dropped her shoulders and tried to feel herself connected to the earth through the balls of her feet. Rohan had finished university and come home with no idea what to do next. He was helping her in the shop but she couldn't pay him. She'd been running a loss for months and could barely afford to restock. The landlord was losing patience. James Broad came back from university and worked in Hunter's timber yard for a time. He refused to go to his graduation. A certificate arrived by registered post, and he showed his mother, the two of them standing in the kitchen in their dressing gowns, James with his mouth full of toast and his mother having to whip the certificate away so it didn't get covered in jam. Later he met the others for a drink in town, and although it was meant as a celebration they weren't really in the mood. They sat out in the beer garden by the river where they'd sat three years before, and soon ran out of things to say. Sophie was the only one who had a job lined up, and she'd failed her course altogether. When Rohan suggested they take the shortcut across the river to the car park Sophie gave him a withering look. In the morning Les Thompson and his men were out early with the mowers. They went straight from the milking to the machinery shed and got things started. The morning had been clear and still, the mist lifting from the fields in waves and burning off before the cows were even turned out. Jones's trial came to court and he was sentenced to eighteen months. There was a report in the paper that no one wanted to read. His sister was still staying elsewhere and his house stood empty. At night the bats flew low over the water and down the lane past the orchard, feeding on insects no one knew had existed before they were carried away. In the evening a police van was seen at Fletcher's orchard. Ray and Flint were arrested.

———

The long days of July were hot. The heather seethed with insect life. On Sunday in the evening Sally and Brian Fletcher ate a meal together. Ordinarily there would be conversation but tonight they were silent. Through the window the caravan was pale against the dusk and the orchard was closing in. The dinner was mostly eaten before Brian spoke. You can't say I haven't been patient, he started. Sally looked at him, pushing the last of the mashed potato on to her fork. There was nothing she could say. Even after that last time, Brian went on, I welcomed him back. The boy's got troubles. We know that. We thought this would help; a bit of stability. But if we could persuade Ray to keep away, Sally said. Ray's always been the problem. There's a hold he has over Phil. I don't think you could persuade that man to go anywhere he didn't want to go, Brian said. Not without a pair of handcuffs. But if we see what happens, with the charges? Ray will have been the instigator. Maybe Phil will just get a caution? Oh, come on, Sally. They were both in the house. They both went into her house and stole from her. It's joint enterprise. It's bloody home invasion. This won't be a caution. She nodded. She knew he was right. She loved Brian dearly and she knew he was right. She knew how much he'd sacrificed to go ahead and marry her, but there were still times when he sounded as though he was the lord of the manor. They did the dishes and settled down to watch whatever was on television. It was something about a murder. The second clutches of goldcrest eggs were hatching in the conifer plantation up at the

Hunter place. When the school holidays started the widower's ex-wife brought one of his children to stay: the youngest, a girl of around thirteen. No one had managed to drop the habit of calling him the widower. The girl spent more time in the garden than when she'd been there with her siblings the year before. She was especially good with the hens, it was noticed, and took longer than needed putting them away at night. Some evenings she sat with her father on a new bench in the garden, sipping at a mug of hot chocolate, and later he sat alone while the light in an upstairs bedroom shone into the gathering dusk and went out. At the end of the month, after his wife had taken the girl back, the same light was sometimes seen on in the evenings, the curtains drawn, the hens taking longer than usual to settle. At the river the keeper waded into the water and cut away at the weeds.

The August nights were cold and in the mornings the first dewy hints of autumn rose from the ground. The swallows were starting to gather along the wires, the first to feel the cold, turning their heads south and waiting for whatever would pass as a sign. In the woods and along the shaded riverbank the ragged robin was in flower. The air was dry and the sounds of the cricket match carried right through the village, the knock and the chatter and the cheers seeming to grow louder each time. By the end of the afternoon word went round that the match was not being lost. More people

227

turned up to watch. The exact score was a matter of confusion, but when Cardwell's last wicket was taken, bowled clean by James Broad with a shout that volleyed right across the river and sent the pigeons scattering from the end of the field, there was a general understanding that the game had been won for the first time in memory. In the shelter of one of the cloughs coming down off the moor a well-made den was discovered, birch and larch branches propped up against each other and the whole thing roofed with bracken until the light barely shone through. It wasn't known who had built the den or what it had been used for, but the ranger took it down all the same. He found magazines. At the office when he mentioned this they wanted to know what sort of magazines. Let's say specialist-type ones, he said. You mean like gun magazines, fishing? No. I think you know what I'm talking about. Adult magazines. Not comics then; we're not talking about *Beano* and *Dandy*? No. Special-interest adult magazines. Oh, like tit-mags you mean? Well. Like I say. These were particularly specialist. In what way, Graham? His colleagues could be very obtuse, some-times. He was aware that they did it on purpose. The best response seemed to be a patience in excess of that which they may have expected. But he had no wish to take this conversation any further. Did you bring any back with you, Graham? For evidence? Can we see them, Graham? Are they in your desk? No, he said. They'll be in the filing cabinet. Have a look in the filing cabinet. Under S for specialist? A for adult? B for bondage? I'm going to conclude this conversation now, folks. Graham pretended to tip his hat, and left the office. He had better things to do. He could hear his colleagues laughing as he closed the office door. Let them waste their time looking through the filing cabinet. On the allotments in the evenings there were queues for the tap and those with water butts looked on and said nothing. The water skidded across the hard ground and didn't always soak down to the roots. There was a sense of the season beginning to turn; nothing wilting yet but a softening in much of the growth, the greens less green and the seed-heads starting to fall. The watering went on after the long shadows had stretched down to the road and been overtaken by the greater shadow of the hill. On a fence-post by the road a buzzard tensed and sprang into flight, settling claws-first on a young rabbit and carrying it away. At the school the boilerhouse was demolished.

Cathy Harris helped Sally clean out the caravan once the police had finished. Most of what they hadn't taken was only fit for throwing away. Cathy asked what Sally thought would happen next. I really don't know, Sally said. I'm starting to think he's just that bit too damaged, you know? He gets himself into these situations. The only time I ever see him looking peaceful is when he's in the hospital, but the only way in is when he gets arrested first. I don't know what more I'm meant to do. The orchard looked hacked and awkward, but Brian Fletcher said he thought the two men had done a good job on the whole. The protest camp had mostly closed down, now that the new quarry was fully up and running. The first excavation had started three miles away from the Stone Sisters, and it was clear that it wouldn't get much closer. Most days there was just the one protester up there, keeping the fire going and repainting the banners. The estate lost more pheasants than usual to poachers, and there was talk of an organised gang. The odd one or two was tolerated, but this was dozens in a single night. In the parlour at Thompson's farm the men hooked the milking clusters up to the next group of cows, the rich smell of cream and shit rising in the late-afternoon air. In his studio Geoff Simmons fixed handles to a new batch of jugs, scoring a cross-hatch at the attachment and sticking each one on with a smear of slip. There were orders to pack and take down to the post office. There was a woman he'd been seeing, a potter from Devon who'd become very friendly at a craft fair and had been up to stay a couple of times. She said she preferred him to travel down to her place. She'd encouraged him into the mail order. He'd hated the idea of a website, and of people buying his pots without holding them first, but she was persuasive. This was starting to worry him. On his lunch break Martin took his sandwiches to the park by the river, and when he'd finished eating he stopped off at the toilets and heard something going on in the cubicle. There was just muttering at first, while he stood at the urinal, and then some other rustling or rattling around. It sounded as though two people were in there, and the thought crossed his mind that it could be two men having sex. He understood that this was something people did. He'd wondered, when they'd first learnt about Bruce, whether this was something Bruce had done. He'd found the thought upsetting, far more than the basic fact of his being gay or whatever they wanted to call it. He'd settled with that. He'd told Bruce, eventually, soon after meeting Hugh, that he'd settled with that. There was silence in the cubicle, and he thought he must have imagined the noises. Which was a concern in itself. And then as he was washing his hands there was the sound of a sudden movement, a bang against the cubicle door, and a kind of wincing grunt of pleasure. He realised, as he walked quickly away without drying his hands, that the idea of the pleasure had surprised him. Because why would it be a surprise. Because whatever else people thought about that type of thing it could only be assumed that they enjoyed it. Else why would they go to all that trouble. Why would they put up with people talking about them. He found himself thinking about whether or not he'd heard what he thought he'd heard for days afterwards. He wanted to tell someone about it but there was no one. He wondered how they went about agreeing to go into the cubicle together in the first place. The wheat fields by the main road were harvested and the woodpigeons gathered for the spilt grain. In the clough in the evenings there was a thin mist following the line of the river, rising like smoke from the water. The weather was closing in.

In their front room the Cooper family watched *Harry Potter*, after a day of walking up on the hill. The twins fell asleep after twenty minutes, one hand each resting in the bowl of popcorn wedged between them. Austin had just been commenting quietly on this to Su when he realised she was asleep as well. He turned the sound down on the film and listened to the three of them. He had a memory of listening to them like this when the boys were babies. They had become so much more in the meantime. He watched the boys' chests rise and fall, their lungs still small and their bodies busy growing. He looked at them. The neatness of their proportions. Their skin. The utter stillness on their faces. The light in the room kept changing with the movement of the trees outside. The people in the film kept shouting at each other, mutely. And Su, turned in towards him, her slight frame slow and tidal in its sleeping breath. He felt as though he were holding the three of them, holding this room, this house. They made him feel at once immensely capable and immensely not up to the task. He remembered all the times he'd lain awake at night, thinking over the locks on the doors and windows, working through what he would do when someone came crashing into the house. And here they all were, safe. The light from the television screen shone across the boys' faces. Austin was holding his breath, as if letting it go would let the moment spill. He felt the contentment in his chest like an aching muscle. He noticed Sam's hand twitch in the popcorn bowl, and wondered what he was dreaming of. He felt Su shift beside him, her cheek turning into his shoulder, and then Lee asked him to turn the volume up because he couldn't hear the film.

When the first siren sounded over at the quarry the workers cleared the area. When the second siren sounded the birds fell silent. In the village, windows and doors were pulled shut. The third siren sounded, and the birds rose into the air, and the explosion came from deep behind the working face, spreading through the body of the earth, a low crumping shudder that shrugged huge slabs of limestone to the quarry floor. The dust rose and continued rising and drifted out through the air for five minutes or more. The first all-clear sounded, and the birds returned noisily to the treetops. The second all-clear sounded, and the workers returned to their places. In the village the windows and doors were kept closed as the dust spread. On the bus back from town Winnie saw Irene and asked whether she'd had her hair done. Irene's hand went up to her head, although she hadn't meant it to. She told Winnie it was only the usual. Keeping it tidy, she said. Well, it suits you, Winnie told her. Irene only nodded, and turned to face the front of the bus. Winnie wondered how she'd caused offence. It wasn't always easy to tell, with Irene. At the bus stop Irene saw Sally Fletcher, who wanted to know about the plans for the next Women's Institute sale and also felt it necessary to pass remark on her hair. What a lovely job they've done there, she said, and for a moment she had her hand on Irene's shoulder, as though she wanted to turn her back and forth like some kind of dressmaker's dummy. Well, Irene said. I do prefer it short, you know. Practical. Later, when Su Cooper said something similar, Irene began to wonder if some elaborate joke was being played on her. She didn't welcome the attention. She wasn't vain about her appearance. She would have to ask Jackie to do a simpler cut, next time. Tidy was all she'd asked for. In the evening she met Winnie for a drink at the Gladstone, as they'd arranged. It was her sixtieth birthday but she didn't want a fuss. At the council meeting there was a dispute about burning the Guy Fawkes at the bonfire party. Susanna Wright said it was anti-Catholic which was more or less the same as racist when you thought about it and she didn't think the parish council should be condoning anything like that. The majority saw it as a harmless tradition which there was no need to drop. After the meeting Susanna was taken to one side and told that as a newer member of the parish council she should wait a year or two before tabling any more motions. There were springtails in the crumbling wood of the fallen ash by the river, moulting and feeding and getting ready to lay more eggs. There was a storm and the felt on the village-hall roof came away. There was so much water damage that the wall panelling down one side had to be taken out. That end of the hall was cordoned off, and a meeting held about urgent fundraising for repairs. There was flooding the length of the valley and some newly cut trees from the Hunters' land came crashing down the river and took out the footbridge by the millpond weir.

Jones came back to the village and kept himself to himself. When the lights were first seen on at his house there were those who felt he should be acknowledged. I'll fucking acknowledge him, Tony said. There was no question of him working at the school again. Once his time on remand had been taken into account he'd only served six months. There were conditions attached to his release but he was allowed to live at home. Those who saw him said he looked gaunt. His offences were said to be at the milder end of the spectrum but in the village they wouldn't be brushed off. Spectrum my arse, Tony said, more than once. Martin said that it wasn't kiddy stuff but teenage girls, and even with some thirteen-year-olds it was hard to tell. There was a silence when he spoke and no one agreed. Tony told him a thirteen-year-old was still a child, and Martin immediately backed off. I didn't mean it like that, he said. The bloody hell is wrong with you? Tony asked. There were sale posters in Susanna's shop window all through December. It was understood to be a closing-down sale, although nobody called it that. She hung fairy lights and paper chains and held a Christmas event. There was mulled wine and mince pies and people sang carols together. The place was packed, although it was noticed that Ashleigh wasn't there. She was having a difficult patch. In the morning there was a new padlock on the door. At the river the keeper repaired a section of path where the flooding had taken out a foot of bank and left the gravel to slide into the water. He'd been shovelling gravel all morning and was glad of the breeze. Richard Clark didn't make it home for Christmas and neither did his sisters. They took it in turns to call their mother's mobile on Christmas morning, and if she stood just outside the back door she could more or less hear what they said. The girls sounded hassled, coming up for air from their hectic preparations. Richard was subdued, speaking from a room that sounded full of carpets and drapes. There was someone in the bed with him, she could tell. She'd always been able to tell, and it tickled her that he was innocent enough not to realise. A rustle of sheets, an impatience in his voice. When the phone calls were done the house and the garden were awfully quiet. Later two of Jackson's boys came and drove her to Winnie's for lunch. They took an arm each as they helped her to the car, and she wasn't sure her feet touched the ground at all.

———

There was talk of putting the pantomime on in the church, while the village hall was being refurbished, but given the tone of recent productions the church council felt it would be inappropriate. Oh no it wouldn't, Jane Hughes said. Well, yes, I'm afraid it would, Clive replied. Her naivety disappointed him sometimes. The pantomime was postponed for the year. That Sunday Jane's family was seen at the church, the son and the daughter home from university and looking uncomfortable in pews they hadn't sat in since they were half as high. The son was taller and broader than both his parents now, and when he did the reading he had to stoop over the lectern, his big hands gripping the edges as though he were about to lift it over his head. They had gone a long way towards home, he read, when they realised Jesus was missing. He was swallowing his words a little. They hurried back to the temple and found the boy there, talking to the high priests. Didn't you know you would find me in my father's house? he said. Jane was standing to one side, waiting to announce the next hymn, watching her son and smiling at the story being told. This is the word of the Lord, he mumbled. Thanks be to God, the congregation replied. They sang another hymn, and during the sermon Jane talked about change and renewal and told them she would soon be moving to a new job in Manchester. The river thickened with silt from the hills and plumed across the weirs. A pale light moved slowly across the moor. The missing girl's name was Becky, or Rebecca, or Bex. If she was still alive she could be close to six feet tall by now. The computer-generated image of her at seventeen was five years out of date, but a police spokesperson said there were no plans to commission a new one. The case remained open, she said. The jeans and the body-warmer and the white hooded top would be too small. The shoes would have fallen apart.

10.

At midnight when the year turned there was a fire in the caravan in Fletcher's orchard. It took a time for anyone to notice, and an hour more for the fire brigade to arrive, and by then the caravan was burnt out and a dozen trees gone with it. In the morning it was still smoking and a smell of molten plastic hung over the village. There was little doubt it had been deliberately set, and not much hope of finding who'd done it. For days afterwards Fletcher was seen pacing through the orchard, inspecting the burnt trees as though they might be salvageable. The softening fields on the south side of the church were thick with feeding fieldfares. Most evenings a fog came thickly down and stayed. Andrew had another incident with his mother. She was cleaning again and she kept on at him to pick his clothes off the floor. He was in the middle of a coding run. He didn't want to lose his thread. She knew she wasn't supposed to come into his room but she kept asking. He was trying to keep his thread but she kept appearing at the door. He would have done it later if she'd given him a chance. He told her he was busy but she said she had a wash waiting to go on. He stood to close the door but she crossed over the metal strip between the hallway carpet and his bedroom carpet. Let me just get them myself, she said. They need washing. She came past him and stooped for the clothes, and he brought his elbow down on the back of her neck. She made a noise he didn't understand. She knelt down and picked up the clothes. Afterwards he said he was sorry but only because he knew that's what people said.

Brian Fletcher was still brooding on the fire and Sally knew to leave him alone. The Fletchers' house was a big one and they each had enough space to themselves. He'd been cut off from the family's wealth but he'd been allowed to hold on to the house. They couldn't afford to keep it up but they did their best. It was a square Georgian townhouse which was out of all proportion with the rest of the street. It had been the vicarage at one time. There were four bedrooms and three reception rooms and a huge kitchen, and it was about three times as big as where Sally had grown up. She had a study for her wildlife books and watercolours, and Brian had a workshop crammed with bits and pieces of cars. It was known they had separate bedrooms. He was taking the fire personally. She kept out of his way while he worked it through. The fire had made him feel targeted. He found a garage in town where he could store the cars. He wondered for a time if his family might be involved, but settled in the end on some associate of Ray or Flint. That type of character is always after someone to blame, he said. After some days of agitation he came to her and asked if she would stay with him that night. It was always done in this way. There was a chance to decline, which made it easier to accept. They each had reasons to protect their own solitude but also nights when they needed to feel safe. They had sex rarely and it never made them feel they'd been missing out. Sally talked all this through with Cathy Harris one time, and afterwards wished that she hadn't. It wasn't something that people understood. In the rains at the end of the month a cast-iron gutter cracked and took down a soffit board when it fell. There was always something to mend and it was hard to keep up. On the moor the sheep were nicotine-yellow against the fresh snow. The falls were heavy and they drifted. Will Jackson kept Tom out of school and took him up to look for lost ewes. They'd brought most of them down the night before but there were a half-dozen they hadn't been able to find. It was likely some would be dead by now, and Will thought Tom was old enough to see. Claire wouldn't like it, and that was fine by him. He got the quad as far up the track as it would manage, and pointed it downhill before they got off. They had brought poles, shovels, sacks, a bag of feed and bottles of milk. They split the load between them before setting off across the hill.

Tom was up to Will's shoulders now and just as broad, and Will found himself working to keep up. He told his son to pace himself. Nothing wrong with this pace, Grandad, Tom shouted back against the wind. Will told him to fuck off, and Tom laughed. They waded on, their boots sinking deep into the settled snow, heading for the narrow clough where Will thought the sheep might have gathered. At the parish council there was disagreement about who was responsible for replacing the footbridge.

The estate was granted a court order against the last quarry protester and she was evicted. Two police officers gave her a lift to the train station with a rucksack full of what she could carry. She asked for everything else to be put into storage and was told this wasn't possible. There was some distress. The police officers didn't think she had much sense of where she would go. Men from the estate took a trailer up to the site and carted everything off for the tip. The reservoirs were quickly filled when the rains returned, the hills soon saturated and the spillways gushing into the river again. Along the footpath and in the corners of fields the first flushes of nettles came up. Winnie was amongst the few left who still cut the tops for soups and sauces. She gathered them with a creeping embarrassment now in case anyone saw. The National Park people put on a fire-safety exhibition at the village hall, most of which was about arson. Following recent events, they said. Refreshing people's minds about securing premises and keeping flammable materials under lock and key. Brian Fletcher took it personally and asked what more he was supposed to have done. There were cutbacks at the BBC, and Su Cooper was offered voluntary redundancy. She spent three long evenings talking it over with Austin. If she stayed there might be redundancies anyway, with far less than they were offering now. If she left now she would always regret it; all the work she'd put in to get this far, all the time she'd missed when she'd been home with the boys. If she stayed some of her best colleagues would be gone anyway, and the workload would be heavier, the whole atmosphere changed. If she left what would she do? They could see it as a sabbatical, take the boys travelling. The boys were too young for that, they couldn't be taken out of school. She could get more involved in village life, do some volunteering, find a hobby. Hobby? she said. A fucking *hobby*? There were no easy ways of talking around this. There was no obvious solution. Fucking hobbies, she said, again, and decided to keep the job. The clocks went forward and the evenings opened out. The buds on the branches brightened. Gordon Jackson took a delivery over to Ruth's shop in Harefield and made sure to arrive after closing. Once he'd unloaded and she'd signed the invoice they both washed their hands and went upstairs. There was a sofa and they undressed and she pulled him down to her. There was never much talking. This didn't happen every time. He only knew when she told him to wash his hands. Months now this had been happening but not often and he was always surprised. She was older than him but she was strong. There were sometimes bruises. Afterwards when he tried to talk she didn't want to. He wouldn't mind but there were things he wanted to know. He wanted to know what this was. Perhaps it was nothing. That would be hard to accept. She lay back against the end of the sofa and rested her feet in his lap. He thought she was falling asleep but she toed at his stomach in a way that made him get started all over again. It was dark by the time he left and he wondered if he'd be too late for tea. From the top of the moor the lights of the cars on the motorway could be seen, soundless and urgent while the village slept.

In April Su Cooper's parents came to stay, and when they walked through the door the boys were all over them. Had they brought sweets, had they brought cookies? Su's father laughed at their directness and bent down to lift up first Han Lee and then Lu Sam. Austin was already outside, collecting bags from the car. Su watched her father, and saw how he struggled with the weight of each boy. Her mother waited, then leant forward to embrace the two boys as they stood. Soon I won't need to bend down at all! she said, as she had done for the last few years. Su embraced them both, and ushered them through to the front room just as Austin appeared in the doorway with all the bags. Where am I putting these? he asked, and was told to take them straight upstairs. There were wild pheasant nests scraped into the long grass at the edge of the beech wood, and when the eggs started appearing they were taken in number by foxes and badgers and crows. The Hunters were having a new drystone wall built at the entrance to their drive, and Liam Hooper had already been working on it for a month. Sean Hooper went over most days to check on the progress, and when he noticed how often Olivia Hunter was coming down the drive with cups of tea and plates of biscuits, or just hanging around asking questions, he made a point of reminding Liam of her age. Liam looked surprised and muttered something about it at least being legal. Sean couldn't help laughing but he told Liam to steer clear. It'd be more trouble than it's worth, he said. At the Women's Institute sale Winnie asked Irene if she was well. She said it with an upward tilt, as though of course why would she not be well, but Irene stiffened at the asking. I can't complain, she said. I'm getting along. And how are you? Winnie said she was fine. She said Irene's cakes and jams had been missed; it had been a while since she'd brought any to the sale. The colour rose in Irene's face and for a moment she didn't reply. I can't be expected, she said. I can't always be expected. Winnie put a hand to her friend's arm. No one's expecting, she said. But if I can help. Irene shook her head and moved back a little, so that Winnie's hand was left in the air. Thank you, she said. I'll manage. I appreciate your thoughtfulness. But, really. A pair of buzzards circled each other high over the moorland by Reservoir no. 5, locking claws and swinging towards the ground in a tumble of outstretched wings. The conservationists had been putting about a plan to control the vegetation in the flood meadows by grazing longhorn cattle, and the Jacksons were asked if they wanted the contract to manage it. The boys were in favour. It would mean putting up a new barn, and getting a bigger trailer to move the stock around, but there'd been a strong suggestion that if they took this on there would be more contracts to follow. Jackson said no. When they tried to explain the importance of diversification he made a big show of how hard he found it to speak and finally spat out the word sheep. We – do – sheep, he said. There was no use discussing it. There was a half moon over the cricket ground and the pale light fell through the leaves of the horse chestnut tree.

In May there was snow on the higher ground, even as the walkers who came through the village started wearing shorts. The new-growth bracken spread across the hills above the reservoirs, pale green and thickening, and plans were drawn up for more spraying and cutting back. At the school the lights in the staffroom were seen on all night, and the next day the word was that Ofsted were coming in. When it was over Mrs Simpson looked as though she'd gone through a month of lambing and Miss Dale had to take a week off sick. Money was found to repair the village hall, and activities moved to the church while the work was carried out. There were objections to yoga taking place in the nave, on account of what Clive said were its possibly occultic origins. There was a discussion. Jane Hughes talked to the church council about how they might best handle her departure, and the interregnum which would follow. The diocese is committed to rural parishes, she assured them, but you will need to be ready for a long period without anyone in post. They were nodding but she knew they weren't taking it on board. She talked about the need to put together rotas of readers and communion servers, the need to book visiting preachers, the options for drawing on retired clergy who lived in the area. She went home and told her husband that these people weren't going to be ready, that maybe she was doing the wrong thing. He told her they would just have to grow up a bit, that they'd struggle for a while but she couldn't always be responsible. She said saying grow up was a bit harsh and he threw up his hands. At the river the keeper dropped the sample bottles into the water from the bridge by the weir. Always the same spot and the same time of day. There were bubbles on the surface as the bottles filled and then he brought the cage up and put the bottles away. He watched a pair of dragonflies come together near the bank. The missing girl had been seen in the visitor centre, listening to one of the audio guides, her eyes closed in concentration and her legs swinging from the bench. She had been wearing the canvas shoes, apparently.

In June the evenings were open and clear. The sun didn't set so much as drift into the distance, leaving a trail of midsummer light that seemed to linger until morning. There was a reluctance to sleep. There was talk. In the meadows Thompson's men worked the baler along the lines of cut grass, the thick sward gathered up and spun into dense bales. Every few hundred yards the tractor paused and there was a tumbling inside the machine and a neatly wrapped bale rolled softly from the hatch into the field. The woodpigeons laid eggs in their nests in the beech wood and in the horse chestnut by the cricket ground. They took turns sitting on the eggs, but there were still plenty stolen by magpies and crows. On the bank above the abandoned lead pits the badgers started coming out of their sett before dark. The sows with cubs were looking for food, and the boars were looking for mates. There were conflicts. There were some in the village still who could remember their grandparents talk of the lead-mining trade, of men who spent their lives clambering down hand-cut shafts to hack away at seams of toxic ore, the fields littered with workings and the smoke from the smelting works settling in everyone's lungs. Mr Wilson went into hospital for a hip operation, and while he was gone Nelson stayed in Cathy's house. In the village hall the well-dressing boards were almost finished. Winnie and Irene sprayed the boards to keep the clay damp, and when they finally stood back and smiled in approval there was a general dropping of shoulders and a cheer and the order was sent out to the Gladstone for sausage and mash. Jackson's boys penned the sheep for worming. Will Jackson was ready with the drench gun and held each sheep by the neck in turn, easing the nozzle in through the corner of the mouth and down to the back of the throat. It put him in mind sometimes of getting Molly to swallow the pink medicine on nights when she'd sweated herself awake. The girl spent a lot of nights awake, it seemed. He wondered if he'd been the same as a child. His mother wouldn't have had the time for it, he supposed. The ewes kept coming down the line and there was soon a lanolin sheen on his skin. Winnie's grandchildren came to visit at the end of the month, and she took them out picking elderflowers in the old quarry by the main road, filling a bin-bag with the foamy white flower-heads and carrying it home on their shoulders. She sat them at the kitchen table and had them zesting the oranges and lemons she'd bought ready, while she picked the flower-heads clean and set them to soak overnight. By the next day they'd lost interest, and refused to leave the television when she added the sugar and fruit juice and heated it gently through. When her daughter came for the children she gave them a bottle of the cordial. It was still warm and the light shone through it, and Winnie knew it would never be drunk. Her daughter hugged her lightly and kissed her cheek and said they'd see each other soon. The children waved from the back of the car.

In his studio Geoff Simmons loaded the kiln for a first firing and took the whippet out for a slow walk. She'd been a runner once but her hips were gone. They walked down the lane towards the Jackson place and the road. He was a bit off the pace himself. He went into the pub and came out with a pint and a bowl of water. He sat on a bench and read the *Valley Echo* while the whippet drank. He knew all the names of the people in the *Echo* but there were plenty he couldn't place if they walked by. They didn't tend to socialise. He'd never expected to be here this long so he hadn't made the effort. He'd been in Devon for a week with the woman he'd been seeing, and she'd talked about him staying longer. He'd told her there were things he needed to get back for. He finished his beer and went in for another. It would be hours before the kiln needed attending. There were other jobs but they would wait. The whippet settled down and slept. By the river Jane Hughes saw Jones, sitting on the bench by the gated cave entrance. Had to stop for a rest, Vicar, he said. It's a nice place to sit, she agreed; sheltered. She sat beside him. There was a commotion in the hawthorn on the other side of the river. Magpies want shooting, he said. They're in there going for the wrens. Jane had learnt not to enter these discussions, and nodded. How's your sister doing? They say she's coming on, he said. Settling in. I told them she could come back here but they thought it best not for now. There was a whine of machinery from the Hunter plantation, and jackdaws circling over the woods. The afternoon was darkening. Jones nodded at the locked gate to the caves. Reckon she might have ended up in there, he said. Who? Jane asked. The girl, he said. They searched it all before they put the gates up though, didn't they? Could never search all of it, he said. Jane watched him for a moment. You know if you ever want to talk, about anything, she said, looking out across the river and keeping her voice light. There was a pause while the river moved over the stones and through the reeds. That's me then, Vicar, he said, standing up. She watched the magpies pull the young wrens out of the hedge while their parents fussed overhead. Jones had started walking away, and turned back. I didn't do it, he said. I didn't do any of the things they said. It was a mistake. Something went wrong with the computer. I'm not like that. Someone put that stuff on there. They can bugger off, the lot of them. He was standing with his body stiff and arched towards her and for a moment she was afraid.

There was swimming in the flooded quarry, and another rope-swing went up. At the parish council a motion was tabled to have razor wire added to the fencing. Brian Fletcher objected. They'll find a way past anyhow, he said. Young people think they're invincible. There's only so much you can tell them. Some of them are only going in there because you keep telling them it's dangerous. Sometimes they just have to learn. The only way they'll learn is by drowning, someone pointed out. Brian shrugged. His was a minority voice, and the razor wire was approved. In Cardwell the cricket was ill-tempered and the match was abandoned. Will Jackson's boy was arrested with some friends from school in a stolen car up by Reservoir no. 8. Tom hadn't done any driving, and insisted he hadn't known the car was stolen, but Will still asked Claire to keep him indoors for a week. In the dead grass around the cricket field the eggs of the skippers turned from white to yellow, and the larvae span themselves into cocoons. At Reservoir no. 12 the maintenance team mowed the grass on the embankment dam, letting a hover-mower glide down the steep face on a rope before hauling it up again. There was a childish pleasure in the work to which none of them would admit. Cathy knocked on Mr Wilson's door before letting herself in with the key. Just in case, she explained, when he asked. He looked up at her from the bed. What do you imagine I might be capable of doing that I wouldn't want you catching me at? he asked. She said she thought it was just polite. She asked whether he needed anything before she took Nelson out. He said he'd love a cup of tea but he wouldn't want to deal with the consequences. She asked how he was doing and he said he'd be fine if the nurse didn't keep dragging him out of bed to do exercises. She probably knows best, Cathy told him. They'll have you walking this dog yourself in no time, she said, putting Nelson on the lead and heading out up the lane, past the cricket ground and the school and left at the church towards the packhorse bridge. When she came to Hunter's wood she rested her hand on the smooth topstone as she squeezed through the gapstone stile.

In September the swallows left, lifting from the wires one morning and heading south, quickly picking up speed as they cleared the valley and strung out into a long steady line. A soft rain came up from the river and blew over the village, sifting through the fields and up to the first of the reservoirs. The river was slow and shallow and when the rain passed the sun bent through the water to the shore. Ian Dowsett stood in the damp shade of a beech tree and whirled a hairwing dun to an overhang on the far side. There was a brown trout in there he'd been watching rise. The dun settled lightly on the surface and sailed away untouched. He reeled it back and waited for a shift in the light to try again. Jane Hughes had moved away at the end of August, and the Harvest Festival service was held without her. It was Susanna Wright's turn to put the display together. She collected produce from the allotments, and made wheat sheaves, and used flowers from the market in town to make two very attractive arrangements. Even with the overabundance of tins and packets, which were sent to the new food-bank, people said it was one of the finest displays seen in some years. After the service Clive found her and asked if it wasn't time she had another go with an allotment. She looked surprised, or embarrassed. After my last attempt? I don't think so, Clive, she said. You'd have more time on your hands now, I believe, he told her. I'm not a retired yet, Clive. So I hope you're not suggesting I'm the other thing. The offer's there, he said. There's other folk'll take it. He turned to go. Susanna told him she'd think about it, and as she thanked him for the offer she touched a hand to his arm. He looked at her hand as though she were wiping oil on to his sleeve. William Pearson was once again asked to step down from the parish council. At night there were fires sometimes in the hills, and it wasn't known who was lighting them or what they were burning.

On Mischief Night a large group of older teenagers from Cardwell somehow managed to lift the entire bus shelter and carry it halfway up the side of the moor. The next day there were pictures of it all over Facebook, and it took the Jackson boys half the morning to bring it back down. Questions were asked about where the youngsters had even got their hands on an angle-grinder, and why no one had heard it being used. Irene said it reminded her of the time her late husband had hidden an entire dairy herd, as a young man. The story was familiar, she was told. There were very few apples gathered in Fletcher's orchard. The trees had been productive and well maintained for a time after Sally's brother had left, and had become a source of pride for Brian. The loss of the trees taken out by the fire knocked the pleasure out of him. He blamed himself for being too lazy to have the caravan removed. Les Thompson was out with the quad bike at four in the afternoon to fetch the herd in for the milking. They'd heard the sound of the motor and were heading towards him by the time he found them, blinking against the low afternoon sun. He turned and let them follow, feeling a push of warm air behind him. He was not a sentimental man but he would miss these girls if he had to give up. He was one of the last dairy men for miles. The prices made no sense. The supermarkets were killing them. On the television there were pictures of floods and storms and fires. The Cooper twins asked if they could join the local football team, which ran training sessions and played on the pitches beside the river in town. Austin drove them down there on a Saturday morning, and did some shopping while he waited to pick them up, leaving Su to have a lie-in at home. He went early to collect them, and watched from the car park as they jogged along the pitch with the other boys, warming down. They didn't say anything when they got in the car, and when he asked how it had gone they said it was fine. The following week they told him they didn't want to go again, and he gave them a talk about how important it was to persevere. The third week they were waiting in the car park when he came back from the shopping, the session in full swing behind them, and they said they were definitely not going again. They refused to explain. They said it was nothing. Lee looked at him pointedly and told him he wouldn't understand. The clocks went back and the nights overtook the short days. The sound of gunshots cracked down from the woods in pairs. At home once Andrew was finally asleep Irene ran a bath as deep as she dared, steaming hot and salted, and winced into it. Her body always felt lighter under the water. The salts had given the water a dark-green tinge which almost hid the bruising on her arms. She rested her head against the end of the bath and listened to the settling sounds of the house. The creak of timber, the water in the pipes, the frantic breath of Andrew's sleep.

On Bonfire Night there was a heavy fog, thick with woodsmoke, the fireworks seen briefly like camera flashes overhead. In the beech wood the foxes prepared their dens. The vixens dug down into old earths and reclaimed them, lining them out with grasses and leaves. In the eaves of the church the bats settled plumply into hibernation. By the river the willows shook off their last leaves. At night the freight trains came more often, a single white light leading and the wagons shadowing heavily behind. The widower asked Clive for advice over pruning his fruit trees and Clive was surprised to see the state that things were in. The plums had silver leaf and needed taking out altogether. The fruit bushes badly wanted cutting back. The timbers he'd used for the raised beds were splitting, and there was no sign of any new hens. It had been a good year for courgettes, he told Clive. He was thinking about keeping bees. Late in the month Brian and Sally Fletcher invited some people to the Gladstone for drinks, and let it be known that it was their fifteenth anniversary. There was a quiet surprise that they felt this worth marking, but there was cheering and applause all the same. More drinks were bought. The two of them left early, and as they made their way home the first snow of the winter started falling, turning in the orange light from the streetlamps and dissolving on the road and not looking like settling any time soon. It had snowed the night before their wedding, Sally reminded Brian. When they'd first set the date they'd been called in to speak to the vicar. They knew there'd been talk about the marriage so they steadied themselves for her to intrude. People didn't know Sally, was part of it. The age difference was something else. There was a feeling that Brian was being taken advantage of in some way. His family had said this directly. They had taken steps to isolate themselves against the risk she might pose. This was the phrase they used. They said they didn't want him to think there was anything personal in it but they had generations of the family to consider. He had no idea what they thought they meant and he didn't much care. None of them had ever let him feel as cared for as Sally did. This was what he'd said to Jane Hughes when the three of them met and it had made her clap her hands with delight. He was embarrassed and told her not to let on he'd said any such thing. She had none of the questions they'd feared she would. She didn't want to know where Sally was from or how they met or what made them think this would work. She'd baked them a fine lemon drizzle cake and she asked if they'd chosen the hymns. She'd only been gone from the village a few months now and the two of them missed her tremendously.

Richard Clark's mother went into the hospital in Sheffield and there were some who thought she wouldn't be coming home. Irene took it upon herself to make sure she had visitors while her family wasn't around. There was a rota. Ruth and Susanna were seen together on the allotments, cutting holly and fir. Jones had hacked his hedge down to knee-height again and was burning off the cuttings in a slow bonfire, spilling wet smoke across the village. Clive was in his greenhouse. The snow started thinly from a low grey sky and was ignored for a time. Towards dusk it was settling, and by the time Jones had shouldered his tools it was clean and squeaking underfoot. There were springtails in the rotting sheets of plywood stacked against the wall in Fletcher's orchard, and the juveniles among them were shedding the first of their many shell-like skins. Gordon Jackson was seen talking to a journalist who'd come up from London to do a piece on the tenth anniversary of the girl's disappearance. The piece was going to be about the impact on the village more than the missing girl herself. Our readers know about the girl, she said. They can imagine how the parents must have felt. I doubt it, Gordon said. She smiled. Well, okay, but they think they can. Her name was Emma. She was wearing a long coat and a silk scarf, knee-length boots. Her hair was very tidy but she kept tucking it behind her ear. He wondered if she might keep the scarf on. He showed her around the farm, took her in for a pot of tea, talked about the challenges sheep farming was going through. There was a perfume came off her each time she fussed with her hair. When she seemed done talking he told her he had to get on. But you call me if there's anything else I can do, while you're here. Eye contact. Careful silence. There was a pattern but it was never routine. Later she texted him and they met for a drink at her hotel in town. She had more questions but he thought it was clear where things were heading. Towards the end of the evening she thanked him for his time and said she had an early start. He went with her towards the stairs and then realised he'd got things wrong. She smiled and said goodnight. He turned away. He didn't know quite what to do with himself. This was new.

Richard's mother was still in hospital after Christmas, and when he came to stay for the week he spent most of his time on the ward. She hadn't taken to hospital life. She seemed diminished by the experience. Some mornings when he arrived he thought she wasn't in the bed at all. He sat with her, and she slept often, and he caught up with emails. The staff got to know him, and offered him tea and coffee, and he marvelled at the care with which they spoke to his mother, addressing her as Mrs Clark, speaking with something like love in their voices although he knew it couldn't really be love. In the valley the rain was constant. The river thickened with silt from the hills and plumed across the weirs. There were scratch-marks in the heaped soil around the badger sett, and a trail of leaves and grass where fresh heaps of bedding had been dragged underground. The pantomime was *Dick Whittington*, with the lead role taken by Susanna Wright. The production committee had chosen a rather modern script, and afterwards there were objections. Clive raised it at the parish council, saying that he had concerns about the use of dick. Janice Green excused herself from the room for a short period, and on returning asked Clive how he would prefer that to be minuted. As is, Secretary, he said. As is. There was rain and the wind was biting. On the reservoirs the water was whipped up into whitecaps. It was a decade now the girl had been missing, and although little talked about she was still in people's thoughts. Her name was Rebecca, or Becky, or Bex. She'd been wearing a white hooded top with a navy-blue body-warmer. She would be twenty-three years old by now. She had been seen in the beech wood, climbing a tree. She had been seen at the railway station. She had been seen by the side of the road. She had been looked for, everywhere. She could have arranged to meet somebody, and been driven safely away. She could have fallen down a hole. She could have been hurt by her parents in some terrible mistake. She could have gone away because she'd chosen to, or because she had no choice. People still wanted to know.

11.

At midnight when the year turned there were fires in three sheds at the allotments, and again they were burnt out before the fire brigade arrived. At the school the lights were seen on early, and when Mrs Simpson walked from her car and came into the staffroom she was surprised to see Miss Dale already sitting there, working on a lesson plan and eating toast. They looked at each other, and Miss Dale asked if Mrs Simpson had overslept. I don't know, Mrs Simpson said. I don't, I don't really know. She seemed confused. The nights were hard with frost. On the high frozen ground a ewe stumbled and died, and the buzzards came to feed. A smell of coal-smoke hung over the village through the days. In his studio Geoff Simmons sat on the sofa and watched the last batch dry. He had left them out too long and they were cracking. The kiln should have been on by now. He had made no sales for weeks and could feel another bad patch coming. He wanted to take the whippet out for a walk but there was too much weight in him to stand. There were plates and bowls in the sink to be washed. She'd said she wanted to see him again and he hadn't yet told her he'd had enough. She wanted to come and stay so she could help him get his living space together. Those were her words. She'd asked whether he'd thought about teaching. It would make for a more reliable income, she said. He was finding her less persuasive than he used to. At the Jacksons' the carers were only coming twice a week now. Jackson was finding it difficult to get out of bed again, but that was more down to the tremendous weight he'd put on than anything to do with the stroke. The adaptations they'd fitted to the shower room went unused. Towards the end of each day Maisie filled a bowl with hot water, added soap and a little oil, and carried it through to the front room with flannels and a towel.

A scrap-dealer came for the remains of the caravan in Fletcher's orchard, dragging out the chassis and wheels and leaving the shreds of blackened plastic on the ground. They were soon covered over by the brambles which had grown high around the walls. The fieldfares had started leaving already. Irene took a long walk back from the bus stop, up behind the post office and round to the top of the allotments. It was warm for the month and as she came over the rise she unbuttoned her coat. In the lane she saw Jones.

She expected him to turn away but he nodded and stepped towards her. Said her name. She stopped. He looked at her steadily, waiting. Weather, he said. It's not what it was, she agreed. He was tracing a line in the limey soil of the lane with his boot. Andrew away on the bus? She nodded. She told him she'd dropped him at the bus stop, that he'd be at the centre all day. Gives me a chance to catch up with some housework, she said, smiling. He nodded. He looked at her, steadily. There's help, he said. I'm not sure as I know what you mean, she said. I can manage the house. He shook his head. No. I mean there's help, if he's hurting you. Irene had a feeling like her legs going out from under her but when it passed she was still standing. She could see Clive on his allotment, digging. He seemed to be looking in their direction. But he wouldn't be able to hear. It's not like that, she said. She was whispering. He doesn't understand. He doesn't mean to. Jones lifted his hat and rubbed his head and put his hat back on. Probably none of my business, he said. But you took enough of that from Ted. You're not obliged. Jones was the last person she wanted to have this conversation with. Where would he go? she asked. He's got no one. He wouldn't understand. Who have you got? he asked. She took a deep breath and pulled her coat together, fastening the buttons. He was right; this wasn't any of his business. She couldn't say anything more. She held up a hand to say it was enough, and she walked on. What was he thinking. What right did he have.

———

From his window if he slid far enough down the pillow Jackson could see the flag on the tower of the church and know the strength and direction of the wind, and in March the first westerly of the year had the flag standing out straight. It had him thinking of the flags on the moor when they were looking for that girl. The allotments committee got the insurance money for the burnt-out sheds, and there were rumblings when the replacements went up. Everyone'll be burning out their sheds if that's what you get in return, Clive said. Susanna Wright took on the allotment plot next to Clive's. It had only been vacant a few months and was in good order. She walked round it with him and started talking about a shed, new paths, a lawn area with a table and chairs. There was a greenhouse but some of the panes were missing and she talked about replacing those. He nodded but he was making a face. You look like you have a suggestion, she said. Clive pulled some shreds of plastic feed-bag from the brambles by the greenhouse and began coiling them around his fist. Not really a suggestion, he said; more of an observation. Susanna waited. We get a lot of new folk taking on plots, he said. They like to do a lot of tidying up. They like to make the place look nice. Make themselves comfortable. Takes a lot of work. Gets so they forget to do the planting. Susanna nodded. There were some pieces of broken glass in the soil beneath the brambles, and she crouched down to pick them up. And that was my mistake last time? It's a question of priorities, he said. You get your plants in at the right time, get the mulch down, do the weeding, do the watering, that's work enough. You do all that, you'll enjoy being here. A plot full of healthy plants, crops coming off, flowers out, that's the best little place in the world. You'll not be worrying about benches or lawns or tidy paths. Water features. Wind chimes, Clive? He looked at her. I see you putting a bleeding wind chime up here I'll be straight over to take it down, he said. She laughed, but he wasn't joking. That's noted, she said. I appreciate it. I don't want to meddle, he said. No, please do. Meddle away. He looked at her, and handed over the coil of shredded plastic. Bins are in car park, he said, and as he turned to go she heard him mutter something more about wind chimes. The clocks went forward and the evenings opened out. The bracken shoots sprang slowly from the hills and unwound towards the sky. The penned pheasants on the estate started to lay, and the eggs were taken to the hatchery to be washed and sorted. Su Cooper was made redundant from her job at the BBC, with a much smaller payment than she'd been offered the year before.

Martin Fowler was working at the meat counter in the new super-market when his daughter called and asked him to come to the hospital, and when he got there he was a grandfather. Would someone tell me why I wasn't told, he kept saying, holding the walnut-faced thing in his big hands. You're here now, Dad, Amy said. We didn't want you worrying. Ruth stepped across and took the child back, kissing him on the cheek as she did so. Congratulations, Grandad, she said. His hands shook with nothing to hold. He looked around the room. Amy's fellow was sat on the side of Amy's bed, looking mostly at his feet. This was the first time Martin had met him. He wasn't sure of the name. None of this was the way he'd planned things as ending up by now. Bloody plans what, he said. He hadn't meant to say it out loud. He coughed, and said he was going out for some fresh air. They called the boy Luke and told Martin he was welcome to come over. Ruth made a point of saying so. Amy and Luke would be at Ruth's house to start with, while the fellow found them a place to live. Why hadn't he sorted that already, Martin wanted to know. But he didn't ask. It was a fortnight before he got over to Harefield, bringing a gift of clothes that would no longer fit. It was as though they'd swapped the child for another. The screw-eyed palmful from the hospital was gone. This one had a whole extra heft to him. Ruth took him upstairs for a nap, and Martin was left alone with Amy. There was an opportunity for him to make an apology but it went past. They sat and he offered to make a tea.

What Irene knew was cleaning. Whatever else was happening or became impossible to understand, she kept up the cleaning. The paid work, of course, but she made a point as well of keeping her own house presentable. Years now since anyone had paid a visit, because of Andrew and the damage he had wrought, and the way she feared he would respond to guests. But she worked to keep the place as though someone was going to call at any moment. Because they might. She might not be able to keep them on the doorstep, or make a show of being on her way out. They might come in and see how his computer equipment had taken over the front room and the hallway and the kitchen, the cables everywhere, the strange system of lights above the doors. They might see the split doorframes, the broken cupboard doors. But they wouldn't be able to say she wasn't keeping the place clean. They couldn't say that. There was a lot she didn't understand. But cleaning she knew. There was a small patch of wild redcurrant on the riverbank below the weir, and when the flowers came out at the end of May she clambered down from the path to gather a basketful. She took them home and for the next week or so was able to sit alone at her kitchen table and savour the rough pink tea they made and remember childhood's first taste of this. It was a way to feel summer's approach. The Millennium Millstones were pushed off their plinths again, and this time one of them split. There was a fight in the Gladstone, and talk it had something to do with Facebook. On the television there were pictures of explosions, fires, collapses, collisions. Broad beans started coming off the allotments by the carrier-bagful, and were shucked into saucepans from their softly lined pods. The gentle cushioning of the broadbean pod was one of nature's senseless excesses. The work was a tedious delight. In his studio Geoff Simmons took each newly fired pot from the tray and smashed it against the floor. He worked at a methodical pace. The rhythm was soothing. He had asked her not to come and see him again and she had not responded well. There was no reason now to keep the work her hands had touched. The whippet was wound up outside the door and making a racket. The pieces of pot were thin and white and clean. It seemed she hadn't understood the worth his work had to him. He smashed the pots very evenly across the floor. It was a careful process. He was never not in control. When it was done he took the whippet for a slow walk and left the door hanging open. What had she expected, was his feeling. The reservoir was low and the river slowed between the gravel banks. Tom Jackson was seen walking out with Ashleigh Wright.

In the morning a mist hung over the fields of the kind that would once have been seen as a cue. Jackson banged his stick on the wall and Gordon went through to see what was wanted. He was checking we'd noticed it's cutting weather, he told the others. I told him we'd already seen. Maisie asked whether he'd set Jackson straight and Gordon said of course not. In his room Jackson looked at the mist lifting around the church tower and felt an ache in his shoulders at the thought of a long day's cutting ahead; the smell of the sap as it fell in the field, the long steady evenings barely turning blue as the swallows came out to feed. He caught himself, and turned on the radio. It was too easy to be nostalgic when it wasn't you doing the work. He sent a prayer through the door to the boys. They'd have a full day ahead. He turned away from the window. Mrs Simpson took early retirement from the school with ill health. There was discretion about what this meant, but it wasn't felt appropriate to hold a retirement do. She was sent a huge number of cards and her children read some of them out to her. Cooper wrote an article about her in the *Echo*. The weeks were long and cloudless and the sun scorched a passage through the days. The family who lived at Culshaw Hall put the estate on the market. At the top end of the beech wood a badger held a hedgehog down on its back and peeled it open. The well-dressing boards stood for just short of a week, with the crowds up on previous years and Jim Stephenson's brass band from the high school playing over the weekend. By Thursday the wind had dried out the clay and the petals were starting to fade. The decision was made to pack up. Richard's mother came home from hospital, and Rachel took time off work. There were care-workers who visited twice a day to help her wash and dress, and make sure she took all her medications, and although they always seemed rushed Rachel soon realised she wasn't needed. Irene and Winnie came in most days, and the talk they had about the village went over Rachel's head. She'd been planning to stay on until Richard came the next month, but in the end she left before he arrived. At Reservoir no. 2 there were divers going down to work on the gate valves at the foot of the towers. The maintenance team watched the screens in the van as the divers made their way through the water. In the white light there were bubbles and plumes of silt and then the first gate valve came into sight. The voice of the diver from inside his helmet was clear and close, as though he'd been standing outside the van all along. On the crest of the dam the men held the ropes and looked down at the dark surface of the water.

One evening in midsummer Gordon Jackson took Susanna Wright for a drive in his Land Rover. She'd mentioned wanting to see the wind turbines up close, and he'd taken that as an invitation to offer. This was how it went. He was never forward. He waited for situations to arise. He'd been waiting for Susanna for years. A quick conversation, a joke, an offer of help. Eyes. But he never said anything. That wasn't him. He was careful in a way he didn't need to think about. He never made a suggestion; never put himself in a position where there could be a refusal. It was the refusals that would get talked about, had always been his sense. The ones who went through with it had more of an interest in being discreet. He only had to steer a situation towards a possibility until the possible became likely and the likely a done thing. A good sheepdog never needs to bark, was how he thought of it. He looked at Susanna now. It had taken time but she seemed interested at last. She was looking out of the window and she had that thoughtful face. He wanted to lean over and kiss her neck but he held back. She was a fine-looking woman and he'd been watching. She'd been on her own for a long time and he'd found himself thinking of breakfasts in her kitchen, nights in front of her TV. He stopped the Land Rover where the new road went closest to the turbines and asked if this was okay. Asked if she was ready. Eye contact, careful silence. There was a pattern. They got out and looked up at the turbine. The wind was down and the blades were turning slowly. The sun was low and the shadows fell long across the ground. He looked at her. He could smell the warmth of her skin and he knew already how it would taste. She stood beside him and told him that she was flattered but she wasn't interested in that way. It was a shock but he kept steady. He didn't pretend not to know what she meant. He nodded, and held his hands up in the gesture of someone losing a small stake at the races. He tapped his nose as if to say that this could be their secret, but she only raised an eyebrow and moved away. She took photographs of the turbine with her phone. When they drove back down the hill his discomfort wasn't so much about the rejection as it was the fear that now conversations would be had and all his discretions begin to unravel. He couldn't afford for that to happen. The days were getting shorter already but they were still so full that no one really noticed. The woodpigeons' eggs were hatching out, and the squabs being fed on crop milk. The sheep had started shedding the wool around their necks and the shearing was due. Will Jackson took his son to bring them down to the pens. The boy knew how to work with animals now. He knew about their distances, and how to lead them from behind. He knew how they understood the rattle of a bucket. The two of them worked together without fuss and had them penned by lunchtime. The shearers were ready. The sound of the milk tanker pumping the morning collection came from Thompson's farm on the far side of the valley, a low murmur through the heavy summer air. Richard's mother died while he was out of the country, and it was two days before he could get back. His sisters had come up and cleared the bedroom by then, aired the house, made arrangements with the undertakers. There was little left for him to do. They told him they understood. They gave him directions to the under-takers', and didn't offer to go with him. She'd died in bed, accord-ing to the doctor, possibly in her sleep. He stayed long enough for the funeral, and saw her buried in the same grave as his father. There are going to be some difficult conversations ahead, he managed to tell his sisters. And now is not the time, Sarah replied.

———

In August the young bats moved away from their mothers' milk and the nursery colonies broke up. Their networks of flight were complex and unseen. They flung themselves through the grazing meadows taking dung beetles and moths while the adults began finding mates. On the baking stone path beside Reservoir no. 5 a slowworm was basking, and was taken by a buzzard to feed to her chicks. Richard and Cathy were seen having lunch again at the new organic pub in Harefield. Questions were asked as to why they'd felt it necessary to go that far. Inferences were drawn. The cricket was cancelled for weather, and the Cardwell team didn't come over for drinks as they had done in previous years. Su and Austin Cooper had their twentieth anniversary. Austin had learnt that Su's reluctance to celebrate dates was sincere and deeply felt, but this year she had surprised him with a card and a booking at a restaurant in town. Susanna Wright had agreed to babysit. When they got into the car to drive to the restaurant, both of them a little damp and flushed from the shower, Su braced herself for Austin's reminiscing. It was what he did. She sometimes saw him, in the middle of some family moment – in the woods with the boys, at dinner with her parents, at the village pantomime, even the two of them in bed together – seeming to close his eyes and store the occasion up for future recollection. He enjoyed the recollection more than the moments themselves, it seemed. But he looked at her, and said nothing. They drove through the village, the sunlight low and flashing through the trees, the smell of summer's tail-end coming in through the windows. She thought about their first meeting, when she was an assistant producer at the radio station and had come to do a piece on the well dressing, and found herself talking to this clumsy, hesitant man with a bag full of cameras and Dictaphones and notepads. How he'd told her far more about the well dressing than she needed to know, but had then asked her about radio journalism and the BBC, and the other stories she was working on. He did a lot more listening than most of the men she knew, especially the journalists. When the well dressing was finished they'd gone for a drink, and when the drink was done they'd gone for a walk, and the walk had taken them all the way back to his tiny terraced house in town. The story had been simplified over the years, but it had never been much more complicated than that. She looked at him now. She wondered if either of them could ever be that impulsive again. They parked the car, and walked towards the restaurant, and she slipped her hand into his. She stopped him, and stretched up to kiss his cheek, and whispered thank you in his ear. He looked surprised, and kissed her back, and they walked on.

In the closing days of summer the eggs of the dark-green fritillaries in the beech-wood clearing turned from yellow to purple to grey before they hatched. There were no swallows left. The nests were still there, crumbling and mud-flaked, and would be there when the swallows returned in the spring. White campion thronged the verges along the road towards town, their neat flowers wrinkling as the seed-heads began to swell. In the beech wood the young foxes were ready to move on. It was Martin's turn to put together the Harvest Festival display at the church, and despite regular promises not to let anyone down he disappeared at the last moment. Irene and Winnie stepped in. The river turned over beneath the packhorse bridge and ran steady to the millpond weir. Lynsey Smith came home from Leeds and moved back in with her parents. It was a temporary move but it took a hired van to bring back all her things. She'd been living with a boyfriend after graduation and it hadn't worked out. He was older than her and worked at the university, and he'd decided the relationship had run its course. He'd told her she was too young to think about settling down. He'd told her she needed some time to find out who she was, to go into the world and have adventures and not be stuck in Leeds with a dowdy old lecturer in public health. He'd told her, when the conversation became a little more heated, that she was too needy and she made him feel trapped. It took her a while to share this with anyone. It made her feel ashamed, she told Sophie. It made her feel that she'd let him down in some way. He texted her sometimes, but when she texted him back he never replied. Sophie told her she needed to let it go. Her parents didn't ask questions but they knew something had gone wrong. Her mother was patient but her father wanted to know what had been the point of spending all that money on university. They offered her work in the shop and it was easier just to say yes. The Workers' Educational Association group stuck with Italian for a second year, and the more dedicated element started a conversation club at the Gladstone on a Wednesday evening. Tony ordered a few cases of Peroni in their honour. Cathy knocked on Mr Wilson's door and asked whether Nelson needed a walk, and he asked her in for a cup of tea. She'd not sat down before he passed her his sponsorship form and told her she'd be sponsoring him for the swim he was doing. She asked if there was a choice and he gave her a look. These poor people don't get a choice about not having clean water to drink, he said. She asked for a pen. He told her he was barely up to four or five lengths, tops, so she'd best make it at least a fiver per. She snorted, and then realised he wasn't joking. She'd sat through his talks about this clean-water charity before, so she went ahead and put herself down for five pounds per length. Don't go overdoing it now, she said. You don't want to go damaging that hip. He poured the tea. Don't you worry. The physiotherapy nurses are good but they're no magicians. There was an unexpected smell about him as he handed over the tea, and she asked whether he'd been smoking.

————

At the allotments in the long days of rain the broad leaves of courgettes and beans were blackened with rot, the cow parsley collapsing into the hedgerows, the ground spread with a slime of autumn leaves blown in from the beech wood. Clive was cutting back the dead growth and raking it into a heap. Jones was digging his plot bare. Ruth and Susanna were talking on Susanna's plot, sheltering under a large umbrella and watching the pumpkins ripen against the mulch. It had been a good first season for Susanna. The tomatoes and peppers in the greenhouse hadn't amounted to much, and the carrots had never even germinated; but there had been potatoes and beans and courgettes and peas, and now these bright swelling pumpkins. The plot was nothing to look at but she had plans for the next year and she felt ready for what was to come. Ruth had been a help. At home Ashleigh had been filling in her university application, and Susanna remembered from Rohan how quickly this last year would go. Ashleigh had broken things off with the Jackson boy so she could concentrate on her A levels, and it didn't look to Susanna as though either of them were much concerned. At midnight the clouds thickened and the moon dimmed. The widower hadn't been seen for months, and Jones helped himself to what fruit there was. There had been a concern that something might have happened, and talk of breaking in the door, but when pushed Jones had admitted knowing the man was away, and being in possession of the key. He'd been offered a lecturing job abroad, was Jones's information, and had taken his daughter with him for six months. For the educational experience. Jones knew a lot about the man, it turned out, but he didn't share anything more. On Mischief Night a girl from another village dressed up in a white hooded top with a navy-blue body-warmer, and black jeans, and canvas shoes, and zombie make-up. She was driven back to her parents, and words were had. There was building work at Culshaw Hall, and talk the new owners were turning it into a hotel and lodge. The dams had their ten-year inspection and three of them were found to be failing, the steel rods in the concrete exposed and the concrete crumbling away. The *Valley Echo* carried a report of the sponsored swim, in which it was noted that Mr Wilson had shown unexpected stamina by swimming twenty-one lengths. Heartfelt congratulations were offered.

In November the rain came day after day and at first people joked about it but by the third week it became uncanny. The moors were saturated and the water rushed off them and was everywhere. The smell of damp earth began to rise from between floorboards and everything was tinged with a dank green light. Les Thompson led his herd across the mud-thick yard from the shed. The sodden air was soon steaming with the press of bodies. From the river-bank up by the fishing pools a heron hoisted into the air, hauling up its heavy wings and letting its feet trail out as it flew along the river. Rohan Wright had been away travelling but he was back again, living at his mother's. She wanted to know what his plans were and he wouldn't be drawn. He spent a lot of time on a laptop, working on his music. Sometimes he saw Lynsey, serving at her parents' farm-supplies place or behind the bar in the Gladstone, and they talked about the others. Sophie was doing another internship in London, arranged through a friend of her father's, and had been trying to get Lynsey to go down and visit. She's moving with a different type of crowd now, Lynsey said. The money they spend on a night out, I couldn't be keeping up with that. In an attempt to meet the county council's target for budget cutting, the parish council agreed to the street lighting being turned off between midnight and five, not without much discussion, during which Miriam Pearson was advised that the expression *black hole of Calcutta* was no longer acceptable. There was an admission charge at the bonfire party for the first time, and nobody seemed to much mind. The predictions of cheapskates lining up along the boundary wall to watch the fireworks were unfounded, and if anything the numbers were up on previous years. Cathy knocked on Mr Wilson's door and asked whether she wouldn't be able to take Nelson for a walk again some time soon. Mr Wilson said he didn't know about that. He stood in the doorway and he didn't invite her in, and Nelson ran circles in the hall. She told him she'd already said she was sorry but she would never have offered that kind of money. He said it was the principle. He said the money was sorely needed and he was sure she could spare it in the long run. She said he had no idea what kind of money she could or couldn't spare and he had no business making assumptions. She said she hadn't thought she was writing a blank cheque. He said it wasn't the money it was the principle and that when he'd been growing up people knew how to keep to their word. She said, David, I can't bear for us to fall out over this. He closed the door, and she went back to her house and sat in the kitchen, and a few minutes later she heard his door slam and saw him struggle up the lane with Nelson. She wrote a cheque for £105, made it payable to a different charity altogether, and put it in an envelope through his door. She knew she was being petty, but she couldn't think she was being more petty than he was.

On a warm day in early December the small tortoiseshells in Sally Fletcher's shed came out of hibernation and were seen feeding on the privet hedge, their wings dulled and ragged and soaking up the watery sun. At the river the keeper thinned out the alder along the banks by the meadow below the school. In his studio Geoff Simmons mixed a glaze and stirred in grass seeds and leaf fragments he had gathered. He stood at the worktable and dipped the newly fired pots in and out of the glaze. There was a rhythm to it that soothed. He held the pots lightly and then brushed the glaze across the dry spots his finger and thumb had left. If there was a way of leaving no marks at all he would take it. James Broad was working in Manchester, but was seen in the village from time to time. He came for the climbing, bringing university friends with bags of ropes and harnesses and plenty of money to spend in the Gladstone, and he always seemed to know when Lynsey would be behind the bar. He was developing a reputation for his climbing. He was known for studying a route with great patience, but then climbing it at such speed that he seemed to be carried up the face by momentum alone. He climbs like a man in furious pursuit, was the way one magazine put it. The less approving said he didn't have the strength to hold one position for any time. His pace of attack meant he took risks which won as much disapproval as admiration, but he hadn't fallen yet. He brought his new girlfriend home just before Christmas and introduced her to his mother, which she hadn't been expecting. She might not be as pretty as that other one, his mother told Cathy, later. But I can at least pronounce her name. She seems nice enough. And she's black of course, but I haven't a problem with that. James took her up to the moor and told her what had happened with the missing girl. She listened, and told him it wasn't his fault. He nodded, and told her people always said that. In the evening they met Rohan at the Gladstone. Lynsey was serving at the bar. On Christmas Eve he drove his girlfriend back to Northampton. His mother told Cathy she didn't really mind. There was carol singing in the church and the sound of it drifted towards the square.

———

Richard's mother had left her papers in no kind of order at all. It took Richard months to even sort through the basics of reading the will, closing her bank accounts, and unsubscribing from the numerous magazines and charity newsletters that kept coming through the door. He was finding himself with longer downtimes between contracts now, and hadn't yet told his sisters that he was no longer renting the flat in Balham that had been his base when he was in the country. He knew that they wanted to sell the house and share the money – Rachel had said they badly needed the money, which he found hard to believe – but he'd told them they should get the house in better shape before they thought about putting it on the market. He talked this over with Cathy one afternoon, and was disappointed to find that he couldn't read her reaction in the slightest. There was a moment when she could have said she'd like it if he was in the village more often or even for good, but she was distracted by something on her phone and said nothing. He realised later that this had also been a moment when he could have asked her if that was a thing she'd like, but he was on the descent into Geneva by then, fastening his seatbelt and returning his seat to the upright position. On New Year's Eve Cathy knocked on Mr Wilson's door and asked whether Nelson wanted a walk. They had tea and cake and then she took Nelson quickly up the lane to the church, down past the orchard to the packhorse bridge and along the river.

When she came to Hunter's wood she stooped to unleash him, resting her hand on the wall where the topstone was worn to a watery shine.

12.

At midnight when the year turned there were fireworks going up from the towns beyond the valley but no one in the village even lifted their heads to look. The fires from the two previous New Years had made people nervous. The village hall was empty and people were standing out by their barns and buildings, half a dozen police officers patrolling and the fire brigade on notice. By half past the hour the tension had eased. A few people set off their own fireworks and a belated 'Auld Lang Syne' was sung. From the old quarry there was an explosion and the empty storage buildings went up. The fire brigade were there quickly but couldn't go near for fear of what materials might be on site. The buildings burnt through, and in the morning a thin trail of smoke was still rising. There was talk about whether the fires might have been set by the missing girl's father, but apparently he had an alibi. The police had checked. You wouldn't want to be the chap who goes and asks the man a thing like that, Martin pointed out. Irene was having work done on the house, now that Andrew was finally settled in his new accommodation. It was a lot of work, and she stayed with Winnie for the duration. There were doorframes to replace, and wiring to repair. Mostly it was a lot of painting wanted doing. Whole place wants freshening, she told Winnie. And she was having the kitchen brought up to spec for the tourist board. She had a plan to bring guests in for bed and breakfast. Because what else am I going to do in that big house all by myself? she asked Winnie. I'll be bored off my feet. Bit of company will do me good.

Cathy knocked on Mr Wilson's door and asked whether Nelson needed a walk, and he was halfway out of the house before she'd even finished speaking. I think we'll both come this morning, he said, Nelson already on the lead and bounding out ahead of him. As smartly dressed as ever, with something extra about him this time; the creases on his trousers sharper, perhaps, or his hair trimmed shorter. They turned left at the church and walked down past the orchard and the lower meadows to the packhorse bridge, and once they'd crossed the river Cathy asked whether he didn't want to stop for a breather. He started to claim there was no need but thought better of it, standing beside the bench and gesturing for her to take the seat first. They sat and listened to the water turning over beneath the packhorse bridge and the crows rising and falling from the sycamore trees. Nelson snuffled around in the long grass on the riverbank. The sun was high and the day was almost warm in the shelter of the overhanging rocks. Cathy tilted her face towards the sky to enjoy it. This was the first day of the year she'd been able to savour being out of doors. She noticed how still Mr Wilson was beside her. He felt poised. They were sitting closer together than she'd realised, and now he lifted a hand from his lap and laid it on her knee. Somewhere a little higher than her knee. It rested there, loosely, and they both looked at it. For a moment they seemed as surprised as each other. She lifted his hand, which was softer and warmer to the touch than she might have imagined, and placed it gently back on his lap. Neither of them spoke for a moment. My apologies, he said. But you won't fault a man for wondering, will you? She smiled, and shook her head. It's just that one does get lonely, on occasion, he said, looking away up the river. I know, David, she said, softly; we all do. The river turned over beneath the packhorse bridge. Nelson hunkered in the long grass, and Cathy reached into her coat pocket for the plastic bags.

Lynsey Smith moved in with her new boyfriend, who lived in one of the new houses on the far side of town. He was older than her and worked as a surveyor for the quarrying company. He owned the house and had two cars, and although it had started as something she expected to be brief she realised she'd grown fond of the certainties he carried with him. He had a tidy home and he could cook and he bought her thoughtful gifts. He encouraged her to apply for the nursing school she'd been talking about since she'd graduated. His name was Guy and she'd met him while she was working at the Gladstone. She told Rohan about it one evening, when he'd come into the bar on his own. He was sort of charming, she said, but he wasn't trying to be charming, if you know what I mean? Rohan nodded. He had no idea why she was telling him this. I knew he was interested, but it was like he was interested in me and not what he could get from me, sort of thing? He sounds nice, Rohan said. I'm pleased for you. I know it looks sudden but it just feels right. Does it look sudden to you? I think you should trust your instinct, Lynsey. Exactly, it just feels like the right thing, all of a sudden. You get to our age and sometimes you just know these things. And it'll be good to move out as well, it's been a nightmare living at home again. How about you, how's things? How's your mum? Your mum, Rohan said, automatically. The Spring Dance was held to raise money for repairs to the churchyard wall, and went off without more than the usual incident. New steps were cut into the embankment leading down to the new footbridge by the tea rooms, and within weeks the earth of each step had once again been trodden deeper than the boards set in place to hold it back. A pair of goldcrests built a nest in the spruce at the end of Mr Wilson's garden, too high for him to see the work of knitting grasses and moss together.

Richard's mother had kept hold of most of her husband's possessions after he'd died, and he was having to sort through all those as well as hers. Cathy had come across to help, and they'd emptied boxes full of paperwork from the wardrobe over the bed. There might be some of this you can just chuck without really looking at it, she said. There were men on the roof, repointing the chimney and re-laying the slates. They could be heard shuffling around precariously. Every now and then a broken slate was flung over the side, falling past the window and smashing into the skip by the front door. There were glimpses of his father all over the paperwork: in his handwriting, in the names of the farm suppliers he'd dealt with, even in the slight smell of engine oil and tobacco. And although it had been almost twenty years now Richard still found himself thinking back to the funeral. He'd only come over for the day, and had felt detached from the whole thing. He'd seen Cathy and Patrick as he was leaving, and that would have been the first time he'd seen them in years, and he hadn't been able to tell if they were awkward about that or just awkward about not knowing how to express sympathy. It was known that he hadn't much liked his father. He'd made it easier by asking Patrick about his work, asking them both about their sons. Cathy had held him, stiffly, and Patrick had shaken his hand. That was the last time he'd seen Patrick. A few years later, his mother had called him to say that Patrick had just peeled over in the street, and been quite put out when he told her she probably meant keeled. You weren't even there, she'd told him. How would you know. Another slate was flung from the roof and smashed into the skip, and Cathy began picking through all the papers spread across the bed. There might be some letters here I suppose, she said. There might be something your sisters will want to see. Before he knew what he was doing, his hand was resting lightly on her back, his fingers trailing down along the thin wool of her cardigan, bumping over the bones of her spine. She didn't stiffen or move away, as he would have expected had he thought about it first. Rather she seemed to soften to his touch, to ease her back slightly towards him. She was old enough for grandchildren now. It should have been too late for something like this. On the roof the men pulled out more broken slates and flung them over the side.

In early May a group of students doing a sponsored walk were lost in a thick fog while coming down from the Stone Sisters. Somehow they ended up around the back of the cement works, and when they were shown where they'd got to on the map they refused to believe it. There were fires started in the Hunters' haybarns and in the bins behind the tea rooms, but there was nothing to link them with the New Year's Eve fires. There was still no evidence that those had been started by the same person. By the beech wood the wild pheasant chicks were hatching. They came out in a crouch and scattered from the nest, scratching around for food and ignoring their mothers' calls. The twins went on a school trip to the visitor centre, and when they came back Lee wanted to know about Rebecca Shaw. He said it quite casually, with his fist in the biscuit tin, and Su had to keep her voice light as she explained. He nodded while she talked, and she guessed he'd heard most of this at school. So what happened to her? he asked. Nobody knows. She was never found. She's not dead then, Lee said, through a mouthful of biscuit. She might be, Su said. It seems likely. She would have turned up by now. Nobody stays hidden for that long. I could, Lee announced cheerfully. Me and Sam worked it out. There's all those tunnels under the hill, mines and stuff. You could hide in there, and come out at night for food. You could come out in a different place every time, and no one would know. You could live down there for years if you wanted. You know, if there was a war or something, or if you were being hunted. That's what she might be doing. Waiting for the right moment to come out and surprise everyone. How old do you think she'd be now, Mum? Su felt cold. She sat down at the table and put a hand to Lee's cheek so he would look at her and concentrate. She told him very calmly that he must never go into any of the mines or caves. Ever. She asked him to promise. Her expression frightened him. He promised they'd never go in again. There was rain and the river was high and the hawthorn by the lower meadows came out foaming white. The cow parsley was thick along the footpaths and the shade deepened under the trees. The river rushed under the packhorse bridge. Richard and Cathy were both surprised by the lack of urgency with which they took each other to bed. If they'd thought about it at all – which Cathy admitted she had a little, and Richard said only that it had in fact crossed his mind – they'd imagined stumbling up stairs, tangling clothes, crashing into furniture. But there was none of that. There was a question carefully posed, and an answer thoughtfully given, and then there were clothes folded over the back of the dressing chair, the bedcovers lifted back and pulled over them both. More slow awkwardness than ever there'd been as half-blind teenagers rushing through things up on the moor. It was no less lovely for all that. It was as though, Richard thought, they'd waited for so long that there was now no need to hurry. He had no idea if this was also what Cathy thought. When she came it was with a low murmuring chatter whose repeated words he couldn't quite make out, her face arched towards the dusty light from the window. Afterwards when he tried to speak she put a finger on her lips and smiled and looked back to the window. There were swallows or house martins restless in the air outside. He realised he should know which they were by now. He knew that she would know. He didn't know if he should ask.

––––––––––

In June it was Austin Cooper's sixty-fifth birthday, and for a treat Su agreed to walk the first three days of the Greystone Way with him, while the boys stayed with a schoolfriend in town. He'd been trying to talk her into it for years, but now she'd agreed he seemed more nervous than she did. In the morning he checked through their bags for a third time, and asked if she was sure she felt up to it. She laughed and said she should be asking him that question. She told him he wasn't getting any younger, and pushed him out the door. At the visitor centre they stopped for a photograph, and then set off up the long low hill. They held hands for a while, but Austin soon found he needed to use both the walking poles he'd brought with him. It took them an hour to reach the top of the first climb, and they stopped to take more pictures. The light was clear and they could see the village and the river and the woods along the main road. Ahead of them a line of flagstones stretched right across the moor, the reservoirs off to one side, the motorway along the horizon, a line of wind turbines turning over on a distant ridge. After you, old man, Su said, smiling and prodding him in the back, and for a moment Cooper wanted to pick her up and carry her into a heathery hollow. But they had a good distance to make before dusk, and there wasn't the time for that manner of thing. He wasn't sure his back would hold. For the first time in a decade there was grazing at the Stone Sisters, the new grass heavy and green and no sign now that this had ever been home to all those young people with their banners and fires and dancing.

Lynsey Smith got engaged, which surprised even her. Things were going well but she hadn't been thinking that far ahead. But she was so comfortable around him, and when he proposed she could see he had no expectation of her saying no, which was enough to make her want to say yes. There was a lot of talk about the wedding, which was coming up soon. The thing was happening very quickly, was the feeling. Very little was known of Guy, but Lynsey was thought of as a level-headed woman who wouldn't do anything daft. Do you have fun together? Sophie asked, when Lynsey worried that it was happening too soon. He's very kind, Lynsey said. He's thoughtful. The well-dressing boards were taken down and scraped clean, the clay and dressing materials dumped in a corner of the meadow. The boards were washed and dried, and two of Jackson's boys hauled them up to the barn at the Hunter place and put them away for the year. Olivia Hunter finished her A levels, with no party to mark the fact. She already knew she was going to fail, and had kept her parents off her back by talking about a year's volunteering overseas. In truth she had no intention of going abroad, but hadn't yet found a better plan. She was spending a lot of time in her bedroom, making YouTube videos. On Thompson's land the bales were finished and dotted the fields in their pale green rounds.

——————

The reservoirs were dry and the spillways rose into the air like chimneys, reaching for a volume of water it was difficult to imagine ever returning. The sun was hot and unrelenting and cracked open the soil. In the beech wood a boar badger stood and watched as a sow turned circles in front of him. They both made low feeding sounds. The boar covered the sow for some minutes, biting the nape of her neck. There was a flurry of scrape-marks in the bare soil. The fledgling woodpigeons were falling from the nests. There were first attempts at flight. In the old quarry by the main road the toadflax was in full flower, low to the ground and buttery yellow in the pale evening sun. Rohan Wright left home for the second time. He'd been looking for work for months, apparently, but it was only once Susanna sat down with him and went through some applications that a job materialised. He asked if she was trying to get rid of him, and she said he knew she loved him to bits but she didn't want him to be the sort of weirdo who still lived with his mother. When Susanna told Cathy about this they both laughed and then Susanna changed the subject abruptly to ask about Richard. Cathy dipped her head to hide a smile and said it was fine. It was good. It was going well. Susanna waited for more. What? Cathy asked. That's it. It's going well. He's a good man. But it's not a big deal. Although. Susanna waited. Although what? she asked. I think he's making more of it than he needs to, Cathy said. I mean, it's all good fun, he's lovely, but I feel like he's on the verge of doing something daft, like proposing or something. Would that be so bad? asked Susanna. Cathy rolled her eyes. I've done being married, she said. I don't want to get into that again. I like not being answerable to anyone, you know? Like, this is my house, these are my boys, this is my time. I feel like he might have something different in mind. Rohan went for the interview, and got the job, and moved in with some friends in Manchester. Swiftly along the river and down the lane the adult bats flew in deft quietness and were gone by the time they were seen.

In August Lynsey Smith was married at the registry office in town. The reception was held at the Culshaw Hall Hotel. James and Rohan and Sophie were all there, and after the photographs they stood on the lawn trying to work out when they'd last been together. Must have been that summer after graduation, Rohan decided. I never graduated, Sophie pointed out. True fact, he said. And look at you now, new-media hotshot. Natural talent; there's no degree certificate for natural talent. Is that what they call it now? They saw Liam heading indoors with a toddler in one arm and an older child holding his hand. He nodded in their direction but didn't come over to say hello. They had to wait for the speeches before they could have any food, and at one point Sophie put her hand on James's glass to suggest he slowed down. The look he gave her was unfamiliar and sharp. He drank on, quickly, and later in the evening Sophie had to ask Will Jackson to take him back to Rohan's house, where he was staying. In Cardwell the cricket match was played right through for the first time in three years, and tradition restored with a win for the home team. Jackson's boys went out and took the lambs away from their mothers and put them in a field out of sight and for three days and nights the racket they made carried over the village. By the middle of the month the evenings were earlier, and chill. The dew that rose in the morning brought with it a smell of must. Richard's mother's house still hadn't been put on the market, and Richard was trying to explain to his sisters that if they wanted a good price they should wait until things picked up. They'd come for a long weekend with their husbands, the children old enough now to be left with friends, and after an evening of eating and drinking and catching up the subject of the house finally arose. Rachel gave out the same heartfelt sigh Richard remembered her developing as a twelve-year-old and her husband, Tim, told the room that everyone was tired of tiptoeing around all this bullshit. Richard asked could he be a little more frank and for a moment Tim didn't hear the sarcasm. Sarah said there was no need for this kind of thing, and Tim said rather sharply that in actual fact there was. Where will I live? Richard asked them. Where will I go? This has always been my home. No one's turfing you out, Tim said. But it's time to talk about money. You were never here anyway, Sarah murmured. They all knew what the house was worth, inflated beyond sense by wealthy commuters and the second-homes market; and he assumed they knew that as a freelancer he'd never get a mortgage of that size. Why are you doing this to me? he said. He left the house and walked up through the square towards the beech wood. He wanted to talk to Cathy but he wanted to calm down first. If they could just leave it a bit longer. A few months, a year. If he and Cathy kept going the way they were they would move in together. It seemed inevitable. After all these years. But it was too soon to mention it now. He didn't want her thinking it was only because of the house. He wanted her to know how much she meant to him. He thought she was ready to hear that. She'd as good as said something along those lines. If his sisters could just back off about the house. He'd said nothing about Cathy, of course. They wouldn't take him seriously if he told them about that.

Lynsey stopped working at the Gladstone, partly because Guy had said he wasn't comfortable with her being up on show behind the bar all hours like that. She'd started a place at nursing college, in Derby. Guy had bought her a newer car so she could drive in each day without worrying about breaking down. It was a lot of driving but she enjoyed having the time to herself. The quarries and the lanes were thick with rosebay willowherb, the purple stemmy flowers curling over and the seed-flights wisping away. The first guests came to stay at Irene's and she told Winnie the weekend had gone well. They weren't all that talkative, she said. I don't think they wanted to chat at all, which was a shame. They spent a lot of time in their room. But they were very complimentary when they left. Winnie asked if there were more bookings and Irene said that since Andrew had made the website for her the diary had been filling up quickly. He must have done a good job, she said. Andrew was in the supported-accommodation place in town, and apparently very content with it. He was doing a course at the college. Irene went to see him most weeks, and he sent her emails. He'd shown her how to do emails. Late in the month Ashleigh Wright left for university, and Susanna was alone in a three-bed house. It was sudden and there was nothing to be done. She made enquiries about exchanging for a smaller place, and even though nothing was available she still had to pay the bedroom tax. She spent a lot of time at the allotment, harvesting the beans and first squashes and preparing the ground for the following year. In the cold evenings Ruth sometimes walked down from the allotment with her for dinner, and when she'd had too much wine to drive she stayed over. In the conifer plantation above the Hunter place the young goldcrests were already feeding up for the winter, fattening.

———

In October the old Tucker place went up for sale, and was on the market for no more than a month. A removal van appeared and the house was cleared. Jones helped himself to what fruit there was. The sound of two-stroke engines came from the Hunters' land, and the whining of chainsaws cutting into timber, and the branchy crash of another tree felled. From the beech wood the young foxes lit out for new territory and were killed on the roads in great number. At the river the keeper took out the crayfish traps. They seethed with claws and bodies crawling over each other. There was a rattle as he tipped them into a damp sack. The eating was a perk although his girls wouldn't touch them. It was true there was a job in stripping out the flesh but the work was worthwhile, he thought. The swallows which had left a few days earlier were most of the way to South Africa by now, and would spend the winter on feeding grounds down there before finding their way back in the spring. Richard had been seen spending nights at Cathy's house, but nobody had felt need to comment. The two of them were entitled, was the feeling. In the mornings Richard was out of bed first, moving quietly through the house, making coffee. Getting into bed again, drawn back for more. They wanted each other in a way he had forgotten was possible or perhaps had never really known. He felt restless unless he was fitting his body to hers. When they'd done this as teenagers, high on the far side of the hill overlooking Reservoir no. 12 and the motorway, the two of them had felt weightless, lifting each other into the air and whispering. Thirty years on they both had more substance but there was no less delight. Her body weighed down on his and he gave himself up completely and only now did he realise how often he'd held something back before. With the others, even when it had been serious, he'd always looked ahead to what would come after. He'd always assumed there would be a moving on. He'd convinced himself it wasn't the case but it was clear now he'd been waiting for Cathy. Waiting for this. The two of them grown old and returning to each other, surprised by the things they could still do. The things they could do better than they'd ever been able to do back then. When she pulled him back against the bedroom windowsill and took him inside her, their fingers laced together and the sash window rattling in its frame, he could see in her eyes she was thinking these things as well. There was no need to say them out loud. This was the way he had thought they would be. Coming to their senses. While she slept he cooked dinner and they ate it and went back to bed. There would be questions about arrangements in the months ahead but for now those questions could wait. As they were falling asleep again that night she told him they should be careful. She whispered this into his ear. He thought he knew what she meant.

———

On top of the moor a wreath of poppies was laid beside the remains of the Lancaster bomber. There were few in the village now who could remember the years of the air-raids; the bombers nightly ploughing the sky and the glow of burning cities from beyond the horizon, and the smell. There was a mishap with the fireworks at the bonfire party, a couple of rockets tilting over in the soft ground after the fuses had been lit and shooting over the heads of the crowd. But no one was hurt, and it was agreed to go on with the display. In his studio Geoff Simmons loaded the glazed pots into the kiln for a second firing. It was raining and there was water running down one of the walls. He had buckets under most of the drips but the rugs were wet. There was a smell of mouldering paper and the pots were taking longer to dry. The whippet was gone and he didn't know what to do with the hours the kiln was firing. He opened the door and let the air blow in and a curtain of rain swayed across the threshold. Nobody came up the lane. The river turned over beneath the packhorse bridge and moved on towards the weir. Nobody much mentioned the missing girl, but she was still thought about often. What could have happened. She could have been hurt by her parents in some terrible mistake, some push or stumble that wasn't meant that way at all, and in a fury of panic they could have carried her somewhere they'd know she was at peace before running back down to the village for help. She could have been hurt by her parents in some deliberate way, pushed or tripped or struck repeatedly from behind, and fallen without getting up again, and they could have taken her up high on the hill and laid her to rest somewhere they knew she would never be found.

Richard and Cathy were in bed together when she told him she didn't think they should carry on doing this. His first thought was whether she couldn't have waited until they were dressed. He'd had enough of these conversations to recognise the pattern but it had never happened in bed. Lately it hadn't even been while he was in the same country; and geography was usually the point being made. Cathy's point was something more elusive. They were trying to re-create something from the past, she told him. It couldn't work like that. They had both changed so much, and yet they still thought of each other as being eighteen years old, and they would come to resent each other for changing. She knew this, it seemed. She could see it would cause a problem. But is it a problem now, he asked. No, but it will be, I can see it, she said. I want to protect us both from that happening. I want to protect our friendship, she told him. He didn't know how to disagree. When he dressed he was suddenly self-conscious and he carried his clothes in a bundle to the bathroom. He ran the taps. Downstairs he told her he wouldn't stay for coffee. He told her again that of course he understood. He said hello to Mr Wilson, who was standing in his open doorway with Nelson, and walked to the top of the lane. There were carol singers going from door to door for the local hospice, carrying candle-lanterns on poles, their breath clouding in the yellowy light and their voices pressing through the low air. For a moment Richard was caught up amongst them, and obliged to join in. *O little town of Bethlehem. How still we see thee lie.*

In the parlour at Thompson's farm, the last cows of the day came in to be milked. The men were tiring. What little conversation there'd been had faltered, and for the last ten minutes there was only the rhythmic slurp and click of the machinery, the occasional snort or stamp of the cows. At the reservoir a heron speared suddenly towards the water and stopped just before its beak broke the surface, carefully straightening and holding itself still once more. In the beech wood the foxes were loud. Mating season was approaching and claims were being made. There were barks and screams and at night the sounds carried the old dread. There was scent-marking and fighting until pairs were established. There were springtails in the soil of the cricket ground, a million or more, moulting and feeding and moving up to the light, and amongst them a female springtail laid the last eggs of her life. The goldcrests fed busily deep in the branches of the churchyard yew. Richard and Cathy were seen up on the moor with Mr Wilson's dog, walking much further than Nelson was used to. He didn't seem to mind. Richard was explaining to Cathy why it wasn't such a bad idea for them to try and make a go of a relationship. They were financially independent; they'd been together before and there was something then that had worked and something they still had now; they were both from the village, and belonged here, and they had an understanding of the place they could share. He'd actually numbered these points, and was counting them off on his fingers. He seemed to have been talking for a while. She stopped him. Richard, she said. This isn't like putting in a tender for a contract. You do know that, don't you? He started to laugh and then realised she wasn't joking and he didn't know where to look. He was still bending back his little finger to indicate the fifth point. It was starting to hurt but he couldn't let go.

13.

At midnight there were fireworks in the next valley and tension in the village and no fires were set. It wasn't until the next day that the old water-board buildings by Reservoir no. 7 were found smoking and charred. On the television there were pictures of a public search for another missing teenage girl, the volunteers strung out in a line across a hillside, their heads bowed. The pantomime was *Cinderella*. It was known that rehearsals had been late and under-attended, and that Susanna had needed to bring new people in at the last minute, and there was as much anxiety in the audience as there was amongst the cast. When Olivia Hunter stepped forward to begin the narration the main lights were left on and there was still furniture being shifted around. She had to be prompted twice in the first few minutes, but was so sprightly with the pleasure of being on stage that no one seemed to mind. Be careful, she announced, bursting with anticipation, here comes the Wicked Stepmother now! There was a long pause and then Les Thompson shuffled on to the stage, stubbled and made-up and minus his false teeth, unable even to remember his first line. The audience took a long time to settle enough for the prompt to be heard. No one had known he would be in the role, and his enjoyment of playing it, wandering in and out of scenes with no concession to the script, made everyone's night. Ruth Fowler and Susanna, who had stepped late into the roles of the Ugly Sisters and worked a long time on their bawdy repartee, were entirely upstaged, and at the end of the show Les was surrounded by people wanting their picture taken with him. At the party afterwards Gordon Jackson got talking to Olivia, and congratulated her for keeping calm amongst all the chaos. He told her it took a lot of maturity to hold it together like that. He reached out without thinking and tucked a loose strand of hair behind her ear.

At the allotments there was little to harvest besides some hardened winter greens: thick-veined spinach leaves, small handfuls of mustard, a yellowing mulch of kale. The frosts had been hard. In the beech wood the foxes were quiet. The earths had been prepared and were warm and well lined, and the vixens stayed down there in the dark. The old Tucker house was refurbished as a holiday cottage, rewired and replastered, the woodwork painted a pale grey-green. The front garden was landscaped for low maintenance.

There were planters with gravel and mixed grasses, and a picnic bench with a patio heater. In the beech wood the trees were traced with snow, the sunlight filtering through and shaking it loose. The river wedged branches beneath the packhorse bridge and poured fiercely over the weir. The missing girl's father was questioned about the fires again, and arrested. At the heronry the nests were rebuilt. On Shrove Tuesday Mr Wilson asked Cathy to come round for pancakes. She had to help him lift the cast-iron frying pan on to the hob, but after that he insisted she sit at the table and be served. The first pancake caught and was thrown on the floor for Nelson. The second one was fine, but Nelson made such a fuss that Mr Wilson put that one on the floor as well. You must think me a soft touch, he said, and she didn't deny it. She quartered the lemons on the chopping board while Mr Wilson made a stack of pancakes and kept them warm in the oven, and when he was done they sat and ate them together. Jean made a very good pancake, he said. Frilly at the edges. You know the way? Cathy nodded, and Nelson came and rested his head in her lap, and she said she'd never known how to get them like that. When they'd eaten they walked up together towards the village with Nelson. For a change they stayed on the main street and headed towards the allotments and the beech wood. At the square Mr Wilson said he'd stop for a drink at the Gladstone and catch them on their way back, and Cathy asked if his hip was feeling okay. He told her it wasn't too bad but he felt entitled not to go traipsing up the moors at this point in his life. As she laughed and turned to go he stooped slightly towards her and made a gesture which must once have been called doffing one's cap. She waved in reply, and let Nelson pull on the lead towards the path through the beech wood and the visitor centre and the high breathless hills.

Cooper was seen outside the old butcher's shop, half-kneeling, with his fist clenched against his chest. By the time Su got to the hospital he was already sitting up in bed. Just a scare, he said, hoarsely, and she told him very quietly that she'd give him an actual bloody scare if he ever did something like that again. The nettles grew up around the dead oak in Thompson's yard, the timber stained white in the sun. A flock of fieldfares lifted from the elder trees on the bank behind the school, climbing out of the valley and heading north-east towards the reservoirs, the hills, the North Sea, Norway. Sally Fletcher persuaded Brian to let her keep hens in the old orchard, and asked Will Jackson to build her a coop. Will told her the hens would scratch up everywhere so to make sure the ground was safe, and she paid the Cooper twins to pick up what was left of the caravan. They filled six sacks with lumps of plastic and the cottony shreds of old cigarette butts. Martin saw Les Thompson at the new supermarket in town, standing at the checkouts with a basket of shopping. He hadn't seen him there before. When Les noticed the price on a litre of milk he asked the young woman to tell him out loud. He looked at her for a long moment and then put his wallet back in his pocket and walked away, leaving his shopping half-packed and the young woman confused. A pale light moved slowly across the moor, catching in the flooded cloughs and ditches and sharpening for a moment before the clouds slid closed overhead.

In April the first swallows were seen, sweeping low over the pastures in the early evening and taking the insects which rose with the dew. And still the sound of a helicopter clattering by was never just the sound of a helicopter but everything that sound had one night meant. Gordon took on some timber work up at the Hunter place, and was seen by his van talking to Olivia on his breaks. Survey stakes went up along the edge of the woodland by the Stone Sisters, and Cooper found a new planning application from a quarry firm. Richard's mother's house went on the market and was sold within a month, and Richard took a weekend to clear it out before dropping the keys at the solicitor's. He thought about calling in to see Cathy on his way to town, but in the end he drove straight past the end of her lane and down towards the quarry and the woods and the bend in the river by the main road. The new bracken shoots were curled tight, waiting for the lengthening days. Mr Wilson died, after a short illness, and Jane Hughes was invited back to conduct the funeral. Cathy took Nelson in to live with her.

———

Su Cooper carried the new issues of the *Valley Echo* around the village in a large shoulder-bag. The bag was heavy, and it took her the whole afternoon to finish the job. Austin had tried to insist he could manage, but he'd already worn himself out getting the issue printed off. She was the one who'd listened properly to the advice he was given after his heart attack, and she was the one making sure he stuck to it. Gentle exercise, a good diet, sleep. Not lugging a bag up and down steep cobbled streets. She was strict with him, as the doctor had said she might need to be. It came easily. She wasn't going to let him bugger himself up again. There was rain and the river was high. The reservoirs filled. Towards the end of each day Maisie Jackson filled a bowl with hot water, added soap and a little oil, and carried it through to the front room with flannels and a towel. When Jackson saw her he made a face that carried as much love as it did disdain. She ignored him, stripping back the covers and unbuttoning his pyjamas, and squeezing out the hot clean flannel. While she washed him he kept his gaze turned firmly to the window and the hills beyond. The fieldfares were gone from the field behind the church.

In the meadows by the river the early knapweeds were up, their thistly pink heads nodding when anyone walked past. In the village hall the well-dressing design was laid out on the boards, pinned into place, and the outlines pricked through into the clay.

Irene watched to see that it was done well, then gave the nod for the paper to be peeled away. In Thompson's fields the wrapped bales were lifted on to a long low trailer and taken to the yard to be stacked and netted. Les Thompson watched with a careful gaze as they worked. At the allotments Mr Wilson's asparagus spears nibbed from the thick black soil. After a week the first two dozen were cut and carried away by Clive, the rest left to grow to their full ferny height, ready for the following year. James Broad fell and broke his leg while climbing on the edges below Black Bull Rocks, and was taken out by the mountain-rescue team. When she heard, Lynsey took the day off from college and went to visit him. He was asleep when she got there and for a few minutes she sat and looked at the dressings on his leg, the bruising on his arms. The movement of his eyelashes. She pulled the chair a little closer to the bed and he woke up. Here for some practice? he asked. She looked at his leg again. Someone needs to change those dressings, she said. But I'm not touching it. You've probably got the lurgy or something. He looked at her. The lurgy? Yes, James. The lurgy. It's a medical term. And plus you smell. The nurse training's going well then? he asked. Must be scoring well on bedside manner. Great, she said. It's going great. How's the climbing? Yeah, fine, he said. Climbing's fine. It's the falling I'm not so good at. She laughed, finally, and when he laughed as well he winced suddenly and stopped himself. She flinched. Ribs? she asked. Very good, Nurse. Yes, ribs. Not broken, but kind of fucked up. She didn't say anything. She stood up and leant over him slowly and kissed his mouth. She hadn't meant to and once she'd started it was difficult to stop. He kissed her back, and his hand came up to the side of her face. She stepped away. She didn't actually wipe her mouth but she might as well have done. Lynsey, he said. James, no. She looked as though she might say something else, but she picked up her bag and left.

The first time Gordon Jackson slept with Olivia Hunter he was reminded vividly of the time on the hill with her mother. For a moment he had reservations. There was a similarity in her voice, although she had less to say. She seemed less certain of what she wanted than her mother had been. But she wanted something, and it hardly seemed fair to explain what his reservations were. Her parents were away and the barn conversions were all empty. He'd been working on Olivia for a time now and things were at a good stage. She was naked almost as soon as they got into the room. She was good to look at, but she seemed uncomfortable with him looking. She knelt on the bed. Her skin was very clear. Taut. He felt himself to be in good shape but looking at her now made him feel worn-down. She held out a hand and reached for his belt. He took hold of her shoulder and laid her down. She kissed him so hard it lifted him off the bed. There was a crushed smell of lavender coming in through the open window, and the sound of a quad bike on the hill. In the conifers there were buzzards bringing food to their nests, the chicks growing quickly and demanding more each day. At the allotments the early potatoes were lifted, pale and smooth as hens' eggs on the warm dark soil.

August was dry and still and a dust rose from the fields and there was a great fear of fire on the hills. The young woodpigeons left the nests and practised their flight, beating up from the trees before cracking their wings into a stiff glide down to the ground. The badgers spent more of the night outside, and ranged closer to the edges of their territory. There was scent-marking, and in the morning small piles of soft scat could be found. In his studio Geoff Simmons wrapped pots in tissue and bubble wrap and sealed them into cardboard boxes. The people who'd ordered them thought they were getting vases or jugs or cups but they were all simply vessels to him. He labelled the boxes and carried them down the lane to the post office. He left the door hanging open all the time now. The Jones house was empty. There was uncertainty about where Jones had gone, and no one could agree on when he'd last been seen. But the house stayed dark and when the leaves fell they blocked the gutter and the rain started spilling under the eaves and staining the render. The post was still being delivered, and could be seen piling up behind the glazed front door. Brief consideration was given as to whether he might in fact be in there, passed. But Brian Fletcher knew where his sister was, and on enquiry was told that he was still visiting her, and so the matter was dropped. What he did with his house was his business, people said. Irene visited once or twice, and tidied the front garden, and arranged for the gutters to be cleared. At the cricket ground the game against Cardwell was lost.

In September Rohan and James came over from Manchester, and Sophie from London, and they met up with Lynsey for the day. They'd talked about it at Christmas and it had taken this long to arrange. The original plan had been to go for a walk, but James was still on crutches so they went for a drive instead. They met at the Hunter place on a Sunday morning, and the four of them sat at the breakfast bar with coffee and croissants. Stuart was working away, but Jess hovered around asking questions and talking about how little time seemed to have passed since they'd been teenagers perching on the same high stools. I don't suppose you've got the time to look at photographs now, have you? she asked. I've got some wonderful ones from your last day of school. They were polite but they said they had to get on. She stood in the doorway and watched as they all piled into Sophie's car. The kitchen shook with quietness behind her. Olivia was already out for the day. She turned, and tidied their breakfast things away. The four of them drove up past the visitor centre and headed for the access roads by the higher reservoirs. They didn't have much of a plan. Sophie asked James how bad his leg was and he said he wasn't a total cripple but he couldn't walk more than a couple of miles. It'll get better though, will it? As long as I don't do anything stupid. Like fall off Black Bull Rocks, that sort of stupid? Yeah, that. As long as I don't do that again I'll be fine. And as long as we don't hold you down and jump on your leg? Yeah, that's not going to help either. Got it. Just checking. Sophie headed up the new access road to the wind turbines, and parked at the top. From here they could see seven of the reservoirs, stepping down towards the village and the river beyond, and in the other direction the motor-way. The wind was up and the car was shaking. This should blow the hangover away, Rohan said, and they all opened their doors. James needed a hand to get steady on his crutches, and Lynsey and Rohan walked either side to keep him sheltered from the wind. They made their way along the ridge. The turbine blades whipped round overhead. The clouds were being scattered ragged in the wind and the light around them flickered. Lynsey put her arm through James's and leant into him slightly as they walked. The three of them moved slowly. Sophie was impatient and kept striding ahead, turning to take pictures of them on her phone and then waiting for them to catch up. The road became a track and the track became a footpath and James started to wince. They could see the old water-board buildings at the top of Reservoir no.

7. They stopped, and he said he thought he'd had enough. There was weather coming from the motorway and they agreed to turn back. Well, it wasn't exactly the Iron Man challenge, but it'll do for a first attempt, Rohan said. We'll try a bit further next time, will we? James was already clenching his teeth with discomfort and didn't reply. Lynsey kept hold of his arm. Next spring, Sophie said. We'll do the whole of the Greystone Way, the four of us. All of it? That's a ten-day walk, at least. Book the time off now then. You're not scared, are you? That's a long time to be away, Lynsey said. She didn't quite say that Guy wouldn't like it, but they could see that's what she meant. By the time they'd got back to the car it had been agreed that they would definitely do it in the spring, but only Sophie really believed they would. They went back to Sophie's so Rohan and Lynsey could drive their cars into town and they had lunch at the pub by the river. The weather had passed and it was just warm enough to sit outside. Rohan talked a bit about how his music was going, and Sophie tried to explain about the start-up she was involved with in London. Lynsey's phone chirped a few times, and the third or fourth time she said she'd have to get home. James suddenly pointed in alarm at something on the other side of the river. There was nothing there, but while Rohan and Sophie turned to look he leant forward and kissed Lynsey softly on the cheek. She shook her head urgently and he smiled. Let's go, he said, taking off his shoes and socks and setting them on the table. He didn't wait for the others to join

him and he didn't count to three, but by the time he'd hobbled over to the water's edge they were beside him, barefoot, Sophie and Rohan taking an arm each and helping him down the bank. Lynsey carried his crutches. Even at the end of a long summer the water was gasping cold coming down from the hills, and they each caught their breath as they made their way across. In the middle they paused. They'd be setting off in different directions from the car park, and three of them had a long way to go. They weren't ready to leave. The water washed around their ankles and turned over beneath the bridge. In the beer garden a blackbird poked at the crumbs beneath their table. The river was cold and it kept moving and they stood and looked up into the hills.

The days shortened and the light grew hazy and thick. Garden furniture was taken in. The teasels along the banks of the river stood brown and tall, scratching stiffly at the air. In the evenings through the beech wood the last small coppers were seen, roosting head-down on the grasses beside the track. The sun angled low over the hill as Les Thompson led his cows out of the parlour towards the night-grazing paddock. He closed the gate behind them and headed back to the parlour for washdown. The metallic smell of coming rain rose up and the air felt charged and tight. There was a tingling before the first fat drops fell and they came as a letting go. Susanna Wright gave up her tenancy in the Close and moved in with Ruth Fowler above the shop in Harefield. They'd been together for months now, and those who'd noticed were only surprised it had taken so long. They'd made no great announcement but neither had they troubled to keep it to themselves. They carried on working their own allotments. On changeover days Irene was kept busy at the Hunters' barn conversions. She bagged the bedding first and opened the windows so the mattresses would air. She mopped and hoovered and wiped, moving back and forth between the three units as the floors dried. She sang as she worked. There was rain forecast but for now the air blowing through was warm and heather-fresh. In the smaller bedroom of the end conversion she stood and said a prayer, as she had done for years now. She felt the old urge to check under the bed. She changed all the sheets and duvets, put welcome baskets on the kitchen counters, arranged fresh flowers in vases and jugs. She pulled the windows to and locked the doors. It was a simple enough job but she made sure it was done well. People knew they could count on her. She pocketed the keys and walked back down the driveway, her feet crunching in the gravel. An hour yet until the bed-and-breakfast guests were due at her place. Time enough to sit. A rare enough treat, still.

———————

At the allotments the first frosts edged the winter crops and broke open the soil. Cathy had thought Richard would be in touch since selling his mother's house, and might even have found a reason to come back to the village. But there had been nothing, and when she called his number there was a strange dialling tone that suggested he was somewhere abroad. He didn't answer until the third time she called, and after they'd spoken for a few minutes she said that she missed him. She'd realised she missed him, she said. The river was high and thick with peat and there were grayling in number for those who knew where to look. Ian Dowsett was out in the channel between millponds, working a weighted nymph around the rocks and waiting for the chance to strike. The cold was already seeping inside his waders. It was hard to stay out in the water as long as he once would have done. The reservoirs were high and the wind funnelling down the valley pushed the water in waves over the tops of the dams. At the foot of the churchyard yew the goldcrests pressed close together against the chill. The missing girl had not yet been forgotten. The girl's name was Rebecca, or Becky, or Bex. She had been looked for, everywhere. She had been looked for in the lambing sheds on Jackson's farm, people moving through the thick stink of frightened ewes and climbing up into the lofts and squeezing behind the stacks of baled hay, and in the darkness outside great heaving lungfuls of fresh air were taken as people made their way across the field to the other barns. She had been looked for in the caves, and in the quarries, and in the reservoirs and all across the hills. It was no good. Dreams were had about her, still. There were dreams about her catching a bus to a railway station and boarding a train which ran out of control and hurtled off the rails. There were dreams where she ran down to the road and met a man with a car who took her to a ferry. Dreams where she ran and just kept running, to the road, to a bus station, to a city where she could find enough places to hide. There were dreams about finding her on the night she went missing, stumbling across her on the moor in the lowering dark and helping her back to her parents. In the dreams the parents said thank you, briefly, and people muttered something about it being no problem at all.

The clouds skated across the face of the moon and the silver light on the fields flushed in and out of the hollows. A blackbird moved under Mr Wilson's hedge, poking around in the leaf litter for something to eat. At the river the keeper broke open the ice on the millpond so no children would be tempted to test it out. He had a good length of scaffold pole to pound down and it took a few strikes to crack through. There were slabs of glassy ice turning on the black water. In the eaves of the church the bats were folded deeply in their hibernation and the air around them was still. In his studio Geoff Simmons washed the day's work from his hands, the hardened clay dissolving in milky streams down the plughole and into the clay trap beneath, the clear water rising to the outlet and flowing cleanly along the open drain outside. The stems of the coppiced willow stools up on the Hunters' land gleamed red and gold in the narrow winter light. There was carol singing in the church, with candles and the smell of cut yew and holly. Molly Jackson sang a solo verse of 'Silent Night', her voice trembling a little while her parents watched from opposite sides of the aisle. When she finished everyone looked down at their sheets to find the words of the second verse. The sound of their singing carried out into the night, down to the river and the school and the cricket ground. The river ran empty and clear, turning beneath the bridge. There were clouds and the evening was dark and people moved through the streets with their heads lowered. From the houses the lights shone warmly and in the square the conversations spilled out from the pub. Car doors slammed and someone called goodnight and the headlights swept across the road, past the allotments, around beyond the beech wood and the visitor centre and away through the hills. The hills were a dark silhouette. The reservoirs were a flat metallic grey. At the quarry the rope-swing hung above the water. From his bed Jackson listened to the singing in the church. All was calm, all was bright.

Acknowledgements

Bamford Quaker Community, Barbara Crossley, Benjamin Johncock, Chris Power, David Jones, Edward Hogan, Éireann Lorsung, Fairholmes Visitor Centre, Gill O'Neill, Gillian Roberts, Helen Garnons-Williams, Jane Chapman, Jin Auh, Julian Humphries, Katrin Moye, Katy Wakelin, Kim Day, Mark Day, Melissa Harrison, Nicky Wilkinson, Nicola Dick, Nigel Redman, Peak District National Park Media Centre, Richard Birkin, *Rosie Garton*, Sarah-Jane Forder, Superintendent Jonathan Morgan, Tracy Bohan.